Preface:

The great British holiday may have chang years: wet and windy works' weeks by the sea givii ostas, only to themselves yield to the limitless possi lobal, internet age. And yet, there remain some cor ounce along the major motorways of the nation, and fields resplendent with canvas homes come into blossom with the school holidays. Then, of course, there are the hire boats.

Each year, thousands of people, from all over the world, are lured by the promise of escape and tranquillity that a canal boat holiday offers. They return, year after year, having discovered that that promise is kept. The waterways remain little more than a shallow, narrow ditch, hidden from the sight of the outside world, and the boats may be little changed from the earliest craft that plied the canals, but it is that very simplicity that attracts the hire boat crews.

One of the most popular ways of exploring the canal network is to take a circular cruise around one of a number of 'rings' that see the crew arrive back at their starting point a week or two after setting off. The ring that still attracts the most boaters is the Four Counties Ring: a circular route of 110 miles and 94 locks that takes the boater through the counties of Staffordshire, Shropshire, Cheshire, and the West Midlands. It's a beautiful route that can be completed in one busy week, although two weeks allows for a much more leisurely journey.

This novel is entirely fictional in all respects, save for its descriptions of the route taken and the basics of what narrowboats are about. You can visit the places, frequent the pubs and enjoy the numerous other features that are all a part of the Four Counties. You can try for yourself a life in a steel box with limited space and amenities. Should you choose to do so, you will never regret it, although I trust that your journey will unfold in a better way than the one described in these pages. It couldn't very well be worse.

Week One

Day One, Saturday.

Gailey to Brewood.

Chapter One:

It was always going to be a challenging couple of weeks. None of the three parties who were getting ready to meet on that bright Saturday afternoon had convinced themselves that it would be otherwise. Although, they were each, in their own way, committed to making it work. It was the right thing to do and the right time to do it, and if their fears proved to be ungrounded, it might actually be a thoroughly enjoyable experience. With that in mind, numerous conversations had taken place; conversations packed with instructions, pleas, requests and demands that behaviours be avoided or toned down. They'd all agreed to make the effort. Not one of them believed they could keep it up.

"Remember what I told you?" Helen Roberts turned to face her husband, Mick, as they arrived at the boat yard and headed towards the designated car park.

"That depends on what it is you want me to remember." Mick mumbled back as he drew the car to a halt next to a gleaming silver Mercedes. "I need an instruction book for all the rules and regulations you've been throwing at me."

"Don't start." his wife softened her tone, knowing the effect that would have on him. "It's important, that's all. Some of the things you say and some of the ways you say them, well ... not everyone understands you, that's all. We're doing this for Steve and Penny. Just tone it down a little and meet Jeff halfway, okay?"

"I'll end up in a bloody halfway house by the end." Mick whispered under his breath as climbed out of the car, concentrating only on not letting the door make contact with its neighbour.

If there was anything that signified the difference between the couples, it was the contrast between the two vehicles and their contents. Helen and Mick's mid-range, five-year-old Ford, looked like a poor, second-cousin to the new Mercedes. The Aldi bags-for-life that filled its boot were even further removed from the Samsonite cases and Louis Vuitton holdalls that had already been unloaded and stacked carefully behind the Mercedes.

"Michael and Helen! So lovely to see you." Alicia Williams dropped her half-smoked cigarette and clacked towards them in her highly impractical shoes.

"Alice." Helen met Alicia and they embraced in a surprisingly genuine way. "It's been too long. Are you well?"

"Absolutely marvellous." Alicia replied. "And Michael, I trust that your journey was okay. We arrived a little early, as is Jefferey's wont. Mind you, the Mercedes simply eats up the miles without any effort."

The embrace between Mick and Alicia was less natural. Mick was a handshake type of guy, if there had to be any contact that is. Hugs weren't really his style, but he let Alicia in and survived the encounter and the double-cheeked air kiss.

"You look well, love." he told her. "You been away?"

"Oh, just a week at the villa with a few of the girls." she replied nonchalantly. "Thought I'd better top up the tan before this holiday. I don't think the Factor 50 will be necessary this time."

"Forecast's reasonable." Mick replied. "Not that that means much. Still, we're not here for the weather."

"Well, good afternoon all." Jefferey Williams joined the group, waving a bundle of papers. "Just signed everything up and we'll soon be on the off. Penelope and Stephen rang a little earlier. They're on their way but running a little late. Morning sickness. Still, gives us a chance to get ourselves sorted. You feeling fit, Mick?"

It was the way that he said his name that always irritated him. Yes, he liked to be called Mick and always had since he was a schoolboy, but it just didn't sound right coming from Jefferey Williams. At least he hadn't called him 'mate'. That would have been too much to cope with.

"Come on, Helen." Alicia Williams grabbed Helen's elbow as they walked away. "We can leave the chaps to do the heavy work. I'll show you around the boat and you can help me with the bottle of bubbly I've got on the go."

"You didn't hang around!"

"Darling, when you've been in the car with Jefferey for most of the morning and spent the journey confirming schedules and route plans, believe me, champagne's the soft option. We've got our work cut out with those two, we need as much help as we can get."

"They have these rather super trollies, apparently." Jefferey informed Mick. "I've asked them to bring a couple around for us. We'll load up and get everything on-board and the girls can unpack while we have the tutorial. Not that there can be much to this boating lark."

"Sounds fine, Jeff." Mick replied, opening the boot of the Ford and deliberately stacking the supermarket bags next to the Williams' premium luggage. "Did you have a good journey up?"

"Splendid. Left nice and early as always, to avoid the jams. The Merc's a beauty though and she's a pleasure to get behind the wheel of. You should look at one. Maybe one of the smaller models?"

"The Ford's fine for me." Mick knew that this was how the conversation would go, but he was on strict instructions to behave so he left the first jibe unanswered. "And how's business?"

"Never better, never better." Jefferey looked around as he answered, tapping his feet impatiently as he waited for trolleys to arrive. "Just secured a major new account and I've got several other irons in the fire, as it were. Hush, hush, of course, but very, very lucrative if they come through."

Mick waited for the reciprocal question about his own job. It was nothing special, but it paid the bills. He'd been at the garage for the past twenty years and enjoyed it. The money was only just above minimum wage, but he and Helen had all that they wanted. A bit more now that the mortgage had come to an end. No, his job was nothing special. It would have been nice to be asked about it though.

"I'll go and check where the trolleys are." he said finally, breaking the silence that had only been disturbed by Jeffery's regular huffs, "I think I saw where they keep them when we drove in. Do I need to do anything about the paperwork?"

"All done and dusted." Jefferey tapped the leather folder that he'd placed on top of the suitcases. "They gave me some guff about my name not being on the booking, but I put them in their place. You have to be firm with people like this. Tell them how it is and what you expect. I think they got the message. And I told them to hurry things along as well. We're on a tight schedule and I don't expect to be hanging around here all afternoon."

Mick mumbled a faint reply and went in search of the trolleys. They were stacked neatly beside the converted Victorian depot that now housed the hire company's offices. Nobody stopped him as he retrieved two of them and wheeled them across the car park. He returned to the cars, justified in having moved things forward in this way.

"The Lord helps those who help themselves, Jeff." he quipped as he passed one of the trolleys to Jefferey who replied with a cursory 'thanks' before beginning to load it up.

"I trust they'll be less tardy in facilitating our departure." he said. "I know how these handover days work. You've got to be there first and not let them dictate the order in which you depart. We've paid our money and we should expect to be treated well. Now, come on, let's get the ship loaded up."

As they trundled across the car park, Mick was tempted to remind Jefferey that it had actually been him that had paid for the holiday. It wasn't cheap either. Okay, so it was their turn, after the Williams' had paid for the bulk of last year's wedding, but even so, an acknowledgement would have been nice.

"Here she is. She's called 'Harriet Knot'." Jefferey stood proudly next the sixty-foot of steel that would be their home for the next fortnight. "Looks to be a little basic, but she'll do. Shall we embark?"

They clambered onto the stern of the boat and were greeted by shouts of 'Ahoy there!' from within. Their wives had used the waiting period to their advantage and were just opening a second bottle of bubbly.

"Steady on, old girl." Jefferey whispered to Alicia, "Bit early in the day for all that, isn't it?"

"Oh, relax, Jeff." Helen laughed as she poured two more glasses for the men. "We're on holiday. No drink-drive laws on the waterways. And we've got an awful lot of booze to get through."

"I'll not be a nuisance then." Jefferey replied coolly. "But we do have quite a lot to do before we head off. Michael, could you please give me a hand with the bags."

"Aye, aye, Captain." Mick replied, downing the glass of champagne before scurrying after his self-appointed leader. "And when we're done, we'll swab the decks and raise the mainsail before weighing anchor."

As they passed the excess of luggage from the trolley into the boat, their wives stored the contents neatly away in the numerous cubby-holes that they'd found when first exploring its interior.

"We'll sort it all properly once we're going." Alicia told Helen conspiratorially. "Otherwise Jefferey will want everything alphabetised and graded by size and weight. Just don't let him see what we've done with it."

"Don't be too harsh on him." Helen replied, "He seems happy to be in command. And I've told Michael to take a step back."

"What, what, what?" Mick flopped down next to the ladies and held his hand out for another glass of bubbly. "My ears are burning. What are you saying about me? All good, I trust? Eh, Alice?"

"Of course, Michael." Alicia laughed and handed him the drink. "Helen was just saying how well behaved you are going to be."

"Scout's honour!"

"Somehow I don't see you as a Boy Scout. But best behaviour it must be or you'll face the consequences. El Capitan will have you walking the plank."

The three were in fits of laughter when that same El Capitan joined them. His face was like thunder and he refused the drink that he was offered.

Chapter Two:

"Can you believe it?" Jefferey hissed out his complaint. "I told them that I expected to be the first off, and there they are, loading up that bunch of students over there and seeing them on their way. I gave them a piece of my mind, and do you know what? They told me that we weren't scheduled to be sent out until next to last. I've a good mind to speak to their boss."

"Oh, Jeff, mate." Mick was properly into holiday mood now and beginning to relax, "Don't sweat it. The kids aren't even here yet and what difference will another hour or two make?"

"That's not the point. One has a certain level of expectation and one doesn't expect to be treated like this. I told them specifically that we required their promptest attention. It's the same as with the trolleys. You can't rely on a certain type of people. It's why this country is going to the dogs. Wouldn't surprise me if the staff aren't immigrants. They have a different mindset to us."

"That's enough Jefferey." Alicia gave him a look that silenced him. "Maybe it's got something to do with your manner. I'll go and see what I can do. Meanwhile, you ring Penelope and see where they are."

Stumbling a little as she disembarked, Alicia took a moment to compose herself before catching the eye of one of the boatyard team, whom she beckoned over. As he approached, she heard a familiar ringtone and looked up to see her daughter and son-in-law walking across the carpark carrying their luggage. She let the call drop, waved and then pointed to the boat that they were on, before turning her attention to the young guy who stood before her.

"Can I help you?" he asked, warily.

"Sweetheart." Alicia drew close enough to him that the swell of her chest was almost brushing against him. "I just thought that an apology might be in order. For my husband. He can be a little demanding."

"Oh, that's fine.", he replied, "No apology necessary."

"You're too kind." she whispered, reaching out to grab his hand. "But I think you know what I'm talking about. Here's a little something for you. Maybe you could see us off a little sooner, especially as my daughter and son-in-law have just arrived."

"I'll see what I can do." he looked down at the hint of purple from the folded-up note that she'd passed him and walked away, his hand already reaching for the walkie talkie that was clipped to his belt.

An hour later, they were on their way. The handover had been fairly smooth, facilitated by Penelope's relationship with her father who she could manipulate in numerous ways according to the circumstances. She'd ensured that he'd listened to what they were being told and that he hadn't made any intimidating or patronising comments as the workings of the engine and the correct management of the boat's systems were explained. She and her husband had been away on narrowboats before, so any gaps in the self-appointed Captain's knowledge could be filled in by them. Of course, if you'd have asked him how it went, he'd have told you a very different story about how he'd led the whole process.

Knowing that the safety of his loved ones was more important than his own desire to make light of everything, Mick had listened carefully to the briefing from the young lad who had been assigned to show them how the boat worked. It was all fairly straightforward and a comprehensive manual supported the briefing. Only when the main information had been imparted did he allow himself to speak.

"So, why's she called 'Harriet Knot?'" he asked, enquiring about the boat's strange name.

"Oh, that's our boss's idea." the lad sighed, having had to explain things just too many times. "All of our boats have a name that's female, because boats are supposed to be that gender, and they all have to have a pun because, well, that's just the type of guy my boss is."

"But," he continued. "they also have names that remind our crews of some of the simple rules of boating. Yours is Harriet Knot because you're not supposed to hurry along on a boating holiday. Harriet Knot, hurry it not? You see?"

"A man after my own heart." Mick laughed. "Have you got a Donna Sinker?"

"Sorry?"

"Donna Sinker." Mick explained delightedly. "Don't sink her."

"Very witty." Jefferey interceded. "I did notice Cilla Void go off earlier. I presume that refers to what you were saying about avoiding catching the cill at locks?"

"That's right, sir." the lad replied. "Same as Cloda Gates, close the gates, and Bertha Gently, berth her gently. I'm not sure what he wants from Maureen Pin, I think he just liked that, but Sharon Locks works okay as a reminder to share the locks. For me, I'd have preferred if he'd chosen to name them after birds or something, but hey, what's in a name."

Both Steve and Mick had racked their brains for other names to suggest, but they let it go when their time came to be pushed off into the cut and begin their holiday.

"God Bless the Harriet Knot and all who sail in her!" Mick had shouted as they left the boatyard and began their journey.

His son sighed and gave Jefferey a knowing wink. He loved his parents and he was proud of his dad, but he was happy to admit that he could be a bit embarrassing at times. That said, if a little bit of embarrassment was the price he had to pay for all the other great times that they enjoyed, then it was worth it. As for Jefferey, well, he was Steve's father-in-law and he was what he was. He was good to Penelope and had now accepted Steve as her choice for a husband, despite his early ambitions to wed her into the aristocracy. As a retail manager, Steve knew that his work was rated by Jefferey as being a bare notch above a shop assistant, but that didn't matter either; he earned good money and looked after Penelope well.

"Okay with you chaps if I take this first leg?" Jefferey raised his voice to be heard above the thumping of the diesel engine.

"Fine with me, Jeff." Mick shouted back, raising the glass of whisky that had replaced the champagne he'd polished off earlier. "Just keep her pointed straight and mind you don't hit anything."

"Dad." Steve sighed as he waited for the next pearl of wisdom to fall from his father's lips. "Cut him some slack. He's a natural at this. You done this before, Jefferey?"

"Oh, there's nothing to it." Jefferey rose to the praise as Steve knew he would. After all, it was text book salesmanship and he was an expert on that. "Used to shift a few old hunks in my army days, and, I guess, it's like riding a bike. Once we reach our destination tonight, we'll plan the driving and you'll all get a share of the duties. Meanwhile, we need to crack on as we're already a tad behind schedule."

That was putting it lightly. On the one hand, their delayed departure from base had knocked the schedule for day one already. On the other, that schedule was a little bit optimistic from Jefferey's part, assuming as it did, that they could maintain a steady four miles per hour all the way. Moored boats put paid to that, as did a narrow cutting that saw the boat bouncing and scraping from side to side, before wedging itself into the rocks along the towpath. Jefferey racked up the revs to try and free it. Mick kept quiet and tried to contain his joy at the foul up. Stephen and Penelope suggested alternative approaches that were eventually taken up and found to be successful. The credit, naturally, went to the Captain.

A planned six pm finish became an actual eight pm one. Fortunately, the weather had been kind to them and a late burst of unexpected evening light had helped them along. They worked together to moor up the boat and Stephen and Penelope were despatched to the nearby village to collect the takeaway that had been ordered. Helen and Alicia, full of the joys of alcohol, giggled and laughed as they set the table. Mick tried his best to disapprove of their behaviour but couldn't help joining in at times. Jefferey sat on his own, maps spread out before him and his scheduled route-plan deeply scored with black lines and amendments.

The arrival of the food drew them all together and they let the kids dish everything up as they toasted a successful first day. Plates of curry and assorted dishes were piled high on the small dinette table and the six of them began sharing the feast.

"Rice, Michael?" Jefferey asked.

"No thanks, Jeff." he replied, smiling as he practised his standard response and not daring to look at his wife before he said it. "Rice is for puddings, with strawberry jam on!"

"Just give him chips." Helen sighed, "And be thankful he didn't order a steak instead of the curry."

Chapter Three:

The remainder of their evening meal having gone off smoothly, idle small-talk dominated the conversation as Helen and Alicia steered the chat where they knew it needed to be. It had been an exhausting first day, what with the journey to the yard and the surprisingly wearying process of navigation. That meant that there was an element of built-in relaxation around the table which in turn meant that they ate and drank and nobody was particularly inspired to say anything out of order.

To round the day off, when the table had been cleared, Jefferey proposed a study of their route before they all retired to bed. Alicia and Helen declined the offer, the champagne finally catching up on them, but the others played along.

"Play nicely." Alicia chuckled as she and Helen departed to their respective cabins.

Mick ensured that everyone's drink was topped up, waving the bottle at Penelope but knowing that she would refuse the offer. He waved it again and nodded to her dad as if to say 'are you sure you won't need some?'. She smiled and snuggled up next to her husband as the lecture began.

"The Four Counties Ring is 110 miles long and contains 94 locks. We are currently here, at Brewood." Jefferey pointed to their location on a map that he'd printed off the internet.

"Please, sir?" Mick winked at his son as he raised his hand.

"Yes, Michael?" Jeffery sighed wearily.

"You said this place was Bree Wood?"

"Yes?"

"Well, I don't want to be rude." he let the opening remark hang before continuing. "But I think it's pronounced Brude!"

Childish chuckles filled the room but were stopped almost as soon as they'd started by the look on Jefferey's face.

"Please can you refrain from such comments." Jefferey sighed. "I'm sure you may be right, however, if we are to be addressing diction and pronunciation throughout this holiday then I can give as good as I get."

"Sorry, mate." Mick slapped his own wrists. "Do carry on."

"Thank you. To recap, having navigated from our starting point at Gailey we have now arrived at Brewood (Mick's pronunciation now accepted). So far, and the reason I chose to do the ring this way, clockwise rather than anti-clockwise, is that we have only encountered the one small stop lock here at Autherley Junction which I hope you watched me successfully manoeuvre through. Tomorrow, we shall encounter more locks. After much careful planning, and a number of conversations with people who've done this route before, I have based my calculations on our cruising for roughly five hours per day. That will give us breathing space and allow us to take our time and spend a little longer in locations that we find to be particularly pleasurable. After all, this is a holiday, is it not. Any questions?"

Nobody said anything. What was there to say? The boat was pointing in a certain direction and they would simply go that way. It wasn't as if there were many difficult navigational decisions to take. You arrived at a lock, you worked through it. You met a junction, you took the left turn. The rest of it was about enjoying the journey. As for rigid time schedules, well, anyone with half a brain knew that 'canal time' rolled on at its own unique pace.

"You've done well, Jeff." Mick wanted the debrief to end.

"Thank you, Michael." he replied. "Let's nip out on deck and have a little tipple and a puff on a cigar? I guess you youngsters will want to turn in?"

Penelope and Stephen were happy for the excuse. They disappeared into the bow of the boat and shut the partition door on their parents. It had been a long day for them and their journey to the boat yard had been hell, compounded by the late start that Penelope's morning sickness had caused. At seven-months pregnant, she'd only reluctantly agreed to come on the holiday but had done so fully prepared for the worst. None of the others had objected to the young couple's choice of bedroom given that it was adjacent to a hatch that opened straight onto the canal. Bodily functions and their accompanying odours were part and parcel of life in such a confined space, but one less to contest with was the sensible choice.

Meanwhile, on the deck, the two older men sat quietly and smoked the small cigars that were Jefferey's worst indulgence.

"It's gone okay so far, don't you think?" he asked Mick.

"Fine by me, Jeff." Mike replied, wondering where this was going.

"Although I think we need to keep an eye on the ladies' drinking." Jefferey continued.

"Good luck with that!" Mick laughed, "I've been married long enough to know where I stand. If you can't beat them, I say, well, we should join them."

"We'll agree to differ on that. But, there is one other thing that we need to discuss."

"Go on."

"Now, I fully understand," Jefferey placed an unwelcome hand on Mick's shoulder. "that in the circles you move, the reduction of names is quite normal. And I don't want to sound too dictatorial about this, but, well, you see, Alicia and I rather like our names. I am Jefferey, not Jeff, and she is Alicia, not Alice. I know that you and Helen don't mind being Mick and Hel, but we don't share that view. Would it be possible to use our full names on this voyage?"

Mick listened carefully and was very restrained in his response. The words going through his head would have been frowned on by Helen, so he waited a while to tame and manage them.

"Aye, you're right." he spoke in his thickest Northern accent, quite deliberately not trying to pretend to be someone he wasn't. "And yes, in the circles I move in, we call each other what we call each other and it's only natural. In the same way that the circles in which you move, it's quite normal to be a pompous and arrogant prat. So, yep, I'll call you Jefferey and Alicia, but do me a favour in return, hey?"

"That certainly seems reasonable."

"Lighten up and stop being a knob. Agreed?"

As expected, no reply was forthcoming. That was what he'd expected and he made no attempt to stop the other as he threw his cigar in the water and stormed into the cabin of the boat. Yes, it was going to be a challenging couple of weeks. But, having paid for it, Mick was certainly going to enjoy it as much as he could.

Week One

Day Two, Saturday.

Brewood to Norbury.

Chapter Four:

The canals and inland waterways of Britain are half-a-world removed from the madness and the pressures of life beyond their towpaths. That's their attraction. And that detachment brings with it more than just the freedom to escape into a hidden realm of tranquillity and natural beauty. It brings the freedom from the pressures of modern norms. This is particularly noticeable in the dress-code assumed by those who navigate the cut.

Those who live aboard their boats wear practical clothing, free of designer labels and purchased cheaply, but to last. Private boat owners, taking their prized possessions out for holiday breaks might also favour such attire. Or they may be seen sporting matching sweatshirts embroidered with the boat's name. They may even, if their boat is a 'historic' vessel, don the outfit of the old bargees as they hanker for a long-gone way of life. Not that it was a lifestyle to be envied. Then again, isn't that the beauty of framing the past? It can be whatever you want it to be, however inaccurate that portrayal.

Holiday boaters are something else. Almost as if they consciously want their holiday to be entirely separate from their other lives, they take the opportunity to wear clothes that they would never walk down a high street in. The norm is shorts. Whatever the weather. Shorts that top the pastiest legs imaginable, and shorts that could rarely be said to fit like a glove. Below the white expanse of flesh, sandals finish the look; sandals worn with socks, no less. Above the waist, things vary a little. Short-sleeved shirts are most popular, although, should the sun be particularly favourable, those shirts are replaced by the sight of more white, flabby and generous desk-bound flesh bellies. The ladies may be a little more discreet. And to top it all off, a hat. A hat that shines with newness and a hat that is being worn by somebody who has never worn a hat before but who knows that boaters wear hats of a certain sort. There's a practical reason for a hat. A number in fact. It shields the eyes from the sun, protects the face from the rain and keeps the balding pate from a burst of sunstroke. Holiday boaters may choose to wear a hat for any of the above reasons, but the primary one remains that it is part of the uniform.

As the sun rose over Brewood on the second day of their journey, Jefferey Williams had set aside the clothes he'd worn the previous day and was resplendent in his newly acquired outfit of shorts and shop-white training shoes. Comfortable clothes, had been his reasoning. And clothes that reflected the freedom that the waterways brought. It was liberating to be free of the social conventions that bound him out there in the real world, and it was invigorating to feel the crisp, misty-morning air flow over his exposed limbs. The others would be up soon enough, but for now, he was enjoying the solitude and the surprisingly pleasant semi-nakedness on his own, as he completed the morning checks that the boat yard had asked to be done daily.

He held in his hand the laminated sheet that he'd extracted from the boat's user manual and had already been down into the weed hatch to check for obstructions when the first sounds of movement came from within the boat. He was topping up the engine coolant tank when the stern doors opened and Mick Roberts appeared.

"Good morning, Jefferey." The new arrival lingered a little too long on the vowels as he pronounced the greeting, making the recipient of the greeting wonder how much of it was simply the effort and how much was ridicule.

"Morning, Mick." Jefferey replied, doing his best to make the greeting sound as down-to-earth as he could. He'd try adding a 'mate' at some time, but, for now, he'd done his best.

"Engine checks?" Mick asked.

"Not yet. Just completed the first couple of jobs. The weed hatch is free of obstructions and the coolant level has been returned to its optimum position. The engine is next. Want to help?"

"Sure."

"Okay, if you can lift that engine cover up, we'll have a look."

"Yep, it's there." Mick chuckled as he spoke.

"Sorry?"

"The engine." he explained. "I've checked and it's there. Next on the list."

"Michael, please, can you take this seriously. The manual says that we need to check the oil and ensure that there is no excess water in the bilge. This is not a game."

"No," Mick replied. "it's a holiday. Lighten up. These boats are built to be hammered by the likes of you and me. And, you seem to forget that what I don't know about engines you could write on the back of a stamp. I'll leave you to check off the rest. I'm smelling breakfast."

Returning to the boat's cabin, Mick saw the rest of the extended family in various stages of getting ready for the day. His wife was already at work in the galley, putting together a proper boater's breakfast that he was impatient to dive into.

"Still on best behaviour." he grinned as he hugged Helen. "Just about."

"You'd better be." she replied. "Now, make yourself useful and butter some bread, then lay the table."

Having been married to Helen for too long to even consider protesting, he set about his duties and was joined at the table by Stephen and Alicia, both of whom were following the newly-discovered clothing regime.

"Bloody hell." Mick laughed as he checked them over. "This is Staffordshire, not the Serengeti!"

"It's loose and comfortable." Alicia replied coldly. "And why shouldn't we wear what we want to? I suppose you're just going to be in jeans and t-shirt all the time."

"Nowt wrong with that, sweetheart. And cheap as chips as well."

"Dad," Stephen intervened. "just let it go, okay. Do you have to have a go at everybody else? It's not like your David Beckham yourself."

"All done." Jefferey came back into the boat with a triumphant grin on his face, making sure that everybody could see the layer of oily dirt that had accumulated on his hands. "She's in fine fettle and ready for a day's cruising. I'll just wash up and then we'll go through today's duties."

"Well, don't be long." Helen shouted across to him. "I'm plating up now, don't let it go cold."

The breakfast was everything they could have hoped for. For the Roberts family, it was proper food that appeared a least once a week on the table. The Williams' were more croissant, fruit and muesli, but they tackled the piled-up plates bravely. Penelope was the only one who really felt that she couldn't make the effort. The morning sickness was bad enough, but the smell of greasy food made it seem twice as bad. She opened the window beside her seat and spent the meal breathing in the fresh morning air.

"Our turn tomorrow." Alicia said as the leftovers from her and her husband's plates were eagerly devoured by Mick and Stephen. "I'll do my special omelettes for you. You'll enjoy them. Now, Penelope dear, you and Stephen do the washing up."

"Yes, mummy." Penelope replied, glad to be excused from the table and casting her husband a wry smile. "Come on sexpot, let's get our hands dirty."

"Penelope …" Jefferey was stopped before his indignant outburst could get anywhere by his wife's hand reaching across to him.

"Relax, Jefferey." she smiled. "Holiday, remember? And Penny's lump should tell you more than anything about what they get up to. Now, how about you get the first surprise prepared? They're in the small locker next to our bed."

That request brightened Jefferey up no end. He'd show them what a stick-in-the-mud he was. And it had been all his own idea as well.

Chapter Five:

"Gather round, gather round." he instructed the assorted family members, having retrieved a packed carrier bag from the bedroom. "I have, as Alicia told you, a little surprise that I hope you will like. If you'll permit me?"

He opened the bag and withdrew a pile of bright blue t-shirts that he laid before him on the small dinette table.

"First, for you, Michael." he passed one of the t-shirts across and watched as Mick unfolded it and read the 'First Mate' legend that was embossed on the back before turning it over to see the embroidered logo on the front which read: 'The Wilberts On Tour'.

"Do you like it?" Jefferey asked.

"It's great, mate." he replied after a brief pause to look across at Helen whose expression told him exactly how to react. "But who are The Wilberts?"

"That's us." Jeffery replied triumphantly. "You see, it's a conflation of our surnames, Williams and Roberts. We're 'The Wilberts' on tour. And I have one for everybody."

He passed around the rest of the t-shirts. Stephen chuckled as he became 'Cabin Boy'. Helen smiled wryly at her designation as 'Chef', and Penelope and Alicia laughed out loud when they discovered that they were simply 'Crew', but that Penelope's t-shirt also identified the lump in her womb as 'Baby Crew'.

"Aren't they just divine?" Alicia squealed. "It's not like Jefferey at all, I know, but when he told me about them I just knew you'd love them."

"Aren't we missing one?" Mick asked warily.

"Ah yes," Jefferey smiled smugly as he held up his own t-shirt, "I thought that I'd take the liberty of being 'Captain' of this vessel. We can swap if you want, Michael?"

Mick refused the offer and Helen squeezed his knee thankfully as he let the moment pass. She knew just what he was thinking and she could pretty much frame most of his responses. He played the game though and stayed quiet.

"Now, with that out of the way," Jefferey produced his folder of maps and laid them out on the table. "it's time we planned today's journey. It's not a long one, but it does involve a lock and a few other interesting diversions. Are we all gathered comfortably? Then I shall begin."

It was nine-thirty when the briefing ended. They had been instructed to prepare for a ten-thirty departure and to use the time preceding to do what they liked. As the day's route was a short one, the briefing hadn't lasted long, although it would have been much quicker had Mick not chosen to pick up on Jefferey's pronunciation of the town where they were scheduled to stop for lunch. That town was Gnosall. It was a popular stopping point as it had shops and pubs that were worth visiting. But it was one of those quintessentially English towns that carried an unusual name. The G was silent. These days, Gnosall was pronounced 'nose all'. In the canals heyday, the working boaters had made it even more complicated by pronouncing it 'Nawzall'. Jefferey didn't quite get the whole thing and made the G a hard one.

"So, we stop for lunch in this small town called G-Nozzle," he explained. "where they tell me that there are two excellent canal side pubs. Something wrong Michael?"

"No, no, please go on." he did his best to stifle the uncontrollable chuckle that was building up in him.

"Thank you. As I say, there are two very good pubs here. I suggest that we reconnoitre each one for a swift drink before deciding which to eat at."

"That's a very good idea." Mick tried desperately to keep a straight face as he interrupted. "That way, we can find which one offers the g-nicest g-nosh. We wouldn't want to end up eating g-nasty g-nibbles."

Only Jefferey was unaffected by the ripple of laughter that surrounded him. He was about to ask what the joke was when Stephen stepped in.

"Dad's right. There's g-nothing worse than g-not enjoying the food. But we should also check outside on the terrace, to make sure we don't have any g-nuisance from any g-nasty g-gnats."

Helen had tried to resist, as had Penelope, but that last comment broke the damn and everyone around the table burst into fits of tearful laughter.

"I simply don't get it." Jefferey shouted, "Will somebody please explain?"

It was Penelope who put him out of his misery. She did it as gently as she could but was constantly interrupted by her husband and her father-in-law who couldn't help but keep the joke running. When he understood, Jefferey thanked them for correcting him and finished the rest of the briefing. He concluded with the instruction that they meet on deck at ten-twenty, before storming into his cabin and turning his phone on to check for e-mails.

The others dispersed at the same time. Helen and Alicia went for a short walk into the village to pick up the Sunday papers. Stephen and Penelope chose to take a wander along the towpath, as much to help Penelope get over the sickness that still dogged her.

"I guess that just leaves me." Mick said to himself. "And I have an appointment with a certain little room that can't be put off. Bombs away!"

They set off five minutes late. It was a delay that Jefferey could live with. The sun was shining and the air was still. The engine started smoothly and they slipped off the mooring rings without a hitch. That made up for the events of the morning so far. They were wearing their t-shirts, which was a positive. The ribbing about his pronunciation of Gnosall continued, but he could rise above that. The only potential fly in the ointment was the e-mail he'd received from a work colleague. He'd have to think about that one, but it could wait. For a little while.

"You see these cuttings?" Jefferey was manning the tiller whilst Stephen and his father sat either side of him on the cruiser's deck. "All of them cut by hand. Straight through the rock and without any thought for today's ridiculous Health and Safety madness. Amazing, what?"

His two companions nodded. Not just dutifully. They actually agreed with him. The sheer labour that must have gone in to driving this waterway through solid rock was testament to an age gone by. But it was the beauty of the surroundings that kept them most distracted. Where the banks of the cuttings rose high above them, interspersed occasionally by high bridges, they marvelled at how nature's ingress back into its disturbed territory had produced a wonderful harmony of the primitive with the semi-modern. The sunlight flickered through the thigh canopies of leaves and the air was kept fresh and cool where the woodland was thickest. As they came out of the cuttings and into open country, the views changed but the feeling remained the same. Vast open spaces were dotted with the very essence of Englishness: small churches, run-down farm buildings, fields of crops, and kingfishers flashing by just above the water.

"You can see why people find this so relaxing." Mick said. "And the pace is lovely. Gives you time to take it all in. Makes you forget the hustle and bustle. And, Jefferey, I'm sorry about having a laugh at your expense."

He stopped himself before adding that he hoped that g-no offence had been taken. Helen would let him off the leash so much, but he knew he was currently on very dodgy ground. He had a little work to do.

"No, that's fine." Jefferey replied. "Would you like to have a go at driving?"

After that, they swapped duties a few times, arriving at Wheaton Aston lock feeling that little bit closer together. Their wives had gathered at the front of the boat. Partly because it would have been unnecessarily crowded at the stern with them all there, but mainly because they wanted to relax and chew through the papers. Penelope found that reading only made her feel worse. She simply watched the world go by instead.

"I'll take us through this first lock." Jefferey told his companions. "You steer her in and I'll tell you what I'm doing so that you're up to speed. Okay?"

Stephen chose not to tell his father-in-law that he'd done more locks than Jefferey had had fish and chip suppers. Mick just went with it, concentrating hard as he bumped and bounced the boat into the lock, before stepping off to close the gate.

"It's like a bathtub." Jefferey told them. "You fill it up by opening the top paddles. Then you close them once the boats in. That's the bath full. Now, we simply need to pull the plug by opening the paddles on the front gate and letting the water out."

The others, bar Stephen, were all on deck now and watched in delight as the boat lowered itself in the chamber, the green-slime covered walls just inches from their sides. Stephen opened one of the paddles, then the two men on the bank opened the gates and let the boat glide slowly out. Another boat honked its horn at them and they saw it heading towards them.

"We can leave the gates." Jefferey said. "Those guys are coming in. Come on, let's head back to ours."

Mick had pulled the boat in at the bottom and, with the two new arrivals aboard, they set off. Alicia had to convince her husband that, despite the hire company telling you to fill up with water at every opportunity, it really was too early in the cruise to stop this time. To everyone's surprise, he let himself be convinced by her.

Chapter Six:

The crew of the Harriet Knot arrived at Gnosall later than expected. The delay had been caused by two factors, one avoidable and one not. The unavoidable one was the having to slow down past the numerous moored boats that were a feature of this canal. Vast lines of them stretched ahead and the rule was that you stayed at tick-over speed when you passed them. It was frustrating for Jefferey who hadn't factored this in. The others were more relaxed about it. Even more so when the first gin and tonics were produced. The avoidable delay may have had something to do with those drinks.

Stephen saw the squirrel drop off an overhanging branch and into the water. He shouted to Mick to stop the boat and they reversed back hard in order to draw parallel with the animal that was flailing helplessly in the water. With Jefferey taking control and trying to perform the impossible task of steering whilst reversing, Stephen grabbed the boathook and stood on the bow of the boat trying to reach the squirrel. His theory was that the helpless creature would grab hold of it and he could lift it up onto the towpath. It almost worked. He was just about to make contact when the back end of the boat slewed towards the other side of the water and wedged itself onto the bank. That sudden stop propelled Stephen into the water where he stood with the boathook at his side held up like a centurion's staff. Jefferey shouted curses at the back and revved the engine to try and free the boat. Stephen put two and two together and decided to get out of the water before that happened. The squirrel meanwhile, watched the whole thing carefully, before deciding that he'd had enough of a swim and climbed out of the water. It took another half-hour to get the boat free and Stephen into the shower and into new clothes. It was a half-hour of silence. Even Mick chose not to make a joke of it all. Not now, anyway. 'Squirrel Rescue' could wait a while before it became the stuff of family legend.

Gnosall was worth the wait though. They pulled up at The Navigation pub, decided that it was fine, despite the fact that it gave Mick the chance to rename it the G-Navigation, and settled on the sun-washed deck that overlooked the canal. They were all in good spirits and the beer flowed freely, washing down an exceptional meal of home-made food. This was what they'd come on a boat holiday for, and it was only the second day. Even Jefferey seemed to relax and begin to enjoy himself. Until the dogs appeared.

"Dirty creatures." he mumbled to himself as the couple with two dogs settled close by to them. "They should ban them from eating establishments. Heaven knows what disease they're carrying. Can't understand why people love them so much. If you're not picking up their doings, you're having to stroke their mangy fur and wipe off their slobber. Disgusting."

"Jefferey." Alicia hushed her husband firmly, knowing that Mick and Helen were already missing the old collie that they'd had to put in kennels for the duration of the holiday. "Live and let live, okay? Dogs are part of the canal life. And I quite like them. At least there are no horrible brats about."

Having helped extricate her husband's foot from his mouth, she herself immediately regretted saying that as soon as she looked at Penelope's face. It was true, she wasn't a children person, but she was pleased that their first grandchild would be on the way soon.

"I'm sorry, Penelope."

"Don't worry about it." her daughter replied. "And I agree with you anyway. Although, I'm sure I'll take a different tack when sprog appears."

"Dogs and sprogs, eh!" Mick laughed. "The Marmite categories. Why don't we move onto politics now and really tighten up the atmosphere?"

"Or," Steve volunteered mischievously. "we could have a round-table discussion about what we're going to call the first of the next generation when it appears. I was thinking, if it's a boy, perhaps, G-Nigel? Or G-Norma, if it's a girl?"

Jefferey gave in to the inevitable and let them carry on. The beer was good and the sum of that and the food and the location were enough to offset his being the butt of their jokes. It would come around to him soon. He'd look forward to that time.

It was late afternoon when they returned to the boat. Common sense said that they should simply stay moored up here. In fact, all the crew bar Jefferey made the same suggestion. But the schedule was the schedule and it wouldn't do to deviate from it so early on.

"Besides," he told them. "it's only a short hop to the next stop. You guys relax and carry on with the drinking. I'll take her from here."

Fewer moored boats meant that Jefferey could finally pick up a bit of speed, but he knew they were only a mile or so from their next stop, so he didn't have to push it. Had the weather stayed faithful, things might have panned out differently. Sadly, an early-evening shower changed the dynamic of the day. And indeed, of the holiday.

Doggedly refusing to give in to a little bit of rain, Jefferey approached Norbury Junction soaked to the skin and shivering. He knew that this was a spot where he had to slow down and he knew that that was what he should do, but he was bone-chillingly wet and extremely frustrated at being forced to stand in the rain whilst the others were clearly enjoying something of a party inside the boat's warm cabin. He pushed the throttle a little past tick-over. Then some more. Then just a tad more.

"Oy!" the shout from the bank shocked him. "Slow down you prat. Tick-over past moored boats. You'll have us all over the place."

He should have apologised and slowed down. He didn't. Why? Well, partly because of who he was, but more because of who the other person was. He knew their type well enough. He knew what the dreadlocks meant and he knew how much trouble that type had caused him in some of the projects he'd worked on.

"It's raining." he shouted back, "I'm awfully sorry, but I need to crack on."

"I don't care how awfully sorry you are. Just slow down. And forget the rain, God made you waterproof."

By that time, the boat was heading away from the shouting stranger, so Jefferey felt confident enough to impart a farewell.

"We're off now, Tinker Man. Why don't you smarten yourself up and get yourself a job, you Water Gypsy? I don't take orders from a numpty like you."

The crew heard the altercation and looked outside at the guy who was shaking his fist at the boat. He did look a bit rough. His boat didn't look much better. It was typical of Jefferey to upset people, but maybe this guy was making too much of it. When he'd gone from view and they felt the boat slow noticeably, they carried on with the impromptu game of cards that they'd started.

Whilst the holidaying crew resumed their game, the occupant of the well-shaken boat, Terry Bottomley, set about planning one of his own. He saw the same thing day in and day out and, maybe it was because Jefferey was who he was, or maybe because he'd had enough of his boat being tossed and swayed by inconsiderate others, he decided to act. He'd thought about the best course of action before, but it had never been as perfectly set up as it was now.

Mungo, Terry's dog, an elderly Staffordshire Bull Terrier, had long ago ceased barking at the people who raced past and caused his sleep to be interrupted. Still, he remained a dog and as such, shared his master's emotions to some degree. Terry reassured him that things were alright, giving him a cheese biscuit and settling him back on his bed. With the dog settled, Terry made a call and waited for the visitor who he knew would arrive shortly. Some things were given priority these days.

That visitor came and went and Terry smiled to himself as he heard the distant sound of the car negotiating the tight road that led away from moorings. It had been easy. Maybe a little too easy. He hadn't told an untruth, not really. That would have been wrong. He may have been guilty of spinning things a certain way, but hey, didn't everyone do that these days?

"Time for a bit of a celebration." he told himself and Mungo. "A little of my finest blend."

He retrieved a tightly sealed jar from the top of his kitchen shelves and began to unscrew the lid. He breathed deeply as the smell escaped. It was a jar that his visitor might well have taken a keen interest in, had it not been labelled in such a way as to divert suspicion. This was where he kept his stash of the purest marijuana he'd ever been able to source, and tonight was a night for it to do its stuff. His neighbours were all back in the comfort of their terrestrial dwellings. Not that they minded him having a bit of smoke every now and then. Their absence added to the peace and quiet now that the sun was setting on a calm evening. A perfect evening to smoke and count the stars. The joint was long and well made. He kept it going for a good half-hour, sitting in his favourite spot in the cratch of the boat, from where, he could see the nothingness that surrounded his home on the water. He was calm now. Calm and satisfied and pleased with himself. But one thing could make it even better. He stumbled into the boat and retrieved the small baggy that held his latest creation. He'd not tried this before, but tonight seemed just the night to do so.

Chapter Seven:

The hire boat had long since scraped itself to a halt on the bank and been carefully moored by Jefferey who had then proceeded to stomp into the boat, ignoring the rest of the crew, and grab a quick shower before changing into dry clothes. The incident with the other boat had wound him up badly and it was an hour before his other family members had begun to help him relax. They encouraged him to see the funnier side of it. With a few glasses of whisky, he'd begun to side with them.

He even joined in their card game for a while, until realising that their alcohol consumption was making it too easy for him and that neither Mick, Helen, nor Steve had retained any interest in winning. Still, it was nice to be settled in the warm and cosy cabin, enjoying the company and the break from the numerous hidden worries that his business plagued him with.

The others struggled on until tiredness overtook them and they'd took themselves to bed, leaving only Jefferey and Alicia alone.

"I suppose it could have gone a lot worse." Jefferey put his arm around his wife and stretched his legs until they rested on the opposite bench seat. "The forecast didn't mention anything about rain. Maybe that was what annoyed me most. I mean, what's the point of weather forecasts if they can't be accurate?"

"Jefferey, darling," Alicia responded to the arm that held her by nuzzling closer to her husband. "You set too much store by things like that. The weather will be what the weather will be. I know you two have differences, but you could learn a little from Mick. Okay, his relaxed attitude to life may be just a little *too* relaxed, but it doesn't seem to cause him much harm. As he's prone to say, 'Get on wi' it'."

Jeffery chuckled at his wife's imitation of Mick. He didn't want to be instructed in life by the father of their daughter's preferred mate, but maybe there was something in what Alicia was saying. Of course, it was leaders like him who helped the less aggressive have a better standard of living, but you had to admit that, just sometimes, it did make sense to just get on with things.

"How about …" he whispered to Alicia. "…you and I have a little bit of bedroom fun? It's been a while and I feel it might just help me to chill out a little? What says my darling wife?"

"I say," she whispered back to him. "that that is a splendid idea. Come on then stud, whisk me off to paradise."

Tired as they both were, despite it only being nine the evening, the promise of a stolen moment of union, long absent in their busy lives, helped them shake off their drowsiness as they tidied a little of the evenings debris away before heading towards their cabin, giggling like school children. Their giggling stopped abruptly when they heard the knock at the door and the visitor who had recently left Terry's boat came calling at their own.

"What the hell!" Jefferey replaced passion with righteous indignation. "If that's that tinker, I'll jolly well give him another piece of my mind."

It wasn't. It was a uniformed police officer who introduced himself as PC James Cartwright before waving his warrant card at Jefferey and demanding access.

"Is everything okay?", Alicia asked him as he settled on the couch next to them.

"I'm afraid,", he explained, "we've had reports of quite a serious offence having been committed. An offence against a certain Terrance Bottomley who lives on the moorings at Norbury."

"Oh, for goodness sake!" Jefferey interrupted. "That's ridiculous. Yes, I went past him a little too fast, but that's not a criminal offence. And certainly not a serious one."

"It's not the speeding that's the issue." the officer remained calm as he resumed. "Although I'm glad that you recognise your own breach of the waterway's rules. No, it's the language that you used. As it stands, Mr Bottomley has accused you of a very serious hate crime. You called him, according to his testimony, a 'Tinker' and a 'Gypsy'. And then you proceeded to use the 'N-word'. Ring any bells?"

"You are joking, right? Yes, I called him a tinker and yes, I said he was a water gypsy, but I did not call him a nigger. He wasn't even that much of a darky as far as I could tell. If he washed we'd know better. If anything, he was more of a Paki."

"Sir." Cartwright stopped Jefferey with a hand. "Can I please advise you that your reaction is not helping. This is the twenty-first century. You simply can't use words like that. The n-word is extremely provocative and your language just now implies a lot of guilt to me. Things aren't as they used to be. These are very serious offences. I'm sure that you have heard of hate crimes. In essence, your language and the tone of your comments might be cause for a charge of assault under new legislation. Now, I need to take a full statement from you before we proceed."

That statement took over an hour to put together. The police officer made it very clear to the Williams' that the seriousness of the offence should be recognised by his attending so soon after the offence had taken place. He was a local bobby, aware of a number of other incidents that needed investigating, but also aware of the priority given to certain categories of crime by his superiors. Jefferey calmed down and played the game, but all he wanted was for the day to be over.

"The way things stand now." Cartwright rose to leave. "Is that we have left it with Mr Bottomley to decide whether he wants to press charges. Or, more precisely, Doctor

Bottomley, given that he has a PhD in Applied Biochemistry and a number of lucrative patents to his name."

"Doctor Bottomley?" Jefferey couldn't resist snorting with derision.

"Yes, Sir, Doctor Bottomley. Seems you may have let his appearance lead you to a premature conclusion. First impressions aren't always accurate. In fact, since retiring from his university post, I think we can safely say that he is happily settled and enjoying an income that all of us would be happy to have. He has acceded to our request to give it a few days before he decides whether to press charges, so, I think you owe him a little respect. Meanwhile, may I suggest that you think about your own conduct and try to make some concessions to how things have changed. These are sensitive times and hate crime is looked on very dimly by the judiciary. I'll bid you goodnight."

Alicia knew better than to try and appease her husband, so she left him with a large whisky and retreated to bed. That whisky became two, then three, each one larger. As the booze flowed so did Jefferey's self-pity. He wasn't that bad a person, was he? He wasn't really a man who hated? Things were difficult enough with work and trying to make this holiday a success. Why did these things have to happen?

Just before midnight, he sighed heavily and took himself off to bed. It hadn't been a great day, but at least they had kept on schedule. That was some consolation.

Week One

Day Three, Monday:

Norbury to Market Drayton.

Chapter Eight:

It was one in the morning and Jefferey Williams, fated Captain of the good ship Harriet Knot, hadn't slept a wink. Worse than that, he was beginning to sober up. Alcohol was a great alternative to sleeping pills, but it had its limitations. The injustice of what had happened to him and the anger that he couldn't dispel against the person of Terry Bottomley, Doctor or not, was more than enough to offset the soporific touch of a single malt. He didn't regret speeding past the boat. After all, they had a schedule to stick to. Nor did he regret his outburst. Whatever happened to freedom of speech? No wonder the snowflake generation was flourishing. They were only words. Since when did they become a crime?

"It's no good." he hissed to himself as he flung the covers aside and slipped out of the bed and into the boat's galley. "I can't let it rest. I need to show that ignorant pikey just what I'm made of."

Throwing on his clothes, he opened the fridge and retrieved the remainder of the breakfast sausages that had been carefully wrapped in foil by Helen. Putting them in his pocket, he grabbed a torch, tied his newly-purchased, and as yet unused, boots securely to his feet and left the boat. If his calculation was right, that the boat had been moving at a brisk walking pace, then Bottomley's boat should only be fifteen minutes away at most. He'd go there, give him a piece of his mind, then be back by two at the latest. You had to act sometimes or people just walked over you. The sort of people whom Bottomley represented simply weren't used to being stood up to. They thought they had the Holy Grail of modern living in their New Age mumbo jumbo, but the world wasn't like that.

The rain had left the towpath muddy. Several times Jefferey lost his footing in the dark and slipped and skidded onto his backside, the mud, grass and worst of all, dog faeces ruining the new trousers that he wore. Deciding to try for a drier route, he clambered over a barbed wire fence and into an adjacent field which offered at least a degree of footing where the farmer had left the hay-like stalks of his latest crop. He ripped his trousers on the way into the field. He ripped his favourite shirt on the way back out. Each tear and each new stain he picked up added to his righteous indignation.

Drawing parallel with the good doctor's boat, he stopped and considered his options. He'd seen the discrete white boxes on the bridge that led over to the moorings and he'd seen the CCTV warning signs that accompanied them. He could try and pick a way past their span of vision, or he could look for an alternative approach. Seeing the shadow of Bottomley sitting there on the front of the boat and seeing the small dinghy tied up near to his own feet, he made the decision to cross that way. A trip across, a good talking to and a rapid departure. What could go wrong?

Well, for one thing, the dinghy was attached to a boat that was between owners and was therefore not a craft that was well maintained. It had been used as a supplementary waste storage depot by the people who'd owned her before and that meant that her floor was thick with stale refuge, pools of leaked oil and diesel and a mix of dank stagnant water and fallen foliage. Jefferey was fired up enough to ignore all of that, although he stepped into the vessel very carefully before pushing it off towards his destination.

The push that he'd given it, combined with the stillness of the water, meant that he slid silently across the width of canal without having to give it any extra impetus. That was a relief. He was struggling enough to stay upright as it was. To have had to reach into the cut and propel the boat with his hand might just have been too much for his balance. The dinghy steered itself towards the stern of Bottomley's boat. Arriving at that point, Jefferey tied it up and used the bigger boat's protruding rudder as a step to help himself get on board. As he approached the door, he heard the dog snuffling about inside. He'd seen it only briefly and it didn't seem to be too much of a threat. Besides, he had the sausages.

"Open up in there." he shouted as he banged on the door.

Nothing.

"I said, open up." he repeated, knocking harder this time.

Nothing.

He was about to shout again when he had an idea. He pulled at the half-sized doors that he'd been knocking on and they opened up for him. He smiled as he stepped aboard and looked into the confused face of Mungo.

"Hello, little fellow." he whispered. "Nothing to be afraid of. I've just come to see your master. Here, how about a little treat?"

The dog took the proffered piece of sausage and demolished it. He begged for more but Jefferey shooed him away as he stepped further into the boat.

"I say, are you listening? I want a word with you, young man. Come here and show yourself."

Waiting in the kitchen and not quite sure where to go from here, Jefferey took a moment to look around at his surroundings. The place was smarter inside than out, but it was still no palace. Functional would be the word he'd use to describe it. Everything neatly stacked and tidied away, labelled and …

"Hello, what do we have here?" he reached for the jar marked 'Rat Poison', and the idea came quickly and demandingly.

"You want to sleep?" he asked the unresponsive owner of the boat. "Then so be it. But you'll wake up to a bit of heartache, I'm afraid. That'll teach you to try and have me arrested."

He found a small bowl and added a little water before breaking up and mashing the sausages into it. Then he tipped a liberal sprinkling of the strange-smelling powder into the bowl and presented it to the dog.

"Sweet dreams." he said as he put the bowl down.

The dog devoured the bowl of food in minutes. Jefferey knew that he shouldn't, but he stayed to watch as the hound's eyes stopped registering their panting pleasure and became hollow and glassy. Confused, the dog tried to make a sound, dribbled and coughed a little, then keeled over.

"Got your attention yet?" Jefferey shouted, making his way to the front of the boat. "Want to come and see what real vengeance looks like?"

Still no reply. Not even as he stepped through the doors and into the bow of the boat where Terry Bottomley sat upright against the cratch-cover, the joint still in his hand and a candle almost burnt away on the table in front of him.

"I might have known." Jefferey snorted. "Your sort are always high on some sort of Ganga-Smack, aren't you? Too weak to face the world so you drop your e's and smoke your whizz and dope yourselves up on all kinds of weird concoctions. Well, you'll have a surprise when you come down. When you see what your negligence did to your buddy. You'll think you left that tin too near to him. That's it! You'll blame yourself. Perfect!"

He prodded Bottomley on the shoulder, then slapped his face lightly. Still no response.

"Well, I want to be here when you see your dead buddy, so wake up, I say, wake up now."

Throwing caution to the wind, Jefferey pushed and poked and prodded the unresponsive man, keen to have him know that he'd been there. He slapped his face again, kicked him a couple of times, then gave him a hefty push on the chest. The last proved too much for the decaying canvas of the cratch-cover which was unable to bear any more pressure and gave way with a slow ripping sound. As it ripped, Terry Bottomley stirred not a jot but simply fell slowly backwards whilst Jefferey Williams looked on in horror as his protagonist tipped past the point of no return and into the canal. The silence of the evening was broken by the splash of Doctor Bottomley hitting the water.

Chapter Nine:

For only the second time in his life, as dirty canal water enveloped the unresponsive form that it welcomed with ease, Jefferey Williams felt that sickening slow-motion helplessness that science simply can't explain. The first time had been when he'd hit a patch of black ice and headed towards, and collided with, a telegraph pole, writing off the day-old company car that he'd boasted about only hours before. This time, it was different. He'd watched his arms reaching out to the fast-disappearing form on the boat, willing them to move faster but knowing, deep down, that he was too late. The sound of the body sliding into the water stopped him in his tracks. He hadn't planned on this. Revenge was one thing. A dog was just a dog, but murder? Which left him with no other option than to follow Bottomley into the cut, where he now floundered as silently as he could, reaching around in the dark for some appendage of the man.

That appendage proved to be a leg, which he pulled towards him, ignoring the numbing chill of the water as he let his hands move up towards Bottomley's arms, which he grasped with relief. When the doctor's head emerged from the water, brown from the sludge it had been dragged through, but otherwise unscathed, he slapped it and shook it but received no response.

"Bugger it!" was the only thing that he could think to say as he dragged the lifeless body to the side of the canal and hauled himself out of the water. He hated to do it and, truth be told, he had no idea really how it should be done, but he tried mouth-to-mouth anyway. He tried for as long as he could, battering at Bottomley's chest with some feint recollection of that being the correct thing to do. It didn't take him long to realise that his efforts were in vain. He had to try another tack.

Checking that the whole scenario remained between just the two of them, Jefferey Williams began to form a plan. Some people would have had the courage to confess. Others might have simply left the body in the water and made a swift exit. Having been visited by the police and having not made a good first impression, he decided on a third way. Bottomley wasn't due to report back to the police for a few days. He wouldn't be missed for at least that time and the silence of his dog wasn't unusual, given its response when he'd boarded the boat. The body would be the giveaway. Ergo, hiding the body made an awful lot of sense at that point.

The dinghy was still tied up to the boat and it was a simple process to bring it around to where the corpse lay. Transferring the body from solid ground to the less-stable craft was no easy process and on two occasions Bottomley returned to the water, from whence, Jefferey repeated his failed rescue attempt. Eventually, the corpse lay in the bottom of the dinghy and, with a sigh of relief, the weary accidental-murderer entered the filthy cut for a final time and pulled the craft after him. On the towpath side, with the dinghy tied back to its rightful place, Bottomley was removed and deposited in a heap amongst the brambles and overgrown grass.

Jefferey Williams took the opportunity at this point to take a breather. He'd never felt so cold in his life, nor had he ever felt so dirty. Every part of him was soaked and layered with a mixture of filth, diesel and oil. His skin stung with the pain of the numerous scratches and bruises that his excursion had ravaged his body with. The next stage of his plan would be the most exhausting, but, with a clear goal ahead, he felt the surge of adrenalin he needed to make it happen. There was a wheelbarrow propped against a nearby boat that showed no sign of its having been used in recent times. Retrieving this and cursing the squeak of its wheel, he lifted the corpse into its belly and set off back home.

An hour later, as the chimes of a distant church clock rang out four times, Jeffery Williams's task was complete and he returned to the warmth of the hire boat that he was beginning to regret being coerced onto. His ruined clothes were in a carrier bag on the deck. If he woke anyone with the shower then his alibi was that he'd nipped out to take the air and fallen in the canal. The crew slept through however and he slipped into bed beside his wife, praying that sleep would come and that when he woke up, he'd find out it was all a dream.

That waking wouldn't be for another few hours. He continued to sleep through the sound of Mick singing his heart out as he showered and shaved, and he slept through the less-tuneful retching and vomiting that marked Penelope's waking. And he slept through the smells of breakfast as they wafted around the boat.

"What happened to those sausages?" Mick asked as he emptied the ingredients for his signature 'Bubble and Squeak Special' from the fridge, the omelette special not having satisfied his hunger. "I'm sure we kept a few back from yesterday."

"Maybe Jefferey had them." Alicia muttered as she plonked herself on the sofa. "He was up late last night. Heaven knows what he was doing."

"Whatever it was," Steve joined the assembled crew, having been out on deck having a cigarette to cleanse his olfactory system of Penelope's morning-sickness. "he made a right mess doing it. Have you seen that bag of his clothes on the deck?"

"Aye." Mick laughed. "I was going to ask about them. I thought they'd been dumped on us by a passing tramp until I recognised Jeff's clobber. Anyone brave enough to wake him for an explanation?"

Nobody was. And, to be fair, breakfast was a much more relaxed affair without him there to share his worldly wisdom. They let him sleep and took their time as they looked out of the windows at the morning shower that had put paid to their early start.

"Hope it clears up soon." Steve offered with a smile. "We don't want to get behind schedule now, do we? Plans are there to be followed. Any deviation from the strict timetable will have serious consequences."

"And that just won't do." Mick joined in with a fairly accurate imitation of Jefferey's voice that caused Penelope to smile but her mother to look away in scorn "Ship-shape and Bristol fashion. That's the ticket. One simply cannot allow the inclement weather to impede on one's agenda."

"I'm glad you think it's funny." Alicia sighed. "You want to try living with him."

"He's not so bad." Helen replied. "And at least he's taking things·a little bit seriously. You two boys should be ashamed of yourselves. Every ship needs its Captain and I'm glad that neither of you are in charge. We'd never make it past the first pub!"

"Oh yeah?" Mick took offence at the comment, coming so soon after he'd treated them to his special breakfast. "Then we'll show you. Come on, Steve, let's get this baby moving. It's only a short hop today. I think we can handle that."

"Aye, aye, temporary-skipper. Let's do the required checks and set sail. Ladies, please excuse us."

Chapter Ten:

With the rain showing no signs of letting up, the female crew members opted to remain indoors whilst Mick and Steve, suitably swathed in the waterproofs supplied by the hire company, cast off and navigated towards Market Drayton. It was, as they'd said, only a short journey that they were embarking on, although there was a lock flight that Jefferey had calculated at one hour and fifteen minutes. The original plan being that Market Drayton had enough going for it to make it worth a longer stop, not least of which was the local brewery with its attached pub.

Despite the soaking they were getting, father and son were thoroughly enjoying the freedom of being able to drive the boat without a certain pair of eyes constantly supervising, and a certain pair of hands adjusting their tiller movements.

"Oh, the freedom of it all!" Mick chuckled as he handed the steering back to Steve. "Go on lad, do your worst."

"I suppose he'll be up and about by the time we hit the locks." Steve sighed. "But, for now, let's get this baby cruising. Too early for a drop of the amber stuff?"

"Not at all." Mick reached into one of the lockers on the deck and retrieved two cans of lager, opening them and passing one to his son.

"Cheers." Steve said as he drank the mixture of ice cold beer and surprisingly warm rain.

"Here's to the A-Team." Mick replied. "And sod the rest of them."

"Don't be too harsh on him, Dad. He tries his best and he treats Penelope really well. He can't help being like he is."

"No, I suppose not. He's just not like us, is he? He lives in some parallel world where the likes of us will always be the lower caste. We need to get him drunk and see what he's like when the guard's down."

"I don't think you do. I've seen it." Steve laughed as he recalled a weekend retreat that he and his wife had enjoyed with Jefferey and Alicia. "She's a proper laugh when she's had a few, but Jeff, well, he starts to loosen up and then he goes all morose. You and I, we're drinkers. We can handle it. He can't. Luckily, the miserable phase only lasts until he's had another couple, then he falls asleep. I told you about the make-up, didn't I?"

Having found out that the best anecdote that he had hadn't been shared with his own father, Steve proceeded to tell him about the last night of their break when Jefferey had succumbed to sleep and the three of them had played a version of strip poker that left them with their clothes on but their target looking very different.

"Every time you lost a hand, you had to apply another touch to Jeff's 'lady-face'. By the time we left him, he was dolled up like a Lime Street tart. We heard the commotion the following morning and poor old Alice had to take it on the chin. He cancelled our scheduled lunch and drove us straight home. Not a word from him the whole journey."

"So, you found a way to shut him up then?"

"Three weeks. No phone call, no texts, no e-mails. Nothing. It was only when Penny had to call him to tell him about the baby that he relented."

"I wish I'd seen that."

"You promise not to tell him?" Steve asked mischievously.

"No, why?"

"Take a look at this."

Passing control back to his father, Steve dried his hands as best he could and fiddled with his phone, bringing up a picture of the decorated Jefferey that caused Mick to choke on his beer and drive the boat into the bank. The phone had disappeared by the time Penelope stuck her head out of the door and asked if everything was okay.

"It's fine love." Mick told her. "Just got a bit out of line and grounded her. We'll be right in a minute. You stay dry inside."

The price they paid for their fun and games was that the jolt to the boat woke Jefferey from his slumbers and cut short any hope they might have had of continuing their relaxed cruising.

"Morning chaps." Jefferey joined them on deck looking very much the worse for wear but hiding it behind a faux-smile. "Top notch work. Well done. Sorry I wasn't able to help you cast off. Had a bit of a wobble last night. Took myself out on deck for a Jimmy Riddle and a smoke in the early hours and somehow lost my footing. Fell in the bloody canal and had a devilish time getting back on board."

Neither of the other men said anything. They were fully aware that any attempt to console Jefferey would only start them laughing. They nodded and stared straight ahead, desperately trying not to catch each other's eye.

"Hair of the dog, eh?" Jefferey pointed to the lager cans. "Think I might join you. Cheers."

With Jefferey surprisingly silent and the rain abating to be replaced by a hint of sunshine, the three men on deck relaxed and let the lager do its work. The lengthy leg of the journey was over as they finished a second can each, but the hard work was now on them.

"I'll cruise her, if you don't mind." Jefferey told them. "Some of these locks are a bit tight and the run-offs can catch you out, so I hear. I'll steer her in whilst you can prep the locks. You okay with what I told you about them? Think of it like a bathtub. Empty it first with the bottom paddles, then open the gates. Remember to put the plug in, close the paddles, when you've shut the gates, and then you turn the taps, the top paddles on. But these are down locks, so they're a lot easier. Give me the thumbs up when you're ready to drop the paddles and ..."

Mick and Steve only heard half of the instructions. They jumped off the boat at the first opportunity, each carrying a windlass, and walked up to the first lock. It was already set so they only had to open the gates and watch as their revered Captain bounced and bumped his way into the chamber.

"You playing pinball there?" Mick shouted, only to see Steve give him a dirty glance.

"It's how their designed." Jefferey's voice echoed back to them. "Even the experts tap the walls on occasion."

"Aye, they might," whispered Mick. "but there's a difference between a tap and your medley of destruction!"

Of course, unbeknownst to the rest of the crew, there were reasons why Jefferey, despite his failing, was keen not to bounce the boat about too much. The additional passenger that they now carried might surface at any time.

"Whoaahh!!" the skipper shouted as Mick and Steve raced to see who could get their paddle open first. "You wait for my thumbs up."

Neither men replied. The boat was safely kissing the front gates and they knew enough to know that it would take itself down and all they need to do was make sure that it didn't get stuck on anything. The likelihood of which was zero, given the huge fender on the bow.

They worked through the flight of five locks in little over an hour. By the time they were on the last one, the three men were working as a team. Their wives, now on the sun-drenched front deck, raised glasses of wine to them and offered encouragement which was only partially sarcastic. Jefferey had time to think about the events of the early morning and began to consider how he could possibly extricate himself from the hole he'd dug. He hadn't really had any option, short of confessing and facing the consequences, other than the route he'd taken. Bottomley, or, more precisely, the corpse of Bottomley, was now tied underneath the boat by short lengths of rope that were only visible as an extension to the fenders that hung down. Strict protocol dictated that those fenders be lifted when locking, but he'd convinced the crew that such a step was unnecessary. He hoped it would remain so.

Chapter Eleven:

"Come on lads." The Captain of the Harriet Knot shouted as they were finishing off in the last lock. "Close those gates and let's head to the pub."

Mick was struggling with the safety catch that was holding his paddle up, trying to free it from the ratchet that it was attached to in order to complete the process. Steve went across to help him and the two eventually freed it up and made their way to the boat.

"They only put those on for the amateurs." Jefferey advised them in his most knowledgeable tone. "You can leave the catch off and it all moves a lot more easily. Quieter too."

Neither Mick nor Steve chose to respond. They opened a beer each and let Jefferey take the helm as they cruised towards Market Drayton. They sensed something a little off with him that morning. More so than usual. But they put that down to his having had a rough night. Maybe it was just the tiredness, but he seemed more worried than they'd ever known him to be.

"Everything okay, Jeff?" Mick asked as Steve left them to join the ladies. "Anything I can help with?"

"I'm fine. Although '*Jefferey*' would help."

"Sorry for breathing!" Mick held his hands up and went to join the others.

Market Drayton would give Jefferey time to think. Their schedule was loose enough that they could hang on there if necessary. He'd find an excuse for them to do so and use the time to work on a more permanent solution to the problem of the corpse, the urgency of which became more apparent as the boat crested through Bridge No.61 and lost forward motion. Those on the front deck were helpless to do anything as the tiller refused to obey its operator's instructions and the boat cruised into the bank.

"Damn!" muttered Jefferey, knowing immediately what the problem was and the implications it carried.

"You all right, love?" Helen poked her head over the roof and shouted to Jefferey.

"Fine, fine." he replied. "Something around the weed-hatch. You guys stay there and I'll clear it."

"You sure?"

"Yes, leave it with me. Two minutes and we'll be on our way."

It was possible that this was just an unfortunate coincidence, and not unusual with bridge holes, but Jefferey didn't want anybody there if it was what he truly suspected it was. And what it proved to be. The propeller was snagged on flesh and bone that would have been repulsive to any other observer but which was merely an inconvenience to Jefferey. He retrieved one of the dog waste bags that had been supplied by the hire company and quickly slipped Bottomley's hand into it. The corpse must have snagged on something and the hand been torn off. Knowing that the ropes had been attached at elbow and knee reassured Jefferey that this didn't spell total disaster. He sealed the bag and threw it deep into the undergrowth.

Ten minutes after stopping, they were on their way again and almost as soon as they'd started, they were pulling into the visitor moorings at Market Drayton and Jefferey had tied the vessel up, noting that its hidden cargo remained as safe as it could be. The six of them headed to the town and enjoyed a relaxed pub crawl that took them into the early evening. The food at the newly revamped Joule's brewery was stunning. The brand having been revived, the new owners had supplemented the brewing business with a purpose-built restaurant and visitor centre. Set close in the bounds of the rest of the decaying town, it was a positive success story for the area and attracted visitors from afar. Market Drayton needed as much help as it could get: the canal was being developed in line with the general gentrification of the waterways, but the high street was as brokenly-British as any.

Stumbling a little from the effects of one too many of the fine Joule's offerings, they'd navigated through the town and managed to stock up on all the groceries that they'd needed. To their surprise, amongst the neglected and failing businesses, they'd even discovered a few independent shops offering very nice homemade goods, the best of which was the obligatory gingerbread man that made the town famous.

"Aye, love. Market Drayton offers no escape for some. He can run, run as fast as he can, but they'll catch him here, that gingerbread man."

Alicia ignored Mick's comments, whilst Helen shut him up with that deadly look that he'd never been able to counter.

The shopping trip completed, their plans for the evening were centred on catching up on sleep. Steve and Penelope watched a film on their laptop, Mick and Helen caught up on their favourite soap and Alicia played solitaire to the accompaniment of a bottle of Chardonnay. Jefferey retired to bed early and was just dropping off when there was a knock on the side of the boat.

Once again, Jefferey felt that sickening feeling in his stomach. A feeling that grew as he clambered out of bed and was greeted by a familiar face.

"Good evening, Sir," PC James Cartwright extended a hand. "Sorry to disturb you again."

"What now?" Jefferey muttered as he reached for the glass of wine that Alicia handed him.

"And how did you track us down? You following us?"

"Nothing so conspiratorial, I'm afraid." Cartwright beckoned Jeffery to sit opposite him on the dinette table. "The hire company have GPS trackers on these craft, so we knew where you were. Please, relax, this is very much a courtesy visit."

"Go on."

"Well, ordinarily, this would be something that we would deal with by telephone, but my Chief Constable has asked me to handle it personally. I believe that you and he are acquainted?"

Jefferey simply nodded, remembering the text he'd sent to Sir George Travis, with whom he regularly played golf.

"Hence my being here." Cartwright continued. "And, as I say, it's to set your mind at rest."

"Really?", Jefferey wondered where this was going.

"You see, we now know a little bit more about Doctor Terence Bottomley and things seem to have taken an unusual turn since your altercation with him. In brief, we received a tip-off from an anonymous source earlier this morning. It informed us that Dr Bottomley was dead on his boat and that we should attend. Fortunately, the character who tipped us off, a certain Thomas Stern, isn't the brightest of operatives. He hid his phone number but we soon tracked down the mobile and, whilst officers attended the boat, I went to see him. Apparently, he and Bottomley were working together to develop some new drugs. Bottomley supplied the brains, Stern, the premises. It was there that I caught up with him and he confessed all. He'd called on Bottomley just after I'd left and found his dog laid out lifelessly on the kitchen floor. The man himself, he found slumped at the front of the boat. He checked his pulse and knew that he was dead, and he knew why when he saw the little plastic pouch that had contained their latest creation. That was the reason that Stern was visiting, to tell Bottomley that their new drug had killed a number of their lab specimens and that he shouldn't try it. Too late, it seems. He fled from the scene and made the call in the early hours of this morning, not wishing his friend to rot away where he was. There remains just one problem though."

"Which is?"

"The officers that attended the boat saw the dog in the galley, dead as a doornail after disturbing a tin of rat poison and eating the contents. But, there was no sign of Bottomley. Our suspicion, based on a large tear in the cratch cover, is that he fell through and into the canal, most likely because Stern had pushed the body against the canvas. It must have given way sometime between his visit and our arrival. We've had teams out dredging, but so far, they've found nothing."

PC Cartwright cradled a freshly-brewed cup of coffee as he discussed some of the finer points of the operation to search the waterways for the missing corpse. Divers would begin their work tomorrow, whilst as many of the local force as they could muster were planning on walking the towpaths until later that night.

"He can't have gone far. And the water's not that deep. Besides, the urgency has faded a little given what we know of the man. I shouldn't really say it, but we do have to prioritise in our work. He'll turn up, but it's all a little odd. If it wasn't so tragic, it might even be one of those things we look back on with a wry smile in the future."

"How very, very strange." Alicia said, grabbing her husband's hand gently. "But a pleasing vindication of you, darling. Seems you weren't so far off the mark with that man. What a shame about the dog though."

"Please, Alicia," Jefferey affected a manner that he didn't feel. "let's not forget that a man has died. Nobody deserves that. I'm sorry."

"You've nothing to be sorry for, Sir." Cartwright smiled as he spoke, "And as for the dog, well, you can set your mind at rest on that score. The officers searching the boat were scared out of their wits when the dog started moving. It seems that the rat poison container only had supplies of Bottomley's cannabis in it. The 'Rat Poison' was a simple but effective way of hiding what the tin contained. The dog was simply stoned. It's recovered now and on its way to a rescue centre. And of course, you have nothing to be worried about. We shan't be proceeding with any action against you and Bottomley's complaint will not progress any further. I trust that gives you closure and that you'll enjoy the rest of your holiday."

As the constable rose to leave, Jefferey wished him well and made a mental note to thank his golfing buddy for a prompt response. He felt a degree of elation at discovering that he hadn't in fact killed Bottomley. That feeling was tempered by a more pressing concern though. What to do with the Doctor's corpse, now strapped to the underbelly of the boat.

Week One

Day Four, Tuesday:

Market Drayton

Chapter Twelve:

The problem was always going to be the locks at Tyrley. That was the thought that accompanied Jefferey Williams as he drifted off to sleep, and the same thought that woke him early the following morning. It was just about feasible that a corpse could float a considerable distance, especially with the locks flowing towards Market Drayton. It was much, much less feasible that that same corpse could somehow work its way down through a flight of five locks. The improbability of that happening was compounded by the unusual layout of the locks which were tightly packed together and which began with a boater's facilities block. Granted, there was a sluice off to the side. That much was evident from the pictures that Jefferey was able to access on his phone. But that sluice was regularly maintained by a resident lock keeper who was unlikely to miss Bottomley's passage past his home. Even if that happened, their remained four other locks that the corpse would have to slip past unnoticed.

With a sigh of regret, Jefferey realised that the only option open to him was to get what was left of Doctor Bottomley into the water above the locks, but how? His first thought had been to take a taxi back to Norbury, hire a day boat, and transport the body back that way. A brief search of the internet soon put paid to that idea as the boat yard's website had a 'Navigation Closure' notice slapped firmly across its home page. The police and the Canal and River Trust were working as quickly as they could to drag the canal for Bottomley's body, but it was expected to be something that would take them until the rest of the week. That slow progress was the only thing that offered any hope. They wouldn't get to the locks for a few days, which brought him some time, but didn't solve the immediate problem.

Stumped, and admitting that fact to himself, Jefferey woke Alicia with a strong cup of coffee and confessed what he'd done. At first, before the coffee hit home, her response was sleepy and useless. When she realised that her husband wasn't joking, she made him retell the whole story again, her mind struggling with both the situation and the need to find a satisfactory solution.

"You're a daft sod." she said as Jefferey fell silent. "You really do get yourself into some stupid situations, don't you? You can't just let things lie like other people. Your pride simply won't let you walk away without getting the upper hand again. Well, this time, it seems that Bottomley had the last laugh. I should ring that nice Constable and tell him what you've done. You and your arrogant vanity ruining another holiday and here we are, floating above a rotting corpse. Thanks a million for that!"

"I'm sorry." Jefferey pleaded. "I know it shouldn't have gone this far, but I panicked. Please, can you think of a solution? I can't go to the police, you know that. For us?"

Alicia passed her empty coffee cup to her husband and nodded to indicate that she wanted a refill. It was just coming up to six a.m. and she'd never been a morning person, but she had enough experience of handling Jefferey's occasional crises that the early hour didn't prevent her coming up with some sort of an answer.

"I'll ask Helen to keep the others occupied for the day." she explained. "I'll tell them that you're having a bit of a tough time and you need a day to relax. Penelope's the only problem. She won't be able to walk far, but that might work in our favour."

"But where would they go?"

"Well, it won't be cheap, but I think I know. Michael and Stephen were raving about Ironbridge earlier, saying that they wouldn't mind checking the place out. We looked on the map but it's way too far, and we don't get any nearer to it on the canal. I'll tell them it's our treat and we'll send them in a taxi. The men can explore the museums, whilst Penelope and Helen relax in the town. I can swing it, I'm sure."

"Okay," Jefferey replied. "but that doesn't solve the bigger problem. It's fine that the others are out of the way, but what do we do about our friend?"

"You brought the collapsible trolley, didn't you?"

"Yes."

"Well, we'll start with that."

As expected, Mick and Steve were delighted about the excursion that was planned, although Helen took a lot of persuading, given the expense that it would put Alicia and Jefferey to. The taxi journey would be eighty pounds each way. To Helen, that was a week's disposable income for her and Mick. They weren't used to such extravagance.

"It's mummy and daddy's treat." Penelope came to the rescue after a brief conversation with Alicia who pleaded with her to ask no questions but help them out. "I like the idea and it looks like it's going to be a lovely day, so we'll take a picnic as well. Let's do it."

"She's right, love." Mick told his wife. "Never look a gift horse in the mouth and all that. If they want to treat us, I'm up for it."

"And," he lowered his voice so only Helen could hear him. "It'll be a Jefferey-free day for us."

That seemed to settle it and the crew duly departed for their day out. Which left a very nervous Jefferey and a surprisingly calm Alicia to tackle the task ahead. Her plan wasn't fool-proof. In fact, it had so many holes in it that, if it were proposed as a plotline in a novel, it would be instantly dismissed. This was real life though, and they had to take the chance.

Chapter Thirteen:

The trolley which formed a key part of Alicia's proposed plan had been put on the boat at the last minute, having been retrieved from the boot of the car after the lengthy delays that awaited the arrival of the boat yard's own equipment. As a collapsible unit, taking it with them seemed a sensible option as it would be perfect for loading groceries onto and it took up very little space in its folded form. It was the trolley that Alicia had brought to help her move all manner of heavy items across the livery yard where she kept a pair of bay geldings. When she'd first arrived with the trolley, a number of the younger people on the yard had decided that it would be fun to take trips in it, so she knew it was up to the present task. All they had to do was load the cargo.

"You're going to have to go in." she told her husband. "I'll keep an eye for passers-by and if anyone asks, you dropped your wallet in the water and you're trying to retrieve it."

Jefferey did as he was told, getting used now to the chill and filth of the water. Prior to climbing in, he'd released all the ropes that held the corpse under the boat and had trailed one down the side to where he would be pretending to seek his lost wallet. The body slipped towards him smoothly with only a little help needed to free Bottomley's dreadlocks from the propeller. The trickiest operation now lay ahead of them.

"Okay," Alicia whispered. "When these cyclists go past, we should be clear. You'll have to climb out, grab the ropes and heave him in. I'll hold the trolley."

Dripping and half-naked, Jefferey dismissed any thought of hesitation and, struggling with the weight of the load, heaved Bottomley out of the cut and into the trolley at the first attempt. He folded the body into a foetal position before Alicia covered it in a layer of logs, purchased hastily from the small marina nearby. Aside from the sight of a soaking wet man in shorts, the scene didn't look anywhere near as bizarre as it actually was. Catching the eye of a pair of walkers who appeared from under the bridge, Jefferey waved his wet wallet in the air and smiled. They seemed to understand what he was so happy about. Either that, or they were simply being polite as they rushed past him. This was, after all, the quintessence of England: one didn't like to interfere and it was usually best to simply look the other way.

The walk to the locks was a fairly short one of only a mile. The heavy trolley slowed them down, occasionally veering off track as it struggled with its excess load, but the image worked perfectly. Those few people who were on the towpath saw only a couple carrying a trolley full of logs to their boat. They didn't seem out of place at all and they were helped by the fact that there was little traffic on the canal due to the closure. A few boats passed them, on their way to mooring below the locks and awaiting their reopening, but most seemed to have stopped in the town. The only problem they faced was an over-eager Spaniel that sensed fresh meat under the logs. Its owner was apologetic as it howled and scrabbled at the trolley. Alicia and Jefferey made some excuse about the logs having been urinated on by another dog. It seemed to do the trick.

With all hands having been seconded to search the canal further past the locks, the facilities block at the top-lock was deserted. Only two boats were moored further along, but neither was occupied. Which was just perfect as it provided a safe resting place for the Doctor and one which wouldn't be discovered until later in the week.

"I'm not going in again." Jefferey told Alicia. "We'll stuff him under one of these boats and hope he stays in place."

Alicia agreed and they manhandled the body out of the trolley, removing any remaining ropes that had been tied to it before easing it into the gap between the two moored boats. It wasn't the likeliest place that a corpse would drift into, but it would be found and the relief of the searchers would allay any suspicions that they might have. However unlikely, its final resting place was just about possible.

"I don't want this with us anymore," Alicia pointed to the empty trolley. "Not now I know what it's been used for. We'll ditch it in the skips."

Piling the logs onto one of the moored boats, Jefferey spent a good ten minutes attacking the trolley to make it look like it had broken. It was very well made and took the two of them to bend one of its main supports by jumping on it. Now useless, it wouldn't look out of place in the rubbish compound where they left it. That done, they walked slowly back towards the town.

The others returned to the boat in the late afternoon. In their absence, Jefferey had taken himself to bed, caught up on sleep and woken up to a long refreshing shower, whilst Alicia had tackled the crime thriller that she'd packed at the last minute. Despite it being a rattling good tale, featuring her favourite characters, her enjoyment was tempered somewhat by the memories it stirred of manhandling Bottomley's corpse. Death and deception were fine on the page. They were less pleasurable in real life.

"Make yourselves decent." Mick roared as he clambered aboard the boat. "You've had your rumpy-pumpy time now."

"Michael." Helen hissed as she followed him. "Will you behave yourself. You're like an over-excited schoolboy."

"You have a good time?", Alicia asked.

"Brilliant." Mick replied. "Quite a way to go, but well worth it. I'll tell you more once we get these opened up."

He waved a bag that rattled with the sound of the bottles of beer he'd brought as a thank-you for the Williams' gesture. Not that either of them would partake. Afternoon was gin and tonic time, which Alicia duly made for herself and Jeff, not skimping on the gin, as Mick poured the beers for himself and Steve.

"Sorry, Mummy." Penelope smiled. "The champagne didn't make it back."

"You need to be careful in your condition."

"Oh, one little drink what harm little he/she/it. It needs to understand that it's a Williams anyway. We're all one-part alcohol at least."

"Don't worry, love." Mick plonked himself down next to Alicia. "We made sure she only had one small sip. The taxi driver was brilliant. He let us sup the bottle as he drove."

"At the price he charged, I'd expect that." Jefferey joined the crew.

"Aye up, here he is." Mick taunted. "Smiler Jeff, the cheery Captain. You two get up to much while we were away? You look a bit tired there. Shagged out even. Eh?"

"You're a very crude man, Michael. We had an extremely pleasant day thank you and I found it nice and restful. Quiet, one might say."

"I'm sorry." Helen passed Jefferey his drink. "He could do with an afternoon nap-nap himself. Thanks for treating us, we had a lovely day."

"You missed all the best stuff though." Steve settled himself in the remaining space. "Cakes and tea and boutique shopping aren't really what Ironbridge is about. Man, you should see the museums there. It brings it right home to you how much the industrial revolution did for the world and how it all started in such a simple way."

"We had a lovely time though, didn't we Helen?" Penelope ignored the jibes.

"We did, love, thank you. It was a lovely day all around. I hope it hasn't put us off schedule though, Jefferey?"

"Not at all, not at all. I'd allowed for a certain degree of flexibility in my plans and we'll be back on track tomorrow. I know it's early days yet, but a bit of a break from the rigours of cruising seemed to be just what the doctor ordered."

Nobody noticed the twitch that accompanied his statement, bringing back, as it did, a memory of another doctor and the inconvenience that he'd caused.

"I expect you'll all be ready for supper?" Alicia asked.

"I will be when it's bedtime." Mick laughed, "But I'm definitely ready for my tea now."

"That would be lovely." Helen kicked her husband. "Can I help, at all?"

"No, that's fine, I've just put together something of a cold collation. Hope that's okay."

Mick wanted to say something but the look he got from Helen was the same look that he'd been scared of since before they married. That look silenced him every time. For a short while at least.

Chapter Fourteen:

The evening meal, whether dinner, tea or supper, depending on which of the crew you asked, was consumed in relative silence, aided by copious quantities of alcohol and only slightly marred by the double-act that was Mick and Steve. The others ignored their querying the absence of iceberg lettuce and its replacement by "a bunch of weeds". Nobody rose to the suggestion that "this ham seems off" which accompanied Mick's waving a piece of Parma ham in the air. Only once did Jefferey feel that he had to respond when the two of them started a conversation between two prawns, replete with head and shell, that he knew it had taken his wife a long time to source and prepare.

"I suppose you think they should be in a little glass bowl with sauce on?" he asked Mick. "But these are how they should be served and very nice they are too. Perhaps a little more adventurousness in the dining department might open your eyes somewhat?"

"Of course, Jefferey.", Mick bowed his head in mock shame, "And you're so right about the sauce. I'm only a humble working-class boy with my dirty hands and dirty mind. Please, feel free to enlighten us on this journey with the delights of nouvelle cuisine, but I should warn you, I'll always think of food as something to be eaten, not to be looked at."

Penelope could feel a hint of tension stirring, so took herself off to bed after eating, the day's activities finally catching up on her. She still had a while to go until junior popped out, but was finding it challenging already. Not that she complained. It was just an annoyance.

"Rummy?" Alicia asked Helen, who readily agreed and cleared the table ready for the game.

"Not for me." Jefferey told them. "I want to make a start on my book, if that's okay. Been looking forward to it since we first boarded."

"Me neither." Mick added, waving a gift-shop paper bag at her. "I've got my own little tome to work through. Picked it up at the museum. A history of the industrial revolution and the engines that powered it."

"Sounds a bit heavy." Jefferey snorted. "Hope it has a lot of pictures."

"Only as heavy as yours. What's that you've got there?"

"Don Quixote. It's something of a classic in literature. One of those works that one simply has to add to one's reading list. A little heavy for some, I'd say, but worth the effort. I'd offer to lend it to you, but I'm not sure it's quite you."

"Good luck with it." Mick opened his own book, "I'm happy with this one thanks. Besides, I don't need reminding that I'm more Sancho than Don. Steve might be up for a borrow though. Hey, lad?"

"Not on holiday." Steve replied, smiling as he saw the confused look on Jefferey's face. "A bit too heavy for me. I'm going brain-dead for this whole fortnight and doing puzzles. Penelope introduced me to them. A bit tacky but they're good fun."

"I'm surprised at Penelope." Jefferey said. "Wouldn't have thought that was her thing."

"She's not all finishing school you know? She does let her hair down at times."

"Besides," Steve continued. "A little humility in self-awareness never hurt anyone. Don't want her tilting at windmills now, do we?"

The comment was lost on Jefferey and would be until he'd moved deeper into Cervantes. Mick got the reference and winked at his son. They'd both read the book several times but neither had the courage to tell their travelling companion.

A sleepy peacefulness filled the boat's cabin as they all settled into their own activities. That peacefulness lasted a good half-hour, a record for Mick and a surprise to his wife and son. It was bound to be broken soon though.

"Here," Mick addressed the room. "It says here that these canal boats that we're on were first designed like this as replicas of the boats used in Bridgewater's mines. Think on that, they built the canals to fit existing boats and we still use the same ones today. Amazing."

That was followed by a brief lecture on how the gauge of railway tracks was directly linked to the axle width of Roman chariots; carts were made to fit the ruts in the roads, and that same measure was used to make railway tracks a certain width. When he moved onto a detailed description of the workings of a blast furnace, it proved too much for the others.

"I'll do the washing up." Jefferey huffed. "No good trying to read when we've got an audiobook playing in the background."

"I think we'll call it a day." Helen added. "And maybe you should bring that book to bed, Mick? I can sleep through the running commentary easily enough."

"I'll give you a hand with the dishes." Steve told Jefferey as the others vacated the room. "I wanted a word with you anyway."

"Sounds intriguing."

"Oh, nothing too serious." Steve replied, "But something that the others don't need to hear."

"Now I'm definitely curious, young man." Jefferey let Steve follow him into the galley where they began the washing-up process.

"I know we're on holiday," Steve began. "But, like you I guess, I still like to keep in touch with work and see what's happening. When we were in the taxi on the way to Ironbridge yesterday, I logged into my work's intranet and scanned through the latest updates on business."

"Very diligent of you." Jefferey passed a dripping plate across.

"You might think so, but Penny wasn't too impressed. She gave me the usual 'you're on holiday' lecture and made me switch my phone off. Which, as a dutiful husband, I did. But not before reading an interesting update memo about 'Tiger Claws'. Something you're familiar with, I believe?"

"Of course. One of our Christmas hits to be. Can't get enough of them into the country and pre-orders are through the roof."

"Which is why the memo seemed strange." Steve replied, stacking the dishes that he'd dried neatly back into the cupboards. "It hinted at a problem with distribution and warned stores to avoid taking any more deposits on them. That's a blow for my own shop. We're the flagship store and we were banking on Tiger Claws to help us hit target. Land of Delight may be the category killer as far as toy shops are concerned, but we still need to have the right product available at the right time. So, what's the story with Tiger Claws? You having problems?"

Jefferey remained silent for an unusually long time. The dishes being finished, he wiped the sink down and waited whilst Steve finished his own duties. Pouring them both a whisky, he beckoned his son-in-law to follow him out onto the deck. There, they watched the sun setting and smoked in silence, Jefferey struggling through one of the small cigars that he'd never really liked but which seemed right for him to enjoy, Steve puffing away on a roll-up.

"Business isn't always cut and dried." Jefferey sought to concoct a satisfactory explanation. "Especially not the sort of business that I run. We source a huge variety of goods, deal with multiple countries to have them manufactured, and then try and co-ordinate the best delivery schedules. The order from Land of Delight is a big one for us. Tiger Claws are widely expected to be the number one must have this Christmas. But yes, we're facing a few delays. The stock's being held up at the port. Nothing unusual, just paperwork, but it's dragging on. I'm sure we'll have it sorted soon. Although, I have to say, it's a bit pre-emptive of your guys to raise such firm doubts."

"That's why I wanted to hear it from you." Steve said. "I've only ever known it once before and that was when Robertson and Co. went bust. You're not struggling at all, are you?"

"If you weren't my son-in-law, I'd ask you to take that back." Jefferey flicked the half-smoked cigar into the canal. "Going bust indeed! I'll tell you, boy, I was making my first million when you were still in nappies. And, at your age, I'd already established Williams of Marylebone as one of the most trusted wholesalers in the country. What have you achieved? You're a store manager for a national chain of toy stores. When my grandchild comes along, you're barely going to be able to afford to keep him in nappies. Penelope should have listened when I advised her that she could have done better for herself. So please, don't lecture me on business."

Steve's first inclination was to throw a heartfelt response back to his aggressor. He wanted to tell him of his impending promotion to Area Manager and of his progress in the Masters he was struggling through with the Open University. He wanted to tell him why he was Penny's first and only choice as a husband, and then go on to share some of the stories that she'd told him about Jefferey's less than perfect parenting skills. Yes, they would find the finances tight when the little one came along, but they would be far from starving. Instead, he put Jefferey's response down to unknown factors and chose to calm the situation.

"I'm sorry you took it like that. No offence intended. It was just unusual, that's all. I wanted to make you aware and see what your take was on it. That's all. Water under the bridge?"

Jefferey took the proffered hand and shook it somewhat reluctantly. The conversation moved onto plans for when the baby was born and, with the whisky hitting the spot, they retired back into the boat feeling more relaxed.

Chapter Fifteen:

Alone in the saloon of the boat, after apologising to Steve for his outburst and wishing him goodnight, Jeffery poured himself another whisky and reflected on the day's events. The success of their morning expedition had been something of a triumph and an opportunity to look forward to the rest of the holiday. Michael had been predictably annoying through supper but in a way that, despite himself, Jefferey was actually beginning to enjoy. Life seemed so simple for him and Helen. They didn't have much. They lived in a small house and earned barely more than a subsistence wage, and they had no social status to speak of. And yet, he'd never known a couple as happy as them. It was their humility that seemed so attractive. That shared philosophy of 'just get on wi' it' had a tempting appeal. It was the simplest of ways of looking at life and yet, it was one that seemed to strip away all the disruptive and diverting social norms that were so much a part of his life. Self-importance ruled the world in which he and Alicia moved. Who you were was measured by what you had. And what you had was never enough.

And Stephen was alright. As down to earth as his parents but with a little more drive to try and improve his lot in life. Retail wasn't something that Jefferey understood in too much detail, but it seemed to be more than just a world of shop assistants and subservient service. Granted, it wasn't a profession as such. Not in Jefferey's eyes, at least. He could spin it with his acquaintances though to make it sound a little more than it was. All in all, he could have done a lot worse for a son-in-law, and, most importantly, Penelope seemed more than content to be with him. Maybe he had been too harsh.

'Don Quixote' beckoned the Captain of the Harriet Knot and he flicked on the small reading light before picking up the immaculately untouched book. Why this particular classic had beckoned him, he wasn't quite sure. It certainly had the kudos of being a work that you wanted to be seen reading but its sheer size was somewhat off-putting. The back cover talked about it being a comedy. Perhaps that had been the attraction. Jefferey had grown up in the era where comedy was dubious British sit-coms and solo performers like Benny Hill. His own parents had drilled into him that this was not their sort of viewing and he'd absorbed that superiority with pleasure. Likewise, The Onedin Line was in and Saturday afternoon wrestling, out. Blue Peter was acceptable but Magpie, due to its not being on the BBC was a little below them. He'd not suffered, he didn't think, by absorbing his parent's values. Nor had Penelope suffered for the upbringing he'd given her. Granted, he could have spent more time with her and been more concerned about her inner peace than her outer image. Maybe, just maybe, with a grandchild on the way, there was an opportunity for Jefferey to discover a more chilled-out part of himself. A part that was able simply to 'get on wi' it'.

And still, Cervantes lay unopened.

It was the peace and quiet that was so unusual. The boat was virtually in a town centre, not far from some busy roads, and yet, it could have been an island alone in the middle of nowhere. Straining to hear just the least confirmation that the world around him hadn't suddenly disappeared, Jefferey was able to catch the occasional rumble of tyres on tarmac and the odd whisper from nature as a late-bird called to its mates.

Refilling his glass from the rapidly-emptying bottle of Glenfiddich, Jeffery set the book aside and leant forward to enjoy the gentle clinking of what remained of the ice that was slowly dissipating. The amber liquid traced teardrops down the sides of the glass which seemed to dance to the tune he was making. Evenings like this were the sort when you drew a line under the past and looked forward to the days to come. The holiday would get better.

Of that, he was sure. He'd try to learn to relax a little and show that he wasn't quite the man they thought he was. Of course, he would need to ensure that things continued in tune with the specified timetable. And he would have to be the voice of reason when the others threw all caution to the wind. But he would try to change, just a little.

Don Quixote now neglected for another day, Jefferey packed the past away in his mind as the gentle hand of the single malt caressed him gently from within. Bottomley was yesterday. Mick was manageable. The Merc was safely locked behind the boat yard's gates. And Alicia was a trophy to be proud of. Why she'd chosen him, he never really understood. They worked well together though and he enjoyed taking her along with him to the round of tedious social functions that were a part of his life. She helped him make the most of them and she sparkled where he stood solidly. All in all, it wasn't that bad.

Then again, the subject of the night's final conversation with Steve was something that threatened to negate the gain he'd made in freeing himself from the curse of the corpse beneath the boat. With one ghost buried, another seemed to haunt him. There *were* problems with Tiger Claws, but they weren't as innocuous as he'd told Steve. The problem was in paying for the shipment. Where the money had gone, Jefferey couldn't quite understand, but gone it had and his own checking up on e-mails earlier that evening hadn't given him any solutions. In fact, his business was barely holding itself together. That was something that he'd have to keep to himself, at least until the holiday was over. Unless, there might be a third way. Maybe the holiday presented an opportunity?

Week One

Day Five, Wednesday:

Market Drayton to Audlem

Chapter Sixteen:

Wednesday's morning briefing took a little longer to complete than had become the norm. There were two reasons for this: firstly, it was a briefing that needed more time, in order that Jefferey could introduce and explain the system that he had planned out as they approached the most 'lock heavy' day of the cruise; the second reason was a factor of that plan and the crew's reaction to it.

With breakfast finished, Captain Williams cleared a space on the table and began to unpack his presentation tools. These consisted of a large schematic diagram of the two flights of locks, carefully numbered and with timings marked against each one. This grand plan was enhanced by the addition of six small Lego characters. The plan itself was greeted with respect by the other crew members, all of whom recognised the time and thought that had gone into it. The introduction of the plastic figures was met with a less respectful outbreak of giggling.

"Bloody hell!" Steve shouted. "Yours is almost life-sized, Dad."

"Never mind that." Mick responded. "Look at you with your builder's hat and high-viz jacket on. You going to break into song with YMCA at any point?"

"I'd better not." he replied, pointing to the spyglass-wielding Admiral who represented Jefferey. "Or Captain Bligh there might make me walk the plank for mutiny."

"They are merely representative." Jefferey huffed as he placed the figures carefully at the top of the drawing of the lock flight. "And they were all I could find at short notice. Now, if the kindergarten outburst has finished, may I please continue?"

Helen and Penelope were on best behaviour and the looks they gave their husbands ensured that silence followed Jefferey's question.

"Good," he continued. "Now listen carefully. We have two lock flights to tackle today. They are here and here."

Muted giggles were somehow restrained as Jefferey extended a pointing stick and used it to illustrate his talk.

"This first, the beginning of the Adderley Locks, is one of only five. A useful way to start our adventures and something of a warm-up for later in the day. As per the other locks we have completed so far, and, as per my careful planning of the best way to navigate this ring, they are all down locks. That means they are easier to manage and we should make good progress through them. Provided, we work as a team."

"Leaving our current location at nine o'clock promptly," he continued. "we should arrive at the first lock by o-ten-hundred-hours. The usual allowance for each lock is fifteen to twenty minutes, however, if we follow my system, I believe that we can get this down to ten or less. So, please listen carefully to your duties."

Positioning the toy characters carefully on his plan, the assembled crew were given a run-through of the role they each had to play. One that saw them move gracefully from lock to lock, some bringing the boat through, whilst others prepped the locks ahead. Despite wanting desperately to interrupt, Mick and Steve remained attentive, deliberately avoiding each other's glances. When the model of Alicia fell over and into the canal, it was a step too far for one of them.

"You shouldn't have had that morning gin and tonic, Alice! Here, let me see if I can help." Mick picked the figure up and, using his own avatar, pretended to give it the kiss of life.

"Do you mind." Jefferey glared at Mick as he snatched the figurines back. "And can you please be so kind as to not molest my wife's figure."

"I should be so ..." a hefty kick under the table from Helen shut her husband up.

"The teams that I have decided will work best." Jefferey tried to control the meeting again. "Is to have Penelope and I together as navigators and co-ordinators. Penelope, in her condition, is best suited to steering the boat, whilst I would prefer to be able to oversee things."

"No surprise there." Steve muttered.

"Now, that leaves the four of you and I thought it would be rather fun if you worked as boy and girl. Stephen, you work with your mum, and Michael, despite your previous crudity, you and Alicia will make up the other crew working the locks. Agreed?"

"I'm not sure about driving the boat." Penelope said cautiously, knowing that changing her father's mind was like turning black to white. "Perhaps Helen might be a better choice?"

"Nonsense, sweetheart. You'll do fine. And remember, I'll be there to help you. Now, if that's agreed, we can move to the rest of the plan. The 'Big One' as I like to refer to it. Or 'Lockus Horribilis', if you prefer."

The anticipated laughter failed to materialise in the pause that Jefferey gave it. Ignoring that Philistine reaction, he clarified the witticism. "The Audlem Flight. A daunting fifteen locks in total and something I want us to do in record time."

"God forbid that we relax." Alicia whispered to Helen who put a calming hand on her shoulder.

"An hour through the Adderley Flight puts us at eleven a.m., with a short jaunt of fifteen minutes or so seeing us arriving at Coxbank Bridge and the first of the main flight by eleven-fifteen."

"Cock spank?" Steve asked in a matter-of-fact way.

"Yes, Coxbank, what's the problem?"

"Okay, so Cock Spank it is. You having that Dad?"

"Not at the moment son, but if I play my cards right with Alicia, who knows!"

"Michael Roberts, you behave yourself!" Helen turned on her husband. "Do not encourage your son and stop being so crude. None of us want to hear it and we're getting pretty sick of it."

"Please." she addressed Jefferey. "Ignore them and continue."

"Snacks and nibbles will be consumed en-route, meaning that we can continue uninterrupted to the end of the flight and do so by two-thirty latest. Okay?"

"That's good." Mick winked at Steve as he spoke. "Because I have a dentist appointment at that time."

"I'm sorry."

"Two-thirty. I have a dentist's appointment."

"And you wonder why nobody is laughing." Jefferey started to pack away the plan. "Maybe it's because you're not funny."

Sadly, although being one of the oldest and corniest of jokes, it was one that none of the others could resist. As Jefferey finished tidying his plan away, they all dispersed before he could hear their uncontrollable laughter.

Despite their reticence to be ordered about by their self-appointed Captain, the crew of the Harriet Knot were all dutifully assembled for departure only fifteen minutes later than the plan had called for. Not much of a deviation from schedule, but more than enough to set Jefferey flapping as first one boat, and then another had slipped slowly past them.

"You see what happens when plans aren't followed?" he muttered under his breath to Alicia who was the only one brave enough to join him as he cast the boat off. "Every boat that passes us will be in the lock ahead of us and will put us farther and farther behind schedule. Give people an inch and they take a mile. I'm trying my damnedest here but getting no support. Can you please control the others?"

"Jefferey.", Alicia turned away from her husband and clambered back into the boat. "Shut-up. Please. Just shut-up."

With nobody to hear him, but with the venom of the words running off his unflappable exterior, Jefferey followed his wife's orders by default. No other boats had passed and he was happily guiding the boat along, enjoying the peace of the morning and feeling quietly confident that his planning would bear fruit.

Meanwhile, inside the boat, the laughter continued, morphing into a plan of action that was both very silly and extremely childish. Just the sort of thing, in fact, that the crew needed to help them cope with the anticipated stresses of the day ahead. The plan became a reality and, with no fanfare to announce his arrival, Mick Roberts emerged onto the deck of the boat just as it pulled up at the first of the five locks at Adderley.

"Dr Roberts reporting for duty." he shouted to Jefferey, who simply looked in silent astonishment at the man who stood before him.

Chapter Seventeen:

It had been Mick's idea initially, but only Helen urged caution as everybody else got on board with it. They'd cobbled together whatever they could from within the boat, raiding cupboards and drawers to find what they needed, and had used their improvised findings to make the transformation. With the Lego figurine as their template, Mick had sat patiently whilst they'd transformed him into a living likeness of the plastic character that had been his avatar at the Captain's presentation. His hair was locked solidly into a black mass thanks to some boot polish and the application of copious quantities of hairspray. From the neck down, a white t-shirt and a pair of plain white shorts had been tackled with a magic marker until every line and detail had been replicated. He was now the lab-coated, stethoscope carrying, identity-tagged Lego Doctor, miraculously brought to life and ready to do as instructed.

"For goodness sake." Jefferey finally managed to speak. "Will nobody take this seriously? I suppose you're all in on this?"

"In on what, Sir?" Alicia jumped out onto the deck and stood next to Mick, her own appearance as changed as his. "Sorry I'm late Sir, please don't spank me!"

Her schoolgirl voice was in keeping with her own transformation into the pigtailed youngster that had been her own figure on Jefferey's plan. Her face was dotted with freckles, her hair sticking out in a faux-plastic manner, and her uniform consisting of a gingham shirt, borrowed from Penelope, and an A-line skirt that had been pieced together from assorted useful items. It was held rigid by coat-hanger wire. The effect worked and Mick and Alicia shuffled around the deck with stiff movements as they watched Jefferey pull the boat in towards the first lock mooring.

"What do you want me to say?" he asked them as he looked ahead at the couple of boats which were in front of them in the queue. "I don't get how you can see this all as a joke. What will others boaters think of us? Are those outfits safe to be doing locks in? It's all one big joke to you isn't it? Well, I'm sorry, I don't get it."

"Don't say anything else, Jefferey." Helen stepped out of the boat and gave him a despairing smile. Fortunately, she and Stephen had been more sensible and conciliatory and had chosen to appear smartly dressed in their 'crew' t-shirts. "It's just the way Mick is. Besides, they'll be suffering for it by the end of the day."

"You simply can't get the staff, can you?" Stephen put an arm around his father-in-law's shoulder. "Still, we'll make sure they pull their weight at the locks."

What with the potential hour's delay that the boats in front presented and the behaviour of the rest of the family, Jefferey could have been excused for having really gone off on one. Almost as if it was simply too much for him to comprehend, his reaction was much more mooted and he simply passed windlasses to the locking teams before settling on deck with Penelope to await their turn.

"You're not angry are you, Daddy?" she asked him.

"No ... not angry," he sighed. "just despairing. I am trying my best you know."

"I know. And it's going well so far. G and T?"

"Why not?"

When Penelope returned with the drinks, she sat next to her father as he watched the boat's crew see the next boat through the lock. Fortunately, the sun was shining and there were as many boats travelling towards them as there were in front. Locking promised to be strenuous but smooth that day.

"You shouldn't take it personally." Penelope told her dad. "You know what Mick and Steve are like. There's no malice in what they do, its just, well … it's their way of living and grabbing as much fun out of life as possible."

"And that makes me the boring stick-in-the-mud?" Jefferey asked his daughter.

"No. No way. You're not boring. Just different. But you could try and ease off on the arrogance a little. This is a holiday after all."

Jefferey thought about his daughter's words as he untied the boat and manoeuvred it into the first lock chamber, taking extra care to concentrate on a smooth entry rather than the sort of bounce and bang that was guaranteed to draw an unwelcome response.

"You know there are times when I'm jealous of Michael and Stephen, don't you?" he asked his daughter as they began to descend. "I'm the one with the fancy cars and the nice house and the holiday villa, but I look at them and they seem so happy and carefree, despite their having none of that stuff. I'd like to be more like them, that's why I sometimes come across as being aloof. I just don't know how to do it. And, when I do think I've grasped the idea, as with the crew t-shirts, I'm not sure whether I'm not making myself seem even more stupid. Trust me, I do try."

"Oh, Daddy." Penelope held her father's hand. "You're great just as you are. Really, I mean it. Yes, you're more serious than them, but you have every right to be. You're under so many pressures and those pressures have given mummy and me so many good things in life. We're not as close as we should be, that's true. But that doesn't mean I don't love you as you are."

"My own parents were very cold. That may explain some things. We never hugged or talked about emotional stuff. I guess that rubs off on you when you're a kid. I tried with you as best I could but I had to be away on business so much. It's not too late is it?"

"Of course not. And when baby arrives, you can use that as an excuse to break the cycle. But you can still be you. I wouldn't have you any other way. The others are great to be with and Steve's family is wonderful, but they'll always be Steve's family to me. I'm happy with the family I was born into. Besides, just every now and then, they really can be a bit too much. Just do what I do. Ignore them! Now, another drink?"

By the time they'd reached the bottom of the Adderley flight, the alcohol, the sunshine and the company had softened Jefferey up enough that he felt that he could begin to enjoy the rest of the day. The sight of his wife and Mick acting the fools and walking from lock to lock with stiff legs and affected mannerisms no longer wound him up. Nor did the way that Stephen and Helen diligently went about their business with a carefree nonchalance and a ready word for all the people they met. He was Jefferey. He was what he was and didn't need to change. Well, not too much.

"I prescribe a good strong whisky." Doctor Mick told his teammate as they skipped together away from the last lock to re-join the boat. "Two shots to be taken every half-hour."

"But Doctor." Alicia replied. "I'm far too young for that. Are you sure you know what you're doing?"

They stopped talking as they boarded the boat, smiling at Jefferey and wondering at the genuine smile that they received in return.

"It's too hot for this lark." Mick said as he slipped into the cabin. "I'll be out in a minute. You coming Miss Williams?"

The presence of Helen and Steve on the stern deck was enough to distract Jeffery from any jealous thoughts. His natural feeling would normally be to worry about his wife's flirtatiousness, but he felt himself able to override that feeling and simply look on it all as being a bit of harmless fun.

"That went better than expected." he told the two remaining crew members. "At the risk of sounding patronising, well done. You all did a good job."

"It was good fun." Helen replied. "Although you seem to be ahead of us on the drinking. I'll have a swift one myself and then make some lunch. Steve?"

"Beer please." he replied before turning to his father-in-law. "Smooth on your part as well. I don't fancy driving in and out of the locks. Penelope okay with it all?"

"We were fine. Had a really enjoyable time. You seemed to meet a lot of people out there."

"Honestly, it's been the best part of the holiday. Of course, dad and Alice threatened to show us up, but it was an interesting way to strike up conversations with others. The guy two boats ahead is an ex-submariner and the tales he was telling us. Whilst the boat behind him is full of yanks. They can't believe this whole canal lark. Mind you, with half our crew dressed as they were, I'm not surprised."

"I don't know how you can befriend people so easily."

"I wouldn't say it was befriending. It's just realising that you're stuck with a stranger for a few minutes so you may as well get to know them. We all move on and that's that. Ships that pass in the night. Well, narrowboats I suppose. And, in the day. Good fun though."

Chapter Eighteen:

Piles of sandwiches and increasing quantities of alcohol were hastily consumed on deck as the boat cruised towards the top of the Audlem flight. Mick and Alicia were now cleaned up and dressed sensibly in their own crew t-shirts. The number of locks ahead was being faced with apprehension, but the promise of a pub at the end was all the incentive the crew needed. On top of which, any time pressures had been negated by the busyness of the cut that day, with a steady stream of boats passing on their way back towards Norbury, and a neatly spaced-out group of boats following each other towards the first Audlem lock. You *could* theoretically overtake the boats in front, but nobody did. As hard as you might try, you simply couldn't rush the waterways and anyway, you'd only meet at the next lock and be ostracised by the other crews. No, slow and steady was the order of the day. A pace that simply cried out to be made the most of.

Jefferey surprised himself by staying on the towpath and holding the boat with the centre-line, rather than tying up and sitting on the deck. Doing this meant that he could engage with the boats either side of him and that was his pet project for the day - he'd try and do what came so naturally to the rest of the family. He'd try and engage in conversations with strangers.

Of those boats, only one was a natural focal point for Jefferey's attention. It was the boat that was being crewed by a family from Boston who were on their third canal holiday in as many years. Jefferey had experience with Americans and had travelled there often. That was a good starting point.

"Not quite the wide expanses of water you're used to." he ventured.

"Hell, no.", the crew member of the American's boat replied. "This ain't even a drainage ditch where we come from."

"You from Boston? I recognise the accent."

"Spot on. You know it?"

And so, the first handful of locks were accompanied by one of those unique and transitory bonding moments that canal boat holidays uniquely create. Jefferey talked about his time in their city. Karl, the skipper of the other boat, talked in glowing terms about his love for England and all things English. Europe was discussed and settled. Immigration was raised and segued by Jefferey who played that subject very cautiously. Then it was onto the canals and the experiences that the Boston crew had enjoyed over the years. It was a perfect conversation for Jefferey at that moment. It helped him to understand how easy it was to make a stranger a friend and it helped him to see his own small, humble place, even on the waterways. Here was someone who lived thousands of miles away and yet, they had a deeper and more extensive knowledge of the canals than Jefferey had been able to garner from his extensive reading.

"The others seem to be working well together." Karl nodded towards his crew and 'The Wilberts'.

"You're right. Makes it easy for us."

"And is that your first one?" Karl pointed to the bulky and prostrate form of Penelope who was lying down for a rest on one of the boats sofas.

"Penelope? Oh, yes. First and only one. We wanted more, but, well, it didn't happen."

"No. The lump!"

"Oh, of course." Jefferey laughed. "Yep, my first grandchild. Hoping it's a boy but I don't really mind."

"Got six myself." Karl replied. "Previous marriages and all that. Heck, it makes you feel old sometimes, but I wouldn't have it any other way. Next step, Great Grandad. Not really looking forward to that."

Which took the conversation onto family and who was who on both boat's crews. Memories of bringing up children and anecdotes about weddings and shared experiences filled up the time between locks and soon the end of the flight was in sight.

Behind them at every lock, just arriving as one of them was heading away, a rough and ready old Springer, crewed by a solitary young man who seemed to have a cigarette perpetually hanging from his lip, puffed and smoked its way to the rear of Jefferey's own boat. It wasn't until the seventh lock that the young lad wandered over and tried to engage his fellow boater in some banter. Beside the fact that Jefferey could barely understand a word that he was saying, to have sought that particular person to be a buddy was, for him, a step too far. He answered what he understood to be any questions politely but made it very clear that he was happy enough to wait until he caught up with the other boat before continuing his attempt at being gregarious.

"Okay." the young guy shrugged his shoulders. "Just being friendly. I'll let you crack on."

"Thank you." Jefferey replied coolly. "I'm not really sure we'd have too much to talk about."

Taking little offence, the other boater returned to his own spluttering relic, from where he began a shouted conversation with the boat that had now pulled behind him. Jefferey was sure he caught the odd reference to himself, but the rest of what they were discussing was lost to the breeze. We were all different, but some were just that too much other to be engaged with. He knew that type quite well. A little like Bottomley in fact. A thought that made him even keener to avoid any conversation. Each to their own and all that, but really, should someone like that be allowed to keep a dog?

At lock number ten, with the pub and the end of the day's journey in sight, Jefferey casually eased the boat into another chamber, being even more cautious now since Penelope's nap was turning into a full snooze. He was relaxed, enjoying himself and confident that he was making a good show of the whole boating affair. A long sip of gin and tonic accompanied the closing of the gates and Jefferey leant casually on the tiller as his crew began to drop the paddles.

"Get forward!" a shout from behind him grabbed Jefferey's attention. He looked behind to see the young lad from the tatty boat waving his arms and running towards the lock.

"Young man." Jefferey shouted back at him. "I will position myself where I feel it best and I am not going to push and shove against the lower gates whilst my daughter is sleeping."

"The cill." the lad pointed as he neared the boat. "You'll catch the cill."

"I'm perfectly okay …" Jefferey's reply was interrupted by the grinding sound of metal on stone and the boat beginning to tilt precariously forward. Not knowing what was going on, he froze where he was leaning against the tiller arm that was, fortunately, resting horizontally across the stern of the boat.

"Drop your paddles!" the young lad shouted to the crew at the front of the lock. "Now!"

Whilst he was shouting this, he whipped his own windlass out of his belt and began to open the top paddles of the lock as fast as he could. Looking up, he saw that his instructions had been followed by the others and was happy that disaster had been averted.

"Sorry about the water, mate." he shouted down to Jefferey, who by now was facing the full onslaught of water that was pouring out of the upper gate and all over the stern deck.

"What are you doing?! I'm getting soaked."

"I'm saving your bacon, that's what."

By that time, Helen and Alicia had joined the young lad and were thanking him profusely. The realisation of what had happened, had dawned on Jefferey now and he could only look down at his wet clothes with embarrassment. He'd not gone far enough forward and had caught the cill at the back of the lock. Had the young guy not corrected the situation as he did, their holiday would very likely had ended with a sunken boat.

Penelope had been woken up by the noise and the banging. She joined her father on the deck and managed to coax him inside to change. She smiled and waved a thank you to the lad who'd helped them out, then waited as the crew organised everything and got them back on the way. She managed the lock fine, but as she was leaving the chamber, the engine began to make a very strange sound, just as the power faded and plumes of white smoke pumped out of the exhaust. Calmly, she killed the engine and let the boat drift to the moorings that preceded the next lock. Stephen pulled the boat in by the proffered rope and the team gathered beside the vessel to take stock of things.

"Typical." Jefferey snorted as he emerged on deck in dry clothes. "Just typical. I might have known I wouldn't be allowed just one uneventful day. I'll call the hire company and get them out here. I'll give them a piece of my mind, believe me."

"Just hold on, Jeff." Mick tried to calm the situation.

"It's Jefferey!" was his reward for being nice.

"Alright, Jefferey, just hold on. You'd be best to take yourself back inside and take a chill pill. Stephen and I will have a look at this."

"Like that will do anything."

"I'm a bloody diesel mechanic!" Mick couldn't help but shout. "I'm not just your poor relation. Now, bugger off or you and I are going to come to blows."

Helen and Alicia managed to steer Jefferey away from the boat and they took an arm each as they walked away to the nearby pub. Meanwhile, Mick called across to a boat moored on the other side of the pound from where a set of tools was borrowed.

"You know what it is?" Mick asked his son.

"Pretty obvious, I'd say." Steve replied. "Water in the diesel."

"Spot on. And no surprise given the soaking the deck got. Come on then, pass me those spanners and we'll sort her out."

Jefferey was finishing his second drink when the boat passed them by on the water. Having bled the engine, drained the sump and returned the tools they'd borrowed, the job had been completed in less than half an hour. There should have been a triumphant look on the face of Mick and Steve as they cruised past. Instead, they chose simply to ignore the man who couldn't help but wind them up.

The locks were completed shortly after and the boat moored up for the night. The proposed trip to The Shroppie Fly pub for food was changed to a meal on the boat followed by Jefferey taking himself onto the bow deck with the classic novel that he was still struggling to begin. Helen stayed with him as the others decided to adjourn to the pub anyway. Penelope and Alicia left Mick and Steve at around ten pm. What time those two returned to the boat was not something either of them remembered. All they knew was they'd had a damned good time, drunk far more than was good for them and been welcomed by the locals with open arms. Although mostly forgotten, due to the alcohol, they'd be reminded of the events of that night later in the holiday and in a way that neither of them expected.

Week One

Day Six, Thursday:

Audlem to Nantwich

Chapter Nineteen:

There was a definite and palpable tension surrounding the crew as they cruised the very short distance from Audlem to their next planned stop in Nantwich. Jefferey had opted for an early start, ignoring the other family members who stayed inside and had a light breakfast, speaking in whispered tones that occasionally generated a conspiratorial chuckle, loud enough for him to hear over the engine. At the two Hack Green locks, he accepted a cup of tea, which he drank as Alicia and Steve saw him through them. Once their duties had been completed, they settled back down inside the boat, leaving him alone with his thoughts.

The original plan, according to the comprehensively-detailed schedule he'd prepared, had been for the six of them to enjoy a full day out together in one of the largest towns that they would pass on their journey. Granted, Nantwich was no metropolis, but there was still enough to do. Those plans were now abandoned, both mentally and physically. Hack Green Secret Nuclear Bunker was to have been the thrilling start to them, but that was now receding into the distance. With the planned stop there abandoned, it was easy enough for Jefferey to let the rest go as well.

"I try my damnedest to make this holiday enjoyable," he thought to himself. "and all I get is idiocy, complaints, criticism and rejection. Well, sod them. They can fend for themselves today."

Besides, the minor problems that yesterday's cruise had thrown their way were nothing compared to those with his business. They weren't insurmountable, not yet at least, but they seemed to get just that little bit worse every time he heard the ping of his phone and received a new e-mail. He'd use the day to sort things out. The others could do what they wanted but they'd do it without him. He had to get things back on track and that meant making a number of difficult calls.

The silence that accompanied Jefferey as he navigated the boat towards Nantwich helped him to plan his best course of action. That same silence within the cabin of the boat was helping the other crew members to slowly thaw the icy atmosphere that none of them was enjoying, but which all of them endured as a necessary period of reflection. Only one member was missing from the party. His absence, a likely contributor to the silence that remained until the boat clunked against the concrete moorings that rose above Nantwich town centre.

It was the mooring process, accompanied by the clinking of metal rings that Jefferey made no effort to mute as he tied the boat up, that finally woke Michael Roberts up. It had been a late night and a heavy night too. Still, despite the hangover, he seemed to remember that he'd had a good time.

"Ay up, everyone!" Mick stood before the others in just a pair of crumped boxer shorts. "When's the funeral?"

"Sorry?" Alicia tried to keep her eyes on anything other than Mick's aged torso and the threat that the boxers presented to reveal more than she wanted to see.

"Somebody's died, haven't they?" Mick looked around at the others. "Either that, or you're all being a bunch of miserable sods. Come on. Let's forget about Lord Jefferey and move on."

"I heard that." Jefferey poked his head into the cabin. "And you can all forget about me today. Do whatever you want. I've had enough."

Mick chose not to rise to the comment but excused himself and disappeared into the bathroom, from where, the sound of him singing as he performed his ablutions couldn't help but cheer the other crew-members up.

"So, what happened to the bunker?" he asked as he emerged shortly after. "I had that down as one of the highlights of the trip."

"Michael." Helen gave her husband the withering look that he'd become so accustomed to after many years of marriage. "Aside from the fact that yesterday's events are best forgotten soon, and the fact that you would have been in no fit state to even walk the short distance to the bunker, our esteemed Captain has changed our plans for us. You'll have to drive down and visit it sometime."

"Sod that for a game of soldiers." He replied. "I'm going anyway. I'll walk it. Steve, you up for it?"

"I am if you are." Steve replied. "But I'm amazed you think you can get there after the amount you put away last night."

"A quick pie and a pint of hair of the dog and I'll be right as rain. Was it a good night?"

"Oh, it was entertaining." His son laughed as he remembered. "I gave up matching you pint for pint early on. Besides, the cabaret was far more fun than the booze. Once it starts coming back to you, you'll know what I mean."

"But yeah," he continued. "I'm up for the bunker. That all right with you Penny?"

Nobody objected to the plan and father and son headed off the boat and into the town to find the nearest pub. Steve held back on most of the details until after they'd eaten. As they began the couple of miles walk to the bunker, he enjoyed sharing a more comprehensive account of events.

Jefferey ignored the others as he made himself a sandwich which he took onto the stern deck, eating it as he watched the gently unfolding activity of the canal. As he washed it down with a glass of lager, his wife and daughter arrived on deck and informed him that they would be out until early evening, baby shopping first, followed by a relaxing swim at the leisure centre. He let them go without bothering to reply.

"Are you planning anything?" he asked Helen as he put his plate and glass in the washing up bowl.

"Not today. I'm happy to sit here and read. I might do some knitting as well. It'll be nice to have a day off."

He told her that he had a lot of work to catch up on and apologised that he'd need to take the dining table for that purpose. Helen simply shrugged and made her way to the bow deck, book in hand, double gin and tonic begun and sun-hat firmly in place to shade her from the day's worst. She wasn't the sort of person to nurture grudges, nor did she overthink the vagaries of the individual personalities of the people her life put her in contact with. People were people. Some you could get along with easily. Others were a little harder to live with. Jefferey wasn't a bad man. Sure, he and Alicia lived their life in a very different sphere to her own, but they were all simply flawed human beings just the same, struggling to labour through life and eke out any joy that was to be had in whatever way they could. Jefferey was just a twerp. She could live with that.

The book that she was keen to make progress on was soon put aside in favour of her knitting, partly because she was struggling to concentrate on it, given the tensions that still cast their shadows over the boat, but mainly because of the constant interruptions by passers-by. The book would always be there. The strangers who greeted her and stopped to chat were a one-off. She could talk to them whilst knitting and doing so enabled her to block out the sound of Jefferey's phone calls and the clatter of his laptop's keyboard. Besides, she missed Herbert, currently begging as much affection as he could in the kennels that he so enjoyed visiting, and most of the people who passed the boat did so with at least one dog in tow.

Chapter Twenty:

The moorings at Nantwich were well-maintained and offered a solid and clean towpath, one that was designed to meet the needs of all canal users, not just those on boats. With the sunshine came the walkers. And with that same sunshine, the boaters were happy to escape the heat of their tin-shell homes and see who else was around. Of course, there were also cyclists. Any good towpath attracted the new breed of Lycra-clad fanatics, sitting astride bikes that had cost as much as a small family car. To them, the smooth towpaths became honorary cycle paths. Not a claim that the dog-walkers and the boaters were necessarily happy to agree with.

"Eh, slow up mate!" the first of many calls from the boat behind her own had begun the interruptions of the day. "Who do you think you are? Bradley Wiggins?"

Helen had recognised the broad Yorkshire accent and poked her head around the bow of the boat to put a face to the voice.

"Sorry, love." her neighbour apologies when he saw her looking at him. "It's just that I get sick of it sometimes. You'd think we were in a stage of the Tour de France the way some of them go flying by. Still, I've got my methods. Watch this."

Helen leaned further over the side of the boat and watched as the Yorkshireman gathered an assortment of items off his roof. They were everyday boating essentials; paint pots and brushes, some well-used and heavily stained rags, and a couple of long poles that could be used to hold a roller.

"The Waterway's won't let me do more than this." he explained as he placed them at various points along the towpath. "I used to have a couple of bright yellow signs that I stuck in the ground at either end of the boat. They said, 'Slow or Go!', and they had a picture of hand pushing a cyclist into the cut. I got threatened with losing my licence for that. Still, this is just as effective."

"What about the dogs?" Helen asked.

"Nothing to worry about there. The paint in the pots and on the brushes dried off a long time ago!"

Helen smiled as the old guy chuckled and returned to the folding seat that he'd set up in front of his boat.

Next came the gongoozlers. The ones who were attracted to the boats by their otherness, but who still hadn't taken the plunge and given it a go. The knitting and the fact that Helen was in the safe space of a hired boat, changed the cursory greeting into a longer conversation.

"You got a little one on the way?"

"First grandchild," Helen would reply proudly. "Due in a few months."

With that door opened, Helen could continue to add stitches whilst the conversations kept her entertained. The weather was a perennial favourite, closely followed by dogs. Then there was the boat.

"How are you finding it?"

"It's great. A different pace of life and the scenery's wonderful."

At that point, the stranger would either identify themselves as another boater, which took the conversation in one direction, or as a curious passer-by which led to different questions. The details of the conversations would never make a bestseller, but that wasn't what this was all about. These were simple interactions between straightforward people and they were a welcome diversion from the limited conversations between the six family members on the crew. The boaters were as diverse a group as could ever be imagined, some boasting about their expensive and well-equipped vessels, others simply welcoming the hire crew to the water and encouraging them to make the most of it. There were the scary young men who you'd avoid at all costs if you met them on a dark night, but who turned out to be intelligent and friendly and all with an interesting story to tell. Then there were the ones who'd opted to trade bricks and mortar for a floating home. They were doctors, teachers, social workers, bar staff, writers even. In fact, the whole spectrum of life was there to be seen, its only common denominator, the shallow ditch of dirty water that was the basis of their community.

Time passed quickly and Helen felt revitalised and peaceful as the afternoon took its last breaths. She was waving at a passing boat when Jefferey emerged from the main cabin, a beer in one hand and a fresh gin and tonic in the other.

"Peace offering?" he smiled as he passed the drink to Helen.

"Thanks, Jefferey." Helen took the glass. "But not necessary. It's time to move on. You have a good afternoon?"

"Brilliant. But I don't agree with you. I was out of order and I want to apologise. I could make the excuse of being stressed out by work, but I don't want to. I was wrong."

Helen didn't quite know how to respond to that. It was something she never thought she'd hear coming from those particular lips.

"But the work hiccup is sorted." Jefferey continued. "Very satisfactorily as well. Not an easy one, but worth the time. Crisis averted and a promising future ahead."

"I'm glad to hear that. I know how challenging your work is. We could never do it. Mick talked about having his own garage once, but we gave upon the idea when we realised how uncertain it might be. You deserve your success."

They chatted away about all and nothing for a short while, finishing their drinks and letting any remaining ill will dissipate in the sunshine. When Helen began to recount some of the events of the afternoon, Jefferey listened carefully and felt himself properly relaxing for probably the first time on the holiday.

"We should go and have a look at this other world." he proposed. "Take ourselves for a little stroll along the towpath and see who we meet. You up for that?"

They locked the boat and hid the key in the place that all had agreed would be the safest. Mick and Steve were likely to be the first back, but with Penelope's condition, that wasn't a given. That done, they strolled past the many and varied boats and onwards towards a small junction where they would still be able to get an ice-cream from the café there. There's would never be a natural pairing, but the canals did that to you. They were a place where everything was stripped away and you made the most of the time you had with the people you were with.

The laughter that they could hear coming from their boat long before they were alongside it, told them that the others had returned. Needless to say, it was Mick's voice that carried farthest but Alicia's shrieking laugh came a close second.

"You go in and join them." Jefferey said to Helen. "I'll sit here and have a smoke. Send Michael out when you can."

"By Jingo!" were the first words that Helen heard as she boarded the boat, coming from the least expected source.

"Helen, love." Mick waved to his wife. "You've got to hear this. We found Jefferey's doppelganger. By Jingo we did!"

"Honestly, mum." Steve beckoned her to sit next to him. "He was brilliant. Made the day for us."

"What about the bunker?" she asked.

"Amazing." Mick replied. "Proper Cold War stuff and brilliantly done. If it all kicks off again, we'll head there. Mind you, I'm not sure the technology still works. Remember those big old phones we had when we first got married? They had them. It was like taking a step back in time. But it was Roger who made it for us?"

"Who's Roger?" Helen knew she'd regret asking.

"I've told you, he's Jefferey's mini-me. As sure as Toddington Heath still stands."

The others burst into laughter, confusing Helen, who demanded some explanation. With Mick close to tears, it was Steve who explained that they'd followed Roger through the exhibits and started to pick up on the expressions that he used. 'By Jingo' was by far the most popular, but 'Toddington Heath' appeared regularly. Added to these, when the sight was particularly special, it was greeted with 'Well, paste my eyes', or if it was unexpected, 'Take me home, Mummy'. Despite his own attempts to make the usual fool of himself, Mick had been thoroughly upstaged by Roger and had failed to embarrass his son even more.

"Mind you." Mick explained. "It was that good that it had me hooked. I've got the visitor guide, which I'll show you later. But Roger, well, he was special. Paste my eyes, he was!"

Alicia smiled at Helen and nodded her head towards the back deck.

"He's fine." Helen answered the look. "In fact, he wants to have a quick word with you, Mick. Give him a chance, okay?"

"By Jingo, I will." her husband replied, downing the last of his whisky before his appointment at the Headmaster's office.

Chapter Twenty-One:

"Mick." Jeffery reached out a hand that was instinctively grabbed and shaken. "Don't say anything. I owe you an apology and I make no excuses. Bygones be bygones?"

"Aye. Why not?" Mick took the cigar that was offered him and let Jefferey light it. "I was hacked off by you, and you know that. Just try and be a little more appreciative in future, yes?"

"Totally agree. This holiday isn't just about me. Helen and I cleared the air, and I want to do the same with you. What say we grab whatever grub the team are cooking then head off for a couple of pints?"

Mick would never get used to the contrived way that that last word was spoken by his companion. Jefferey could just about get away with 'snifters' and a 'buddy' if he was being really friendly, 'pints' and 'mate' sat uncomfortably on his tongue. Still, the idea itself was sound. Last night's excess had worked its way through his system and the afternoon's walking had made him ready for another session. He'd quite look forward to it actually. Stephen was, like him, a pub person. Jefferey, by nature, wasn't. It could be fun.

They started in the first pub that they came across. Nantwich had its pick of some great hostelries with a huge range of beers and the town's layout made it simple to plan a mini pub crawl that would more than satisfy the most hardened real-ale fanatic.

"To the rest of the holiday." Mick raised his pint of Titanic Plum Porter and clinked it against Jefferey's.

"Indeed, indeed."

"And to Jeffery who has decided to take the stick out of his backside."

"And to Mick for fixing the engine."

The beer flowed freely and the conversation was surprisingly easy. Despite their differences, they shared a lot in common and Mick was one who never ran out of things to say. In fact, he was the sort of person who you could listen to for hours on end, full as he was with a bank of memories that meant he could name every classmate in every year of his schooling. And even tell you where they sat in the classroom.

They were properly relaxed by the time they sat supping a lighter beer, a lot more slowly, in the fourth pub they visited. Jefferey had held his own and they were still shy of the point of wobbly drunkenness.

"I want to make amends." Jefferey told Mick as he placed the next round in front of them. "By way of apology."

"No need, mate."

"I want to. Honestly. At least let me ask you?"

"Go on."

"Okay, as Helen may have told you, I was a bit tense because of something at work. Well, I fixed all that today, but in doing so, I was presented with another opportunity."

He paused to compose himself and make sure he had Mick's attention.

"You ever hear the expression, 'Capital makes capital'?"

Mick nodded.

"Good. Because I want to give you a share of this opportunity. Now, I know that ... and don't get me wrong when I say this ... that, well ... you and Helen aren't awash with cash. That would be right?"

"We've got enough thanks."

"No, don't take this the wrong way. The thing is, I want to offer you a chance, but I understand if you haven't the capital to invest. Thing is, I've been given a chance to buy into a business opportunity that should see a 100% return in less than a month. I can't put the money in myself, for a number of reasons, but mainly because it might be seen to conflict with other investments I have. I don't want to upset certain people. But you, well, if you can come up with the funds, you'll be quids in."

"How much are we talking about?"

"Well, that's just it. It's a ten-thousand-pound hit. Not the sort of money I imagine you have lying around. I thought I should offer though."

"And when do you need the money?"

"Immediately, I'm afraid. Like I say, don't be upset. I felt I should ask, that's all."

"What makes you think I'm upset?" Mick leaned closer to Jefferey. "I ain't got a penny of debt, my mortgage is paid off and I've got a few quid of my own stashed away. Granted, not ten grand."

"I'm sorry." Jefferey finished his pint. "I should never have asked. I just thought that a quick return like that would mean you could spoil the baby a little when it comes. For someone like me, lines of credit are easy to open. I understand that they may not be so available to you. Well done on paying off the mortgage though. I wish I was in that position. Anyway, let's move on."

Whether it was the thought of being able to surprise the family with a small windfall, or whether it was the gauntlet that Jefferey had gently laid down at his feet, Mick wasn't sure. Either way, by the time that they had reached the final stop on the drinking tour, he was ready to fight back.

"How do I get you the money?" Mick asked.

"Sorry?"

"The ten grand. How do I get it to you? Cash isn't practical. A transfer?"

"Well, yes." Jefferey eyed Mick up cautiously. "You want the bank details?"

And that was that. The five minutes that Mick had stolen to log onto his internet banking account had netted him a loan of seven thousand pounds, far too easy but that was the way things were these days. A transfer of the three thousand that he had in an account that only he knew about and which had grown steadily with little 'foreigners' he'd done for friends and neighbours followed. Before they returned to the boat, the money was in Jefferey's account and Mick was looking forward to a big payday.

A few celebratory drinks saw the two new best friends singing as they stumbled along the towpath and continuing to sing as they entered the silent boat cabin, each trying to tell the other to hush.

"Mum's the word." Jefferey shook Mick's hand.

"By Jingo, it is." Mick replied. "I'll see you in the morning."

"You best of buddies now then?" Helen asked as her husband clambered into the bed beside her.

"Sorry, Love. I thought you were asleep."

"I was worried about you. Couldn't sleep until you came back. Everything sorted now?"

"We're good. He's not such a bad guy. Matched me pint for pint and we had a good laugh. He'll always be different, but I think I can cope with him now. You proud of me?"

"Of course." Helen snuggled closer to Mick. "Just be a bit careful with him. There's something about him that still makes me nervous. I don't know that you can trust him."

"He didn't try anything on with you today, did he?"

"Don't be stupid. Of course not. Unless you count trying to make me part with my savings for one of his dodgy schemes to be trying it on."

"What do you mean?" Mick felt the soporific effects of the alcohol instantly dissipate.

"Keep this to yourself, but he wanted me to invest in a get-rich-quick scheme he had. I told him no and he was fine with that. I had a word with Steve later on and he did some checks on Jefferey's so-called business empire. Seems it's not as solid as he makes out. Still, I didn't give him a penny. You just watch out that he doesn't tap you for some. You'd be better putting it on the 3.15 at Haydock."

Mick muttered a brief reply that appeased Helen enough that she kissed him and turned over to go to sleep. She was gently snoring an hour later. Mick heard it all. Sleep was evading him that night, and for good reason. What had he got himself into?

Week One

Day Seven, Friday:

Nantwich to Wimboldsley Wood

Chapter Twenty-Two:

As the end of their first week aboard approached, the six family members, despite the few hiccups that they'd endured along the way, were beginning to understand and buy-in to the canal way of life. There had been dramatic events, days of busy activity and numerous times when conversations had led to familial relations forging ever-stronger ties. But, those aside, the majority of the time they'd spent cruising had been a simple process of tootling along at walking speed through a world-away-from-the-world that had to be experienced to be appreciated.

The canals were no great natural asset. Their birth had been a strictly commercial venture, brought about by capitalist speculators and pick-wielding labourers. From humble beginnings in the Duke of Bridgewater's mines, the network of waterways had grown at an exponential rate as they criss-crossed the country and moved the supplies to where they were needed to start the industrial revolution. There were variances in the lock mechanisms, the ways in which individual canals exploited or ignored the contours of the land, and in the style and width of the waterways themselves, but one constant remained as a reminder of those humble beginning: the boats were all a variation on the original ones used to remove the coal from those first mines.

Having been almost lost to history with the advent of the railways, it was post-war activism that saved the canals and rebranded them as a unique leisure facility. Progress continued in reinstating long-abandoned arms, but the bulk of the network was functioning again, not a stranger to its past, but certainly a half-removed cousin. The furlough period between death and rebirth had been exploited well by the forces of nature and that was the single-most notable feature that defined their new identity. Even a hard-hearted suburbanite like Jefferey had had to admit that the unplanned beauty of overhanging trees reflecting against the water and offset by the flash of kingfishers in flight, was a sight worth seeing. Nor was it the exception. Their journey so far had taken them up the 'modern' Shropshire Union Canal, built to speed up transit times rather than to drive through the major urban centres. Despite being the most obvious of man-made waterways therefore, it was now a smooth thoroughfare through truly unspoilt English countryside, the passage from stop to stop being remembered for what surrounded rather than for the waterway itself.

Ask anyone who's experienced time on the canals and the world they'll use to describe the experience is 'escape'. Time on the waterways was a physical escape from the mad and hectic world that existed sometimes only a stones-throw away, but it was also a mental escape from the pace and the pressures of modern living. It was an escape to a more primitive way of life where the trappings of stuff were traded for basic necessities of life and the busyness of deadlines were traded for acceptance of rigidly defined pace. Most simply enjoyed the escape and recharged their batteries whilst aboard. Some were not content with just a taste and chose to make their home on the cut. Peace, places and people were what made the canals something special.

That sense of peace had relaxed Penelope so much that she found herself freed of the morning sickness and the other negatives of pregnancy. At the same time, she now felt the wriggling lump in her belly with joy and expectation, looking forward to the day when it would emerge.

"You sure you're up for this?" Steve asked as they began to unload the fridge and prepare breakfast for the crew.

"Of course." She replied. "I wouldn't have offered our services if I thought I'd be serving puke as a side order. We're good. And it's nice to be with you whilst the others sleep. We should enjoy it. Being with them all the time is a taster of what it will be like when sprog arrives and demands our attention twenty-four seven."

"It'll still be a lot easier than trying to manage the Alpha-males on this trip." Steve sighed. "I'm beginning to wonder if we really are the kids in this set-up."

"Let it go, Steve. It's been a week now and no-one's killed anyone. Granted, it's been close at times. Daddy will chill out now, I'm sure. And we've always got Mick to lighten things up."

"You don't think he's a little too much at times?"

"Oh, yeah. Of course I do. But give me your dad reading the local paper aloud to all and sundry any time when the alternative's to be ordered about as part of a merchant fleet. Mind you, your mum's been really good to me and I'm even beginning to get some hints of affection from Mummy. She was almost in tears when we were buying baby things yesterday. And not just about the price she was paying."

They continued to chat away as they put their breakfast offering together, broaching the subject of buying their own boat one day, before agreeing that the new arrival would put all such plans on hold for a number of years. It would be a pipe-dream for them. Something to work towards.

"We've met so many different people." Penelope mused. "Every stratum of society seems to be reflected on the boats. But, there isn't a sense of competition or conflict out there. They all seem so chilled and happy just to get along with each other. It's a strange world, but an enviable lifestyle."

"So, you wouldn't miss the flushing loo? Or the constant running water? The electricity and the central heating? The space to move about in? The baths? The security of bricks and mortar?"

"Don't be daft. You know I would. Just maybe not quite as much as I'd previously thought I would. It's nice to think about though, and it makes you appreciate the home comforts that we have."

They paused from preparing the food to give each other a cuddle that began to develop into something more.

"Aye up! Less of that!" Mick's voice burst any bubble of passion that might have been forming. "You've done the bun in the oven thing, now you're on breakfast."

"Morning Dad." Steve sighed.

"Morning Michael." Penelope gave her father-in-law a peck on the cheek, somewhat forcing him off guard.

"You're a bit perky this morning, Penny. Baby not giving you grief today."

"I'm as right as rain." She smiled. "And your sausage and bacon butty should be ready in a moment. Would you like to take a seat, Sir?"

"Ay, Steve, I'd say that's a pleasant surprise, hey? Take me home Mummy!"

"By Jingo, you'd be right."

"Please.", Penelope put the plate in front of Mick. "Can't we have a bit of a break?"

"He hasn't even started on the secret thing yet." Steve added. "That'll be today's topic, I guarantee it. As sure as Toddington Heath still stands."

Penelope's reply was to push her husband into his breakfast slot and stick his own sandwich in front of him. It was easier than simply telling him to shut up.

Silence reigned as the two Robert's ate their breakfast, broken only by Mick's deliberate and loud slurping of tea. Mick, Helen and Steve had never been conversational eaters. Food was to be eaten and words only got in the way of that process. There was plenty of time to talk after. Penelope, however, had been brought up in a different environment. One that now gave her an advantage.

"So, Mick." She smiled as she spoke, knowing that she wouldn't be interrupted. "Steve was telling me about that night at the Shroppie Fly. It appears you had a fun time."

Steve gave his dad a guilty look and held up his hands in admission.

"I knew you could play." Penelope continued. "But I didn't know you sang as well. And composed. Quite a man of many talents."

"Aye, well ..." Mick washed his breakfast down with the last of his tea and held out his mug for a refill. "I'm not sure you'd say it was composing. I can't even remember the words. Still, it got me a few drinks. Besides, what about your dad? I didn't think Jefferey had it in him. He was the instigator last night."

"Mea culpa!" Jefferey uttered as he joined the family. "Just one of my old songs from the army days. We had a laugh, didn't we Michael?"

Mick was stopped in his reply by Helen.

"There's nothing funny about being woken up by a pair of drunken louts." She muttered as she pushed in next to her husband. "You two should be ashamed of yourselves. I've never heard such words."

"And as for you, Michael Roberts." She continued. "I dread to think what you got up to at that other pub. Steve tells me you had a captive audience. Well, you just remember that your surnames Roberts, not Jackson. You're a mechanic, not a musician. And besides, I thought I told you that the accordion stayed at home?"

"I borrowed one." Mick confessed. "You know how it is? There were a bunch of musicians in there and well ... we had a few jars ... I said I played, and ... it just went from there."

"Well, it can just stop there." Helen buttered a slice of toast. "Anyway, good morning to the rest of you, and thanks for doing breakfast. Alicia still not up?"

"She'll join us shortly." Jefferey explained. "Has to put her face on and all that. So, are we ready for a fun day today? Half a day's cruise and then one of the highlights of the trip, a towpath barbeque. Sound good?"

Chapter Twenty-Three:

Plans for the day were completed as the crew finished their breakfast. Regular glances out of the window at the overcast sky and the occasional drop of rain that spattered onto the towpath kept Jefferey wondering if the main event of the day might be a non-starter. It had been one of the first things he'd planned once he knew they were set for this holiday and had been vigorously researched in all aspects prior to their departure. Everything was in place, but the weather didn't auger well for the plan. Aware of their Captain's excitement about the afternoon's jollities, none of the others had the courage to raise the spectre of it being rained off and the conversation moved onto more mundane topics.

With politics threatening another day of tension and sport drawing a blank from most of the crew, baby talk and brief reminiscences about the journey so far saw the conversation lifted into a safer and lighter place. Needless to say, it was only a matter of time before it would be brought back down by Mick and Steve.

"I thought the barbeque was a secret?" Mick whispered to his son who burst out laughing.

"Me too." Steve replied. "Better check with the Commandant. Jeffery, have you printed any invites? Come to the 'Secret Barbeque'"

"What are you talking about?" Jefferey looked quizzically at the two men. "Is this one of your silly jokes?"

"Can't tell you." Steve whispered, pausing before continuing. "It's a secret!"

That set Mick and Steve off and it was a good five minutes before the rest of the crew had been brought up to speed on the final piece of their trip to the bunker yesterday. It was silly and childish and a joke that didn't have the legs that Mick and Steve attributed to it, but it made them smile every time they thought of the ten-foot by ten-foot sign that was placed beside the canal and announced 'Secret Bunker' with an arrow pointing off to the location.

"Look." Mick showed them the photo he'd taken. "You get it? It's a secret bunker, but it's got a big sign showing where it is. Funny, no?"

"Very amusing." Jefferey forced a laugh. "But more a reflection of the quirkiness of the English than a rib-tickler in itself. Very good."

"Sorry I said anything." Mick mumbled, turning to his son. "Wish I'd kept it a secret!"

By the time Alicia had arrived and settled herself over a bowl of muesli, the majority of the washing-up had been done by Helen and Penelope, whilst the engine checks had been completed by the men. She'd told them to carry on and ignore her. She wanted a leisurely breakfast and a lazy day. The shopping trip and swim had been lovely but had taken it out of her.

"You sure you're okay?" Helen asked.

"Oh, I'm fine, sweetheart. It'll just be nice to have some me time today. Jefferey can be a bit challenging in too large a dose. I'm not sure we've spent this much time together since we've been married."

"He was a lot better yesterday. I saw a more relaxed side of him."

"We'll see how long he keeps it up for, shall we? He's on rocky ground in my book and I expect to see him change. Not that that's likely."

With that, Alicia took her tea and settled herself back in her own cabin, picking up a copy of Vogue just as the engine started and she felt the boat moving away.

Given the overcast conditions, Helen and Penelope opted to remain inside the boat, the older knitting away as the younger flicked through one of the many parenting books that she'd felt obliged to study in minute detail. They all said much the same thing, but it was as well to be sure as a first-time mother. Thus are the fortunes of writers made.

Steve was permitted to navigate for the first leg of the journey, having been given only one instruction, which was to make sure that he didn't miss the junction with the canal that they were due to join. He cruised at a much slower speed than either of the older men, but he was happy to take it easy and look around him as he steered away from Nantwich. With the boat under new command, Jefferey and Mick sat out on the boat's well-deck and took in a view of the journey that they'd not been able to enjoy so far.

"Looks different from here." Mick offered by way of a starter.

"Different indeed." Jefferey replied. "And you know what the big difference is?"

"No? Don't tell me, it's a secret!"

"Very good. Tres witty. No, it's the noise. Or lack of it. Back there at the stern, you've not only got the boat in front of you, but you've also got the engine throbbing away beneath you. Here, well, it's just so much more peaceful. And unobstructed."

He was right. Once you let go of the worries about the person driving the boat, the well deck was the perfect place to be to take in the sights and the sounds of the waterways, and to replace the rattling of the engine with the gentle splash of water against the bows.

Don Quixote sat expectantly on its owner's lap. Mick was thumbing the pages of the free waterways newspaper that he'd picked up from one of the pubs. Unusually for him, he was keeping the contents to himself. That reflected his interest in the 'For Sale' adverts as well as a wary reluctance to treat Jefferey as he would the other members of his family. On the one hand, the profit from his investment might well be converted into his own boat. On the other, he may have blown what little savings he had. Either way, the newspaper was engrossing and his mechanic's mind was beginning to understand the technicalities of the narrowboat.

Thumbing the unopened classic, the silence that surrounded them presented the perfect opportunity for Jefferey to begin to tackle Cervantes. Peace of situation was, however, not peace of mind, and worries about the barbeque took precedence.

"I hope that sun comes out." Jefferey sighed. "I was looking forward to today."

"We've got brollies, haven't we?" Mick put the newspaper down.

"Of course. But that's not the point, is it? I pictured today in my mind and had it all set out. Rain wasn't a factor and battling stoically against the elements wasn't part of that plan."

"You try and manage things too much." Mick replied. "Never forget that you're English. We're a nation that works around, not with, the weather. So what if it rains, we'll barbeque anyway. Under umbrellas if we have to. Come on, cheer up, you miserable sod!"

"You're right, we don't need to worry about the …what the…?!!"

Mick looked ahead to see what the problem was but it was Jefferey who leapt up and began shouting at Steve who was turning the boat hard into the junction and making quite a good job of it.

"What are you doing?" Jefferey shouted.

"The junction." Steve pointed to his left. "Come on, you guys need to get off and sort the lock out."

"It's the wrong one! That one takes us to Llangollen. You want to turn right at our junction."

"Well, paste my eyes lad, he's right!" Mick joined in, not quite as seriously as Jefferey. "Unless you fancy a trip to Welsh Wales? It's the next one."

Steve muttered to himself as he slammed the boat into reverse and tried to counter his turning manoeuvre. It wasn't as simple as that and he ended up having to do a full pirouette before he was back on the Shroppie and facing the right direction.

"Hey, Dad!" he shouted down to his audience at the front. "Why not tell me there are two junctions to choose from next time? It might help."

"Sorry, Son." Mick replied. "Thought it would be fun to keep it a secret."

"I'll secret you, you prat." Steve whispered as he settled back to cruising.

Chapter Twenty-Four:

When the correct junction appeared just after a scary moment of squeezing the boat between two moored-up work boats at Barbridge, Steve tried his hardest to make the turn without incident. He got a huge amount of satisfaction from blowing the horn as he began the turn, knowing that it would be ear-piercing to the guys at the front who were already standing up and waving at him, just in case he missed the turn. He let the boat move gently around, flitting between reverse and forward gear to ensure that he approached the bridge as dead-on as he could. It all worked perfectly until the last second when a light gust of breeze caught the boat sideways-on and threw everything off kilter.

Despite moving hard into reverse, and actually making it worse by doing so, Steve smacked the front of the boat against the bridge that formed the entrance to the tunnel, bouncing off that side before hitting the other. A short burst of forward thrust saw him safely through the junction, but by then it was too late. They'd rib him for that for many a long day. One of them could do the next one.

"Everything alright?" Penelope popped her head out of the back doors.

"We're good." Steve smiled. "It'll give them something to have a go at me about. The wind caught us, that's all."

"Ah, poor baby. You want me to drive?"

"Don't make it worse woman. And anyway, what are you doing coming out on deck without a beer? Come on wench, back in there and fix it."

It was all said playfully. They were still at that stage in their marriage where nothing was too serious. Penelope obliged and sat with her husband as the began the cruise along the Middlewich Arm of the Shropshire Union.

Mick and Jefferey, despite the flaws in Steve's navigational skills, opted to stay at the front of the boat until the first lock appeared, set high above a marina and already in motion with a constant stream of boats.

"We'll get these." Jefferey informed Steve as he passed a windlass to Mick and the two clambered onto the towpath.

With more boats coming up than were going down, Steve was soon in the lock chamber and being lowered down.

"I told you about that catch thing." Jefferey said to Mick. "That's only there for the amateurs. Health and Safety gone mad and all. It's a damned sight easier just to flick it over and wind the paddles without it on."

"I'm not sure, Jeff." Mick replied. "They say you're supposed to keep it on."

"Oh, suit yourself. I know how I'll do the locks and if you want the noise of the ratchet, that's your call."

They boarded the boat again opposite the marina and let Steve continue the journey, happy to do so now that the sun was out and their wives had joined them on the bow.

"Sorry about this morning." Alicia said. "I was just tired. It takes it out of you this boating. And the whole thing has a sleepiness about it, don't you think?"

"Canal-time, Love." Mick told her. "That's what they call it. Bed before nine and a struggle to get up in the morning. Don't complain, I'm loving it."

Once that first lock was out of the way, the Middlewich Branch wended its way slowly eastward, interrupted only by another single lock that the team worked rapidly through. From there, it was plain sailing to the final destination for the day. Little was said as the family members relaxed and watched the world go by, taking in the stunning beauty of that particular waterway. Built as a link between the Trent and Mersey and the Shropshire Union canals, the Middlewich Branch was something of a super-highway in its time. It didn't need to pass through towns and villages as it was an entirely functional through-route; the legacy of that history being that it was simply the most stunning and unspoilt stretch of waterway that they had so far cruised along.

Not only was the waterway a delight, but the views surrounding it were breathtakingly simple: pure, practical, and wholly natural farmlands straddled the canal, giving way, at times to high banks that looked away far into the distance, revealing hilltops and mountains that were vast distances away. Where it had been developed to account for leisure traffic, the extended towpaths were replete with grassed areas for resting and relaxing, simple moorings on concrete-set rings and, best of all, purpose-built barbeques set around picnic tables.

"We should stop at one of them." Mick suggested.

"I thought about it, Michael." Jefferey replied. "When I was planning the route. But, and forgive me for taking somewhat of a punt on this, I think we'll be better off in the spot that I've chosen. Besides, you never know who's used those barbeques before and what sort of germs they may harbour. And we don't really need to use those public utilitarian ones. Not when you see the alternative."

"Don't tell me you're finally going to reveal the monster in the wardrobe?" Alicia asked.

"Indeed, my love, indeed. You shall have your space back tonight. Prior to which I shall, as you say, reveal my latest surprise to the crew."

"Not been keeping more secrets there Jefferey, have you?" Mick's question was as irreverent as it was irrelevant.

"Yes." Jefferey sighed as he responded, thinking more and more that Mick was becoming more like a schoolchild with every passing day. "It is my secret and I will reveal it. And no, there isn't a sign in the bedroom that says 'Secret Surprise – This Way'"

"I think we've had enough of that one now, Mick." Helen looked up from her knitting as she spoke. Her words brought back the silence that they'd all been enjoying. A silence that continued until they slipped through Wimboldsley Bridge, at which point Jefferey declared that their destination was near and that he'd moor the boat up. Mick stayed at the bow, jumping off as the boat stopped and tying the front off to one of the rings there.

"Bloody hell, Jeff." he said as he turned to look at the view. "I'll let you have this one. It's amazing."

And it was. The bank on which they moored was raised high over a rolling, tree-lined valley through which the River Weaver meandered on a rambling course. The others disembarked and took a few moments to enjoy both the view and the peace that came with the cutting of the engine. There were only two other boats on the visitor moorings, neither of which were showing any signs of life.

"Sometimes," Steve spoke to the crew as he put an arm around his wife. "Everything comes together just right. The sun, the views, the cruise here and the promise of a barbeque. You did well, Jefferey. Now, perhaps a beer or three?"

"You're not relaxing just yet, honey." Penelope told him. "Get the kitchen stuff sorted first, then you can chill."

"Yes, dear." Steve mumbled as he went indoors again.

"He may not be Gordon Ramsey," Penelope explained. "But he makes a mean coleslaw and can knock up some stunning barbeque sauces. Give him half an hour and all the trimmings will be ready. Meanwhile, Jefferey, you'd better get it over with."

He didn't need asking twice and with an excited nod, he jumped onto the bow of the boat, slipped into his and Alicia's cabin, then returned carrying a big cardboard box.

"Ladies and gentlemen." He announced. "Allow me to introduce you to the Firestorm 5000. The Rolls-Royce of flaming food preparation. Michael, shall we attempt to tame this little beasty?"

Chapter Twenty-Five:

Whilst the two men selected a spot in the sunlight and began the process of unpacking the numerous parts that made up the very compactly-packed cooking machine, the ladies scooped up folding chairs from the boat's roof and laid claim to a sizeable chunk of the towpath. Half an hour later, a triumphant cry from the master builder was greeted with stunned looks from everybody else as they gazed on the monster machine that seemed to have appeared from nowhere.

Mick was the first to make a comment, asking if Jefferey now wanted him to go off and find a pig for the hog-roast, but that was tame compared to Stephen's response.

"Well, take me home, Mummy!" he shouted as he emerged from the galley and stared at the barbeque. "By jingo and paste my eyes, that's some piece of kit. I'll get the hosepipe and we can start filling her up. Hey, who'd have guessed? A hot tub on the towpath!"

"Thank you, gents." Jefferey was fine with the ribbing. "I'll grant you, it may be a bit bigger than I expected. Still, we won't go short of food."

"Talking of which," Steve said. "My work is done in the kitchen, so, I'm having a few beers and relaxing now. Mind you, given the amount of food in the galley, it's not a bad thing that you've made that monster. When are we expecting the rest of the five-thousand to arrive?"

It was now mid-afternoon and a couple of other boats had eyed up the mooring spot and decided to call it a day, pulling their boats in and tying them up before chairs and sun-loungers were put in place. Each of the passing boats had waved a cheery greeting to the family and each in turn had received a welcoming wave. A few of the crew members from the other boats drifted along to greet the family and, if they were honest, to gaze on the wonder that was the enormous barbeque, but most chose to stay in their own space and use the location and the warming sun to recharge their batteries.

"We should invite them over." Jefferey suggested, only to be greeted by a response from Mick that immediately poo-pooed the idea.

"I don't mind chatting with them." He said. "But they can keep their hands off my grub and my booze. This isn't a community event y'know."

The others were in general agreement. This was a family barbeque and a time for them to enjoy a rare moment of togetherness without any pressure to do anything but get progressively more drunk and to graze on the vast array of food that the Firestorm 5000 was delivering to them. Had it been a scene in a Hollywood movie, it would have either been deleted or used as a brief filler to bring the running time up. It was just one of those lazy afternoons where nothing much happened and which soon turned into a relaxed evening of good humour and banal chit-chat.

The tiredness that they were all succumbing to was a welcome balm that eased any concerns that they had. Even Mick, occasionally reminded of the money he'd been fooled into investing with Jefferey, was able to forget about the consequences of what he'd done and put off the inevitable explanation that Helen would demand. Of course, it might pay off. He wasn't banking on that. But it wasn't like he had any choice. He'd asked Jefferey if he could change his mind, when the two of them were building the barbeque, but had been told that it was now too late. The investment had been made.

"I think," Jefferey told the group as he finished the remains of his first bottle of wine. "That I shall go for a little wander along the towpath. Anyone coming?"

When the others declined, he simply shrugged and left them to it. They were about to move on to Scrabble and he was happy to absent himself from that game. Especially if

Michael and Stephen were amongst the players. He could do without the guaranteed 'tits' and 'bums' and 'farts' that he knew they'd readily sacrifice a high score to place on the board. He knew well enough that that was where it would lead.; they'd tried to play once before and he'd told himself, never again.

"I say." Jefferey stood beside the last boat to have moored up and admired its polished paintwork and gleaming brasses. "She's a beauty, isn't she?"

"Well thank you, kind sir." the owner replied, getting up from his seat and walking towards his visitor. "She's my own design, built for me from scratch and fitted out by a team of guys that I know in a local yard. Of course, the engine's a classic Gardner. One can only compromise so much to the modern age."

"I must confess." Jefferey admitted. "I'm no expert in all things boat. Is a Gardner a good engine?"

"The best." the proud reply. "Come aboard and I'll show you. I'm Roger, by the way."

The two men entered the boat and Jefferey let Roger lead him through to the engine which occupied its own separate compartment in the back third of the vessel. That whole space, immaculately clean and smelling of hot oil, was taken up by a gleaming engine that looked as shiny as if it was built yesterday but which carried a brass plaque that identified it as being over seventy-years old. Roger then proceeded to talk Jefferey through the workings of the engine and the history of its renovation. It was all a bit over his head but he didn't mind. Roger was his type of friend.

When they emerged from the boat and were back on the towpath, Roger continued to chat away about the features of his pride and joy. Once the boat talk was over, the conversation moved somehow to golf, and then on to the various destinations that they'd visited on business travels abroad. Time flew and more wine flowed as they chatted away, occasionally getting a glance from the family who were pleased that not only was Jefferey not close by their side just now, but that he also seemed to be entering into the spirit of the holiday at last. It was gone ten when he returned, a beaming smile on his face and a slight stagger in his walk. Only Mick had remained outside and he and Jefferey closed the barbeque down and cleaned it up as best they could before joining the others inside.

"You seemed to have a good time there?" Mick asked.

"Splendid chap." Jefferey replied. "Seems we share a few business acquaintances. And his boat's a beauty. Nice to just have a chat. Lovely guy."

Mick didn't say anything else. He was tempted to ask if the new friend might have had money to invest, but he resisted the temptation. Meeting strangers was bread and butter to him and he didn't need telling that the best moments in life were shared with other passers-by as they stumbled their way through their days. It wasn't Jefferey's world at all. If it started to become so, then maybe there was hope for him after all.

Week Two

Day One, Saturday:

Wimboldsley Wood to Wheelock

Chapter Twenty-Six:

Ask any seasoned boater about the challenges that the British weather presents and it will be the wind that they least like having to deal with. Rain is simply part and parcel of the experience, easily managed with waterproofs and a decent hat, and not unwelcome either, since it keeps the waterways topped up. Sunshine is generally a positive, although for those who live in their tin cans and feel the inside temperature rising to sauna levels, it can soon outstay its welcome. Ice is what it is. Some battle to crash their way through it, but when it sets in hard, you can't win the battle and have no choice but to stay where you are. The wind though, that's a different beast altogether.

Aside from the fact that sudden gusts can seem to come from nowhere and catch you out, the wind, when it comes in all its fury, seems to smile at the choice that it presents to canal users. Those who don't need to move on can simply wait it out, checking that their mooring lines are secure before hunkering down inside. Those who want or have to move, have a choice to make - sit out the gusts and catch up on their navigation schedule when things are more settled, or take the punt and do the best they can to stay on course. Of course, irregular or new boaters don't always see that choice. After all, it's only wind. Not a frame of mind that the working bargees of old would entertain, knowing that their precious horses were at risk whenever their boats were caught by a side-on gust.

It was the wind that had woken the crew of the Harriet Knot as they began the second week of their cruise. The boat had knocked and banged against the bank as their mooring lines loosened, and their location was high enough up for them to hear the howling around the craft that was impossible to ignore. It was also the wind that generated the first excitement of the day as the crew were gathered over breakfast and half-deciding to sit it out until later.

"What the hell do you think you're doing?!" the shout was loud enough to be heard over the sound of the wind and the boat's engine. It caused the male members of the crew to rise as one and head out of the boat to see what was happening. The women weren't inclined to follow, being less nosey than the men and generally less excitable.

"Hey, look at this." Mick chuckled as he led the other family members out of the boat. "Looks like the cabaret's started."

The others joined him on the deck and took in the sight. A smaller boat than theirs was sideways on across the canal further back on the moorings. The young couple on the deck were frantically switching from forward to reverse in an attempt to straighten themselves up, but their efforts were proving to be futile and all they were managing to do was press the bow of the boat harder onto the gunwales of the nice, shiny boat that Jefferey had been so enamoured with. It was Roger who had shouted and who was continuing to shout.

"You shouldn't be on the cut if you don't know how to handle a boat." He kept up the tirade as he walked carefully down the side of his boat toward where the damage was being done. "And stop revving the engine! Every time you move forward, you're taking more paint off. Just get a grip."

The couple who were trying to bring their boat under control tried to ignore what was being said. Yes, their boat was banging against the side of Roger's and yes, they were fairly new to this whole boating lark, but, they were doing their best. Their apologies were unheeded and, to be fair, unnecessary. Sometimes things like this happened.

Mick and Jefferey, assuming that their assistance would be welcomed, took the initiative and joined Roger on the gunwales of the precious vessel, the three of them pushing the other boat away with their feet. It wasn't as easy as they'd thought it would be, since every time they thought they'd done enough, another gust would bring the two boats back together with a gentle thump. After several attempts, their combined forces had removed the danger and the other boat straightened up before settling firmly onto the opposite bank where the wind ensured that it was well and truly grounded.

"Throw us your centre rope." Steve had split from the others and was standing on the deck of Roger's boat and calling across to the stranded strangers who responded to his request by doing as he'd asked.

The rope was long enough to reach Steve but the first two attempts to get it to him were unsuccessful. Each time, the rope uncoiled, looked set to be on course, but then fell that bit too short and flicked the side of Roger's boat before falling into the water.

"I say!" Roger watched what Steve was doing and was sufficiently concerned to stop looking at the damage done to the side of his boat and shuffle back to the stern deck.

"Do you not think they've done enough damage?" he asked Steve as the rope was prepared for another throw.

"Come on, mate. They need a hand. I'd get you head down if I was you."

The warning came in time but it was ignored. More concerned about the further damage that a length of wet rope could do than his own safety, Roger felt that rope whip onto his thigh just before Mick leapt onto the deck and secured it with his foot.

"I've got it." he told his son. "Come on, let's heave them in."

"What on earth do you think you're doing?" Roger rubbed his stinging leg and spoke directly to Steve.

"I'm helping them out. They're stuck over there. Come on, give us a hand."

"I will not give you a hand." the reply caught Steve by surprise. "And I would kindly ask you to let go of that rope and disembark my vessel. They can sort themselves out."

"Come on, pal." Mick intervened. "We can't just leave them there."

"We jolly well can. And you, Jefferey, do you want to be a part of this travesty as well?"

Jefferey looked at his new-found friend, then at his family members, then across at the young couple who were wondering what the delay was.

"Yes, I think we should leave them to it. Throw the rope back and let them sort it out for themselves. They've damaged Roger's boat enough and I agree we should leave it now."

"You big, long streak of piss!" Steve whispered under his breath. "I'm not leaving them there. Come on Dad, let's get this done."

"You're right, son." Mick took the strain and began pulling, despite the gentle shoving that he was receiving from Roger, who would never make a particularly good enforcer.

"And you ..." Mick continued. "...you can get your hands off me or you'll be in that water. It's only a rope. It won't sink your stupid boat."

"Now, now," Jefferey tried to assert his authority. "That's simply not on. Roger has a right to protect his property and Stephen, you shouldn't have interfered."

Had they not been putting all their energy into pulling the rope that they held between them, either Mick or Steve or both would have been likely to have taken a swipe at one or other of the two men who stood idly by. Their efforts paid off and the other boat cleared itself from where it was grounded and was able to make use of a lull in the wind to straighten up and begin to pull off. Stephen pulled them even closer to Roger's boat, ostensibly so that he could hand them their rope, but secretly willing that they'd make contact again. They didn't and, with a heartfelt thank-you the young couple headed away.

"Please leave my boat." Roger addressed Mick and Steve.

"With pleasure." Steve replied. "And I hope that a few chips in your paintwork are just the beginnings of your troubles. You're unbelievable. And you, Jefferey, well, why don't you just pack your things and move in with your lover boy?"

"Come on, Steve." Mick put an arm around his son's shoulder, led him back to the boat and ushered him into the cabin. "You go and finish your breakfast. You deserve it. You did well, and I'm proud of you."

"Not you." he barred the doorway as Jefferey clambered aboard. "You and I are going to have words. What the hell do you think you were doing?"

"I don't know what you're talking about." Jefferey tried to push past but Mick refused to let him off the hook.

"You just don't get it do you." Mick leaned in close as he spoke. "Steve was doing his best out there and you should have supported him. I don't care how buddy-buddy you think you are with the other bloke, Steve's family and he should count on your support."

"Well, I happen to disagree. Roger has a very nice boat and should be entitled to keep it that way. Those youngsters should never have been allowed on the water and Stephen made it worse."

"Oh, Jeff, you really are sailing close to the wind. I've told you, Steve's family and you let him down. You either apologise to him or you and I are going to have to take this further. I'm getting sick of you and your pompous ways. Now, get in there and make sure you say you're sorry. I can't bear to look at you just now."

"Well, you'll be pleased to know that you won't have to shortly." Jefferey hissed as he entered the boat. "You'll be pleased to know that I have to go to London on Monday and I'll be away for the night. You should like that. Never mind the fact that I'm going to make sure your little investment pays off. So, don't you dare talk to me about family."

Mick turned away and lit a cigarette as he willed himself to calm down. Jefferey, needless to say, didn't apologise to Steve, nor did he get the opportunity to as Alicia had caught some of what was said.

"What do you mean, you're away on Monday?" she asked her husband.

"Yes, sorry you heard it like that, I was going to tell you all." He addressed his reply to everyone. "I need to sort out some business and have to visit the shipping agents in London on Monday. I only found out this morning. I will take the train and stay over. Don't worry, it won't interfere with the holiday too much."

"Sometimes, Jefferey," Alicia muttered as she started clearing the table. "I wonder why I bother with you. And, as for what happened out there with the other boat, I think we're all better not knowing and trying to move on. Is that okay Stephen?"

"Whatever." Steve shrugged his shoulders.

"Let's just move on." Mick told them all as he joined them. "We're going to have to work with the wind today, so, we need to get going. You do what you want Jeff. We're trying to enjoy a holiday here."

Chapter Twenty-Seven:

Preparations to leave their current mooring spot took a lot longer than expected. The delay was down to the Firestorm 5000. It was indeed, the ultimate in barbeque standards, but it was never designed to be portable. Once it has been assembled, disassembly was never a part of the designer's brief. Funnily enough though, almost as though it were a metaphor for the relations between them, it was the Firestorm's stubbornness to yield that helped diffuse the tensions between the family members. It could have fuelled more dissent, but Mick and Steve didn't get too many holidays and they were determined to steer this one back on course.

"Well, Jefferey," Mick stood next to the barbeque with his hands on his hips. "any thoughts on this one?"

"Hmm…I'm not sure. The legs will come off fine, at least, up to the last strut. But the rest of it is never going back in the box. My error, I'm afraid. Perhaps the Firestorm was something of a sledgehammer to crack a nut."

Stephen had absented himself from the barbeque problem. It would take a little longer for he and Jefferey to forgive and forget. He chose instead to check the weed-hatch and tick off all the other pre-cruising essentials. He had the boat ready to go and sat watching his dad and Jefferey as they thought about how to make the barbeque small enough to be transportable. In the end, their collective decision was very much a compromise. The Firestorm 5000 would have to be strapped to the roof of the boat as best they could. To do that, both Mick and Jefferey had to work together to lift the monstrosity up, place it as securely as possible between the roof furniture and a lifebelt, then tie it with some spare ropes that were provided by the hire company.

"It still looks a bit high." Mick said.

"We'll just have to be careful." Jefferey reassured him. "From my calculations it'll fit below the bridges, just about. We should be fine. Come on then, let's head off."

The calculations that Jefferey had made were not particularly scientific, involving only his standing on the towpath and measuring his height against the apex of the monster barbeque. It was a calculation that worked in theory, but which failed to take into account the varying heights of towpaths and bridges along the waterways and, more importantly, any variance in water levels. Still, it was a calculation that proved itself accurate as the cruised slowly under the first bridge, clearing the brickwork by a good inch or two.

"Told you we'd be okay, Michael" Jefferey announced triumphantly as they continued on their way.

"It's a bit tight though." Mick replied. "We'll need to keep an eye in it. So, where to today then?"

Jefferey was about to reply when the Firestorm played its first trick of the day. The movement of the boat had set up a series of vibrations within its structure and these caused the drop-down lid to slide open. Not a major problem in itself, since it was designed to retract into the main body of the barbeque, but not really what the team wanted as the winds continued to blow. Having opened itself up, the barbeque willingly received the first of the gusts of wind that filled it like a tacking sail and which caused it to rise slightly against the ropes that held it in place. Before Jefferey had time to impart the day's itinerary he felt the full force of the wind hitting the barbeque and was powerless to stop it. Slowly, despite his best efforts to shift the tiller, the boat moved off it course along the centre of the cut and headed uncontrollably towards the towpath. Revving the engine to compensate and continuing to believe that he could make the correction, Jefferey watched helplessly as his efforts proved fruitless and the stern of the boat edged closer and closer to the opposite bank, where it bounced off a huge boulder, scraped under an overhanging tree, then sat itself unmoving on the soft mud which enveloped it.

"Bugger!" Jeff muttered as he killed the throttle.

"Bugger indeed." Mick replied as sympathetically as he could and barely able to hold in the laugh that so wanted to come up.

"What's the matter?" Helen popped her head out of the bow doors and shouted down the boat to the others.

"We've gone aground, love." Mick told her. "The wind."

Setting aside their recent difficulties, the family convened on the stern deck to consider a plan of action. Moving the boat was a necessity, of course, but it was also a particularly time-bound one as it now straddled the canal and blocked the navigation.

Jefferey was all for pushing the bow of the boat off the towpath and straightening up the boat that way. Fortunately, Penelope was able to persuade him that that would only result in the whole of the boat becoming grounded on the far side.

Helen proved to be her usual practical self and instructed Alicia and Penelope to climb out of the bow and take up stations on the towpath to warn any oncoming boats. She then ordered Mick and Steve onto the roof to remove the barbeque, which was still picking up the full force of the wind, and dump it on the well-deck.

"Be careful with that." Jefferey shouted to them as they set to work, but neither chose to hear him.

"I think, Jefferey," Helen continued to control the situation. "that you should have a go with the barge-pole and see if you can shift her that way. Just be careful."

Not a person used to be ordered about, Jefferey was surprisingly compliant and began the process of wedging the pole deep into the soft bank and applying all his weight to the end. Mick and Steve dumped the Firestorm 5000 onto the bow, making sure that it made enough noise to irritate Jefferey, before clambering down the gunnels on the towpath side, where they began to rock the boat to help free it up.

There were a few moments when the men felt the boat yield to their efforts, but they were soon offset by the wind answering them with a touch that negated their efforts. Offers by Mick and Steve to take over Jefferey's task were waved away as he strained and pushed at the barge-pole, determined to be the one who got them out of this mess.

Alicia shouted to the crew that another boat was approaching, running towards it as she did so with her arms waving frantically. The driver of the boat understood what was happening and slowed to a stop just behind the grounded stern.

"Bit of a problem, what, what?" Roger shouted to Jefferey, who turned and recognised the boat he'd so admired the night before.

"Gust of wind." he explained. "Seems to be well and truly stuck."

"Well, you need to get shifted. I'm on a schedule here."

"I'm sorry, Roger, I'm doing my best. Any suggestions?"

Jefferey was a little surprised by Roger's impatience. Sure, they hadn't exactly known each other long enough to be bosom-buddies, but he did feel that the two of them had bonded in some way.

"I suppose I'll have to pull you off." Roger shouted across.

"Can you not wait until we've got the boat free?!" Mick couldn't resist the open goal that had been set up for him.

"Please," Jefferey gave the two men who clung to the far side of the boat a withering look. "This is not the time for your silly comments."

He shouted back agreement to Roger and ordered Mick and Steve to the stern deck where they followed Roger's instructions and reached across for the bow rope, which they then attached firmly to their own boat.

"Ladies," Roger called across to Alicia and Helen. "Can you please hold the bow rope of your boat and pull it to the towpath as I resolve this issue at the back end. Once she's free, you need to pull her in."

The two women gave Roger the thumbs-up and he engaged reverse on his engine and let the rope that attached him to the other boat take up the strain.

"I'll keep pushing here then, Roger?" Jefferey asked, only to be greeted with a non-committal shrug from the other.

Roger gently increased the thrust on his boat until it was straining away noisily gradually putting more and more pressure on the vessel that continued to fight the wind and the ground that held it. Slowly, the hire boat began to yield. Jefferey increased his efforts with the barge-pole, pushing it further into the silted bank. With a loud scraping sound, the stern of the grounded boat gave in to the inevitable and was released back into the main channel of water, more quickly than Jefferey had anticipated.

"There she goes!" Roger shouted.

"I'm free!" Steve added with a yelp.

"Guys!" father and son turned to where Jefferey was standing but were too late. The man on the end of the pole had pushed too hard and too far and was now at the point of no return. As the boat moved back towards the towpath, the barge-pole remained set where it was. The thing holding the two together, Jefferey, had only one place to go. The physics once again defied him and Jefferey teetered for a moment before giving in to the inevitable and dropping into the murky waters with a loud splash.

As Jefferey hit the water, Steve had the presence of mind to catch the pole as it fell back towards the boat. They wouldn't want to lose that, after all. It would cost a fair few quid to replace. Mick meanwhile, had one of those 'too-stunned-to-move' moments. He knew this wasn't a life-threatening situation, but he didn't know quite what his course of action should be: laughter was the default, but he retained a modicum of human sympathy, even for Jeff. That said, the decision was pretty much made for the remaining crew as the boat was now being dragged closer to the towpath with Helen and Alicia guiding it in.

"Well, don't mind me." Jefferey shouted to no-one in particular and he stood, waist-deep in the canal and wiping weeds off his face. "Roger, a little help maybe?"

The plea was ignored as Steve undid the rope that held the two boats together and coiled it back on Roger's bow. Once there, a brief wave told the others that Roger was keen to move on, so Steve jumped onto the towpath and they watched as the other boat accelerated past them, creating a wave that knocked Jefferey back onto his backside.

"Sorry, old chap." Roger shouted. "Got to crack on. You'll be okay to walk it."

Jefferey said nothing. He simply watched Roger cruise away, his cheery wave the final death-knell to any friendship he thought they might have. With the canal clear, he did the only thing he could and walked slowly through the water and back to the towpath. At one point, the water reached the top of his chest, but that was as high as it got. The others shouted encouragement to him as he made his way to them, Mick and Steve reaching out hands to lift him back onto dry land.

"If either of you," Jefferey muttered to them as they helped him out. "Say a single word, then I shall not be accountable for my actions."

Uncharacteristically, the two obeyed the instruction and walked back to the boat as Alicia and Helen did their best to dry the creature from the deep off. Once out of sight, they collapsed together as the pent-up laughter inside them released itself.

Chapter Twenty-Eight:

Before setting back off and whilst Jefferey took a shower and changed into clean and dry clothes, the rest of the crew considered the Firestorm 5000 and just what to do with it. It couldn't go back on the roof. Yes, the wind was dying down now, but it could easily pick up again. Nor could it stay where it currently was, since its bulk was taking up the whole of the free space on the well-deck.

"We could just ditch it." Alicia suggested, a certain gleam in her eye at the thought of Jefferey discovering what they'd done when it was too late.

"No, Mum." Penelope could sense the tension between her parents and didn't want anything else to fuel it. "How about we put it on the back of the boat"

With no other alternative, other than to have it as a bedtime companion in one of the cabins, it was this suggestion that they agreed to and the bulky barbeque was carried from the front of the boat to the stern deck, where it was strapped to the handrail with the same ropes that had held it onto the roof.

"He's not going to like it." Mick muttered. "You can hardly move the tiller all the way around with that in the way."

"And he's not going to like this either." Steve smiled as he pointed to the half-dozen dents and scratches that the Firestorm has picked up in its travels.

"I don't care what he likes." Alicia replied. "Now, let's get moving again and I'll go and tend to his own bumps and scratches. The biggest of which will be his pride. You guys stay out here while I calm him down. Penelope, you want to help your mum?"

Helen said very little as her husband and her son navigated the boat away from the towpath and on towards the next lock. She was there as a peace-keeper. Her two companions on deck knew that they had to be on best behaviour. For now, anyway. There would be plenty of time to milk this one later.

"Now that," Jefferey was in a surprisingly good mood as he came back out on deck, clean, dry and refreshed, and holding a bottle of wine in his hand. "Was what you call an almighty cock-up. So, if you two gentlemen would like to get your own wisecracks out of the way, we can crack open this bottle of wine between us before we crack-on with the next lock. You've got five minutes.

It was more than enough for Mick and Steve who accepted the hall-pass willingly and exchanged the baton of banter with increasing mirth.

"Roger certainly pulled you off good and proper, didn't he?" Mick braved the look from Helen as he spoke.

"Yep, Roger tossed you right off there." Steve added.

"Aye, he shafted you good and proper there." Mick continued. "You could say, he shafted you with your own shaft."

And so it continued, the phrase 'Rogered' featuring prominently in the chatter.

The wine did the job though and Jefferey's five-minutes of persecution were soon over and the process of working through the final lock on this stretch of the canal was begun.

"If you and Stephen are okay to do the lock." Jefferey asked. "I wouldn't mind sorting this barbeque out. I think I know where we can store it."

They agreed and jumped off the boat as it joined a queue of several others waiting to descend. Roger was the first in line, but he was already entering the lock when they arrived so they decided to stay well back. That Roger should have gained so much time on them was not unexpected. What did surprise them was that he had a wife on board and she was now working the lock for him.

"He must keep her in a cupboard." Mick suggested.

"Or chained to the sink." Steve added.

"Didn't see her offering to help us though." Helen joined in before saying that she was probably inside polishing Roger's brasses and instantly regretting the opening she gave to the men.

Whilst they waited to descend, Jeffery and Alicia untied the Firestorm 5000 and carefully lifted it over the handrail to let it rest on the safety arm that protruded from the boat's stern and which kept the propeller away from danger. That arm was capped-off with a fender which added further protection. Jefferey looked at the barbeque in its new home and was satisfied that it would fit there quite nicely, although the clearance was tight. They tied it in place and tested it.

"That should do the trick." Jefferey said. "And it's out of the way now."

They were waved into the lock at that point and Jefferey made sure that he took his time and executed a perfect entry into the chamber, conscious that the slightest tap on the sides would draw more banal comments from Michael and Stephen. His faultless approach didn't save him though, as Mick couldn't resist congratulating him on 'pulling-off' the manoeuvre.

They'd done enough locks by now to understand how they behaved. As this was a down lock, it was simply a question of nosing up to the gates and keeping the boat there as the water was released. Down locks were certainly the easy of the two and the most predictable. Which made it all the more surprising that Jefferey forgot some of that behaviour. At the point at which the lock gates are ready to open, the boat in the chamber would be drawn backwards towards the rear of the chamber. It wasn't something you really needed to worry about since the danger of the cill was well passed and the fender on the rear would take up any forces should the boat touch the rear wall under the gate.

Concentrating more on the junction ahead, Jefferey watched as the crew members prepared to open the gates, giving them a thumbs-up as he did so and pointing to the right, where the boat would have to turn into a blind junction. As he made sure that they had got the message to go and check for oncoming boats, the boat began its drift backwards, unheeded. Expecting no more than a light bump, Jefferey turned the tiller at right angles just to be on the safe side and looked up to ensure that a leak wasn't going to give him a second drenching of the day. Had he looked down instead, he would have seen the boat edging closer to the rear of the chamber and the fender compressing as it hit the stone. That compression hadn't been accounted for in his calculations so the first thing he became aware of was a gentle crunching sound as the Firestorm 5000 met an immovable barrier and was crushed by the weight of a twenty-ton steel boat behind it. The fender reached its maximum compression shortly after and the boat began to move forward again. It had only been exposed for a brief moment, but the barbeque had made the most it. It was now a good six inches thinner than it had been before. Maybe now, it would fit on the roof.

"Sod it." Jefferey muttered as he put the boat into drive and headed out of the lock. He wouldn't mention it to anyone. Besides, he had other things on his mind as he edged slowly out into the junction, praying that the simple right turn onto the Trent and Mersey Canal wouldn't become another opportunity for him to make a fool of himself.

Mick and Steve left the gates of the lock open, having been asked to do so by a boat that was waiting at other side of the junction. Their prayers, despite all their best intentions and some semblance of sympathy for Jefferey, were directed the other way. They ran eagerly out from under the bridge and up towards the next lock, keeping a close eye on Jefferey as he turned the boat. The wind could have answered either prayer. It chose to favour the man at the helm this time, breezing gently across the port-side of the boat and guiding it safely in the right direction.

"Well, paste my eyes and take me home, Mummy!" Mick shouted as the Jefferey came towards them, a smile on his face. "Come straight in."

The latter instruction was unnecessary, since the gates of the lock were wide open, but Jefferey acknowledged his crew members with a thumbs-up. He glanced briefly behind him and could make out the line of boats heading further North up the canal, thankful that they were no longer in a queue as the others all seemed to have gone that way. Maybe now, things were turning a little in his favour.

Chapter Twenty-Nine:

"Gently does it." Jefferey shouted up to Mick and Steve as they began to work the top paddles of this first of the upward locks that led them onto the Trent and Mersey. "And be sure to keep an eye out for my signals."

"Okeydokey, Skipper." Steve saluted as he replied.

"And, Michael," Jefferey continued. "Will you please stop faffing around with that safety catch and flip it out of the way."

Mick chose to ignore both the man on the boat and the instruction. It was still a bit early in the day for Jefferey to have regained any credence as far as boating ability was concerned. Instead, he chatted to his son, keeping a left eye on the boat to ensure that it was ascending smoothly. As they chatted, the wind began to die down and the sun appeared. Despite the morning's shenanigans, perhaps the afternoon would be a little more enjoyable.

"By Jingo!" Steve explained as he boarded the boat. "You had that one nailed there, Jefferey. Thought we were in for a bit of a cabaret as you turned it, but all credit to you. A perfect manoeuvre."

"Aye." Mick joined them having closed the lock gate. "You couldn't have done any better, as sure as Toddington Heath still stands. And, it seems that your friend Roger can now become a distant memory. He went the other way. Can't say I'll miss him."

"He was a bit of a prat, wasn't he?" Jefferey sighed as he resolved to move on. "And Stephen, I'm sorry about not supporting you last night. I was wrong."

"Forget it, Jefferey" Stephen replied. "Water under the bridge and all that. Talking of which, have you dried off now?"

"Very witty, young Stephen." Jefferey responded. "But the bigger question is to you, Michael. Who on earth were those three people you were chatting with? They seemed to greet you like a hero."

"Bloody funny that one." Mick chuckled. "I've got no idea who they were, but they seemed to think they knew me. They wanted to shake my hand and take a selfie with me. Hey, I wasn't going to stop them. Still, I don't know what it was all about."

"Maybe," he continued. "They mistook me for someone famous. Tom Cruise maybe."

"More like Tom Thumb." Steve patted his dad's head as he replied.

Another bottle of wine kept the navigators in good spirits for the next leg of the journey. One which consisted of just nine 'canal miles' of four locks and five miles travel. It should only take them a few hours, after which, the promise of a fish and chip supper/tea was enough to make them look forward to mooring at Wheelock.

Inside the boat, Helen, Penelope and Alicia spent the time working their way through a bottle of gin (Penelope making only the very smallest dint in it) and keeping out of the guy's way. At first, their retreat inside had been an escape from the tension. Now it was simply a relaxed time of chit-chat and baby talk and plans for the rest of the journey. Plans to at least salvage something out of this rare time that they had together.

"You have one of those smart-phone thingies, don't you, Alicia?" Helen asked during a lull in the conversation.

"We all have them." Penelope laughed. "You really should get with the technology, Helen."

"Why do you want to know?" Alicia asked.

"I wouldn't mind going to church tomorrow." Helen explained. "I missed it last Sunday and I think a prayer or two might be in order after some of the things we've been through."

"I'll have a look what there is near Wheelock." Alicia told her, taking her phone from her handbag. "I'm sure there will be something. In fact, if you pass me that map, I may not even need to use Google."

The map was passed and Alicia smiled as she saw both their location and the nearby town on the same page.

"I thought so." She told them. "There's Sandbach, there, and there's Elworth. I lived nearby for a few years, many moons ago. Long before I met Jefferey in fact. Elworth has the most delightful little church. I'll check if it's still open and what time the services are."

"But," she continued, waving her phone around frantically. "I'm struggling for a signal in here. Excuse me for a moment and I'll see if it's any better on the front of the boat."

"You holding up okay, love?" Helen waited until Alicia was gone before reaching out a hand to hold her daughter-in-law's. "Baby not suffering too much with the tensions?"

"I'm fine, Helen, thanks." Penelope couldn't quite hold back the tears. "I grew up with them and I know what they're both like. I'm not going to let them affect little-un though. Besides, it's not all bad. Daddy's main problem is that he works too much. Proved by his trip to London on Monday. And Mummy, well, she's just Mummy. I think it's a marriage of convenience at times, but again, what's that to me. What really matters is that Stephen and I are making our own way. He's so like Mick at times."

"Yes, well I'm sorry about that. Hope it's not all the time?"

"Oh, Mick's a sweetheart, Helen. I'd rather have him and his unfettered ways than the stilted social paranoia of my lot. Besides, if he ignores you when you ask him to shut up, you can always get the job done with a decent stare."

"It was his idea." Helen explained. "This holiday. We would have loved to have been able to treat you to something more exotic, but we do have to watch the pennies. He was so excited about us all being together as a family and about the cruise itself. He's not one to

..ar grudges if he can help it, but Jefferey's pushing it a bit. We need to give Mick a bit of a lift if we can. He'll blame himself if he thinks we're not having a good time."

"Agreed." Penelope replied.

"What's agreed?" Alicia re-joined them. "Are we going to stage a mutiny and take control of the ship?"

"No, Mummy." Penelope sighed. "We're just agreeing to make the best of the time we have left. You in?"

"I've never been out, honey. The men are the men and we are what we are. Why stress it? Besides, we've always got gin and tonic!"

"Now, Helen." She continued. "Good news. The church at Elworth is alive and well. They have a 10.30 service tomorrow which looks like it might be a bit of fun. I might even join you. We can get a taxi from Wheelock. Sound good?"

"Great. But I didn't have you down as a church-person."

"Well, maybe there are some things about me you've still to learn. Besides, it will be nice to take a stroll down memory lane. We can carry on into Sandbach and have lunch afterwards. Penny, darling, you want to join us?"

"I'll see how I feel, Mummy. If that's okay."

"What say we brave the elements then and take the crew some food up?"

Which, after another bottle of gin was opened, they eventually did, handing the cold platter to the others just as they exited the second lock.

With the alcohol flowing and the food a welcome respite, the whole family managed to squeeze out onto the stern of the boat and enjoy the afternoon's cruise. A few glances were aimed at the Firestorm 5000 but no comments were made about the damage it seemed to have sustained. They'd let it ride for now.

Chapter Thirty:

Aside from Jefferey's repetition of his instructions for Mick to stop using the safety catch, the next lock was negotiated swiftly and the rest of the family chose to stretch their legs and walk towards the last one that they needed to work through today. Jefferey kept the boat at a snail's pace to accommodate their stroll, and even allowed another boat to overtake him.

"Take her up." he shouted to Helen and Mick who were the ones with windlasses this time around.

Husband and wife complied, chuckling away as they whispered something about being constantly nagged by the voice of God. Perhaps He heard and wasn't happy about His Name being used in vain. Perhaps He didn't like being compared to Jefferey. Or perhaps, it was simply something that was bound to happen. Either way, Mick finally succumbed to Jefferey's commands and whipped the paddle up without engaging the safety catch. Momentarily distracted by a swan swooping in low behind him, he lost focus for one second and the inevitable loss of grip on the windlass was followed by that freewheeling length of steel catching him on the forearm at full speed.

"Bloody bugger!" he shouted as the lock paddle clunked itself firmly down. "Bloody, bloody buggering bugger."

Jefferey's enquiring shouts from within the lock chamber were ignored as the rest of the crew gathered around Mick who was now rolling around in agony and clutching his arm.

"Michael." Helen shouted to him. "Stay still. You'll roll into the water. Now, let me have a look."

You didn't need to be medically qualified to pronounce a diagnosis on the arm that they were offered to examine. It was already swelling up and anyone could see that it wasn't quite as straight as it should be.

"It's his fault." Mick shouted. "Him and his bloody useless suggestions. I'll brain him when he gets up here."

"Now, Michael." Helen tried to console him. "Don't worry about all that. I think your arms broken. We need to get you to hospital."

"Bloody marvellous." he replied. "Absolutely bloody marvellous."

"I'm on the phone to the Ambulance people." Penelope surprised them with her prompt actions. "They wouldn't normally attend, but I've explained about our being on a boat and not having any transport. She's just checking if they have any paramedics about."

"Hold on a second." She returned to the call. "Oh, that would be wonderful. Thank you. yes, lock number 67, just outside Sandbach. Yes, we can walk to the main road."

She finished the call and explained to the others that a paramedic would be along shortly. They were to meet him on the main road.

"Steve," she told her husband. "You see El Capitan through the lock whilst Helen and I walk with Mick. Moor up just past the lock landing and we'll be back as soon as we can be. Mummy, I think you should stay with Steve."

The paramedic was already waiting when they got to the road. He took one look at Mick's arm and ushered him and Helen into the back of his car, which he then set racing towards Leighton Hospital in Crewe, leaving Penelope to walk back to the boat.

The remaining crew members had just finished trying to enjoy their fish and chips when they heard a taxi pull up and saw Mick and Helen emerge, the former with a fibreglass cast on his arm which was secured with a sling.

"Nobody." Mick hissed as he walked through the boat's cabin. "Say one word. They've given me a sedative and some heavy painkillers. I'm taking them and going to bed. I'll see you all in the morning."

They let him take himself through to the far cabin, and waited until they could hear the sound of his snoring before anything else was said.

"They were great at the hospital." Helen talked them through what had happened. "Despite Mick still not being able to avoid his stupid quips, they ushered him through x-ray, confirmed the break and set to with the cast at record speed. They even sorted a taxi out for us, on their account. He'll be fine tomorrow. But the arm will take a couple of weeks."

"Now," she continued, "despite everything that's happened, I'm famished. Any of that fish and chips left?"

Week Two

Day Two, Sunday:

Wheelock to Church Lawton

Chapter Thirty-One:

With Mick expected to be absent from the breakfast table, given the strength of the painkillers he'd been prescribed, the rest of the crew opted to forgo a Sunday fry-up and opt for simply toast and cereal instead. They worked around each other in the small galley, each helping themselves to what they wanted, and few words were exchanged between them. Having eaten, they sat in that same silence for a while longer until Helen decided to that enough was enough.

"What's done is done." she told the others. "No point crying over spilt milk. And Mick will be fine. He's not one to let something like a broken arm ruin the rest of this holiday. Besides, I had a good talk with him last night whilst we were at the hospital, and he only blames himself. Your being away tomorrow may help things Jefferey, but the two of you are man enough to move forwards, I'm sure. This is a holiday for Stephen and Penelope as much as us, we should think more about them."

"We're fine, Mum." Stephen took the last slice of toast. "It's all a bit of a laugh really. Something that we can tell sprog about when he's old enough."

"Or she." Penelope reminded her husband that the scans had been inconclusive.

"It, then! I'm not worried, as long as it comes out in one piece."

"So very thoughtful, Stephen." Alicia whispered. "You'd better be there for Penny when the time comes."

"I am worried about Mick though." Helen steered the conversation back to where she wanted it to go. "There's something going on that I really can't get a grip on. I can usually read him like a book, but things are happening that don't square up."

"What sort of things?" Jefferey's attention was firmly on Helen as he spoke, a slight hint of guilt in his voice as he wondered whether she was party to the special investment opportunity that Michael had partaken in.

"The people who keep greeting him." Helen's answer changed Jefferey's fears into curiosity. "Even at the hospital last night. It wasn't too busy, thankfully, but a couple of the people there kept looking at Mick and whispering to themselves. It was like they knew him, or something about him. Even one of the nurses asked if they could shake his hand. How can he know these people, when we're so far from home?"

"You know Dad." Stephen offered an explanation. "Once met, never forgotten. They're probably people who know him through his bowling. He gets around with that and his name appears in the papers occasionally. It might just be that."

It was true. Mick devoted much of his spare time to bowling and had played for his county on more than one occasion. In season, every night he'd be out on a different green, leaving Helen to her reading and giving Steve a chance to rib his father whenever possible about the time he spent with Bo Ling, his Thai bit-on-the-side.

"Morning, everyone." Mick startled them all as he opened his cabin door and greeted them, dressed only in a pair of boxer shorts. "Apologies for my state of dress but I'm going to need a hand. Alicia, you want to help dress an invalid?"

"Michael!" Helen chastised her husband. "Don't be so crude. Just grab a dressing gown and join us if you must. I'll help you get dressed later."

"So, why were my ears burning?" Mick asked as he sat down next to his wife.

"We were trying to fathom your mystery life." Steve answered. "Wondering why perfect strangers kept recognising you. I offered bowling as an explanation but it's a bit of a lame one. I mean, ten's a crowd at one of your matches."

"It's funny isn't it." Mick ignored the jibe. "First, the locks at Middlewich, then the hospital last night. I'm going with the celebrity thing. There must be another handsome stud of a man who's making it big. Who knows, I might be able to make a few bob as a looky-likey!"

"More like a looky stupid." Helen muttered as she poured Mick a bowl of cereal and thrust a spoon in his good hand. "Now, do you need mummy to feed you or will you be alright?"

Fortunately, it was Mick's left arm that had suffered the break. Right-handed, he wasn't as incapable as the others thought he might be.

"I'm surprised you're up so early." Jefferey tried to break the ice between the two of them. "Arm not hurting too much?"

"It hurts like buggery." Mick replied after clearing his mouth with a long swig of tea. "No thanks to some people around this table."

"Steady on old chap…"

"Forget it, Jeff. I'm only joking. It was my stupid mistake." He paused before continuing. "Although a mistake that I made because I listened to you. It had better be the only time it happens."

Knowing that he was referring to the money he'd lent him, Jefferey chose not to rise to the bait but instead to rise from the table.

"Don't go just yet, Jefferey." Mick emphasised every syllable of the name. "You haven't heard why I'm up nice and early. And you need to as it concerns you. Sit down for a few minutes."

"Right," Mick addressed all the family members once Jefferey was back in place. "call it a mutiny or just call it a slight change of plans but here is today's revised schedule, as determined by me. His Lordship can take a day off with his planning. This is what we're going to do, like it or not. Helen and I will go to church, after which, we shall have a leisurely lunch and I will get hammered enough to forget my woes. Whilst we do that, you Jefferey, can take full command of this vessel, something that I'm sure you will thoroughly enjoy, and take her for today's cruise to Church Lawton. Steve can help you, whilst Penny and Alicia have a lazy day."

"I rather think we'd like to join you in Elworth." Alicia interrupted. "I know Sandbach quite well and would love to treat you to lunch. Penny, sweetheart?"

Penelope declined straightaway, using the baby as an excuse but really more concerned about her husband having to endure a full day under her dad's command.

"And this is a group decision?" Jefferey asked.

"It is now." Mick replied, challenging the other. "Unless you want to make a case for my risking breaking the other arm?"

Huffing as he left the table, Jefferey accepted that their plans would go ahead, and began the process of checking the engine ready for departure. Alicia booked a taxi. Helen and Mick giggled and chuckled like school-children from the privacy of their cabin as one tried to dress the other who was feeling surprisingly frisky.

In the taxi to Elworth church, Helen grilled Alicia about her time in this neck of the woods and what had led to her leaving the area. The answers she received were fairly vague but interspersed with the pointing out of some old haunts that they passed. Mick sat in the front seat of the cab, trying to make small talk with the driver who preferred his passengers to be seen and not heard and who was trying to listen to the radio. Maybe Mick wasn't as popular as he'd been led to believe he was.

"Drop us here, please." Alicia checked her watch and noted they had a little time to spare before the service began. 'Here' was the entrance to an estate of modern houses, several hundred yards from their destination.

"Let me show you something." Alicia led them into the estate. "See the end of that road there? When I lived here, all that was beyond that was green pasture. They were starting to dig it all up when I was leaving, but it was beautiful. I used to come down here and walk through those fields, with the only thing disturbing me being the cattle."

"How long ago did you leave?" Helen asked.

"Oh, I wasn't even twenty by the time I headed away. I'd left home and hitch-hiked from Southampton. The last lift I got, well, he tried to get frisky with me when he pulled into Sandbach services. I did a runner, found myself in the town and kind of liked what I saw. I got a job in the record shop the day after, found a flat-share and that was that. Happy times. Then again, I could probably tell you similar stories about a hundred towns in the UK. I was a bit of a nomad before I met Jefferey. Still, we'd better be going, the service will start soon."

Chapter Thirty-Two:

They arrived at the church just in time. Lively music was playing in the background and a loud buzz of chatter had risen up like a swarm of bees over the packed pews. The website that Alicia had seen should have given her a clue to how surprisingly vibrant this little parish church was. There were pages of details of events that were taking place and the photograph of the vicar, Jonathon Mackintosh, showed him to be a fun-loving guy who had used a picture of himself in full make-up as Widow Twankee. The transformation from dying village church to prospering evangelical worship centre had been a slow and challenging one but Mackintosh had never given up and the harvest days were upon them.

"This doesn't look too bad." Mick whispered to Helen. "Thought it was going to be a bit fusty, but we might be okay."

The Methodists were the Roberts' preferred group. At home, their own Minister was a young and vibrant leader who was doing wonders with the old chapel. The children had been educated in the old school building, but this had now been demolished and replaced with a modern 'community' facility. Pupil numbers continued to rise despite their home town now having a population of numerous faiths, and none at all. Positive OFSTED reports and even more positive pupil outcomes were enough to offset any parent's fears of indoctrination.

Of the two, Helen was the more committed believer, but Mick had a steady and certain faith as well as a love for the old hymns that drew him to her side most Sundays (bowling permitting).

As the congregation heard the familiar final chords of the worship song that had been playing in the background, they quietened down and waited for the service to begin. They needed no encouragement as, each week, Reverend Jon, as he liked to be called, preferred to start things off with a bit of a bang. This week was no exception and only the three newcomers were caught off guard as an electric-guitar-wielding apparition leapt out from the side of the nave playing a rift that would never be found in a hymn book. Strutting and thrusting in time with the music in a poor imitation of Mick Jagger, only the clerical garb gave him away.

"Ooh," Helen nudged Alicia. "He's a bit dishy, isn't he? Glad you came now?"

Alicia would normally be up for a bit of banter with Helen, but she remained strangely silent, giving just a cursory nod as she stared towards the front of the church. Ignoring the applause and the hand-clapping all around her, she retrieved the order of service that had been handed to her on arriving at the church and checked the details again. It was the vicar's name that intrigued her. It didn't make sense. Surely it couldn't be who she thought it was?

Mick did his best to join in with the singing at the now-obligatory 'time of worship' but he couldn't understand why each chorus had to be repeated ad infinitum. He made a point of singing every song just once, then standing silently. When the hymns were sung, that was a different matter. Despite the modernity of the church, they were the old Wesley classics that he loved and which were here played at a jaunty tempo.

"See, now that's a song!" he told Helen, as the last bars of 'And Can It Be' faded away. "Proper music, proper words and sung once. That'll do for me."

Whilst the service was forced to follow the minimum of the Church of England prescribed routine, it pushed the boundaries and was never stuffy or rigid. On top of which, the Reverend Jon knew that a sermon over twenty minutes long was no good. He finished his in fifteen, even after digressing to make a few ad-lib jokes.

"Dishy and funny." whispered Helen, still wondering why Alicia was so quiet.

When the service was over, the expectation of the regulars was that they'd enjoy a cup of tea and a chit-chat in the newly-rebuilt hall attached to the Victorian church. Knowing that not everyone would want to linger, Reverend Jon took up his position at the door of the church to say farewell to those who were leaving.

"I'll be out in a minute." Alicia told Helen. "You go on ahead."

As with the previous night at the hospital and the feeling she had about Mick, Helen sensed that something wasn't right with Alicia. And that something seemed to be related to the vicar. She went with Alicia's suggestion, but made sure that after they'd been through the obligatory handshakes and welcomes, they lingered near to where the vicar stood so that they could observe what she was doing. It was almost as if she wanted to avoid the vicar. Something she almost managed as she took an opportunity when he was distracted to bolt for the door, not realising how brief and ineffective that distraction would be.

"Cheryl?" the vicar asked as he caught Alicia's reluctantly offered hand. "Cheryl Atkins. It is you isn't it?"

"I'm sorry." Alicia replied. "I think you're mistaken. My name's Alicia. Thank you for a nice service."

Alicia almost ran to join the others, but the voice behind her made her turn back.

"Please, don't dash off." the vicar beckoned her back. "I'm sorry if I embarrassed you. Must be a case of mistaken identity. Forgive me and I hope I haven't caused you any hardship."

"It's fine, vicar." Alicia managed to compose herself, fully aware that both Mick and Helen were watching intently. "And thank you again for a lovely service. Your church is a credit to you."

She offered her hand again and let the vicar clasp it firmly. Only when he'd let go did she feel the piece of card that had been placed there. She stuffed it in her pocket and walked boldly away from the church.

A taxi dropped them off at a small pub in the town centre, where they secured a table and ordered the set Sunday lunch. Mick's painkillers were wearing off but the presence of a decent pint was enough to take his mind off that. He drank his first, ordered his second and joined the ladies who were already seated in the dining room and working through a bottle of wine.

"Cheers, Alicia." Mick raised his glass. "So kind of you to pay for lunch. You don't mind me putting a few of these on the tab?"

"Not at all Mick.", she smiled as she replied. "You've earned them."

"Ta, Alicia," he grinned mischievously. "or should that be Cheryl?"

Chapter Thirty- Three:

The leisurely pace of the lunch that the three crew members were enjoying sat in sharp contrast to the hectic activity aboard the boat. The short hop from Wheelock to Church Lawton was only five miles, but those five miles included eighteen locks. The number of locks hadn't, at first, factored in Mick's calculations. He simply had to get away from the boat and its skipper. That said, when he realised how many locks he'd be missing he merely saw it as another positive gain and something of a retribution for the pain he was enduring.

Jefferey's protestations to his wife about the unfairness of the workload had fallen on deaf ears. He knew better than to try and argue the point and had quickly resigned himself to a hard day's cruise. Under Alicia's instructions, he was to navigate, whilst Steve, under Penelope's command, was to do the locks. She would offer moral and practical support by providing the two men with cups of tea and food as she felt the urge to. Steve too, made no counter-argument. He was that little bit better trained than the other husbands aboard the Harriet Knot.

If all went according to plan, and if they chose not to stop for lunch, Jefferey reckoned that they could be at their destination by four p.m. A number of the locks sat close together, meaning that with traffic coming the other way and Steve going ahead to set them where possible, they could work in a way that made the task simpler. Being up-locks, they were, by nature, that little bit harder to negotiate, but they wouldn't let that get in the way.

"Nice going, Stephen." Jefferey brought the boat in to pick up his son-in-law as they ticked off the last of the Wheelock flight and set off towards Hassal Green. "Just goes to show that three can be a crowd sometimes. We'll soon have the rest cracked."

"It's not what I expected to be doing." Steve opened the first cans of lager for the day. "But it's okay nonetheless. Probably the best option as well. Can you imagine how insufferable dad would be?"

"He's a good man, your dad." Jefferey took the proffered drink. "I know that you and Penny think that we have issues between us, but I respect Michael immensely. And you too."

The shock of the compliment was a little too much for Steve, who chose not to respond. Instead, he settled down next to Jefferey and let the warm sun (a pleasant bonus) add to his general feeling of relative peace. When his dad had broken his arm, he'd genuinely believed that that would be the end of the holiday. It hadn't gone quite as they'd expected, that was for sure, but there were still some enjoyable moments and it certainly beat having to go to work every day. Besides which, the whole canal boat experience was something that he was really buying into. He was a man for whom the mad pace of modern career-building left little time for rest and relaxation. Here on the cut, you had no choice but to embrace the escape it offered. And it wasn't just an escape from the practicalities of labour. It was also an escape from the social conventions that were so binding. You could be a rocket-scientist or a cleaner, a famous rock star or an unknown taxi driver. None of that counted for anything on the canals. You were just another person and everybody had value here.

"Come on, lad, locks ahoy!" Jefferey's shout snapped Steve out of his daydreaming. "Just two pairs along this stretch then young Penny will be furnishing us with lunch. Let's show them what we can do."

Steve dutifully left the boat and began to set the first lock. He liked Jefferey's use of the plural, given that the actual work was being done by him. Still, he'd only get bored if he was simply driving the boat. Locks were an opportunity to do something and to have a nice chat with other boaters as well.

After the first two locks, he pointed at the nearby pub.

"No time for that Stephen." Jefferey replied to the question that hadn't been asked. "Time and tide and all that ..."

"I'll walk ahead then." He sighed. "Take my mind off what I'm missing."

Circumstances worked in their favour at Pierpoint Locks, both being exited by oncoming craft just as they arrived. They headed out onto the next section just after one o'clock, and used the gap between the locks to devour the lavish cold spread that Penelope presented them with.

"Are you boys playing nicely?" she asked as she passed the plates of food through from the inside of the boat.

"We have been on best behaviour, mummy." Steve put on a mock infant's voice. "And we did do lots of locks and we did drive the boat and we saw some swans and some ducks and some geese and ..."

"Shut up and eat your lunch." Penelope replied wearily, settling down next to them and working her way through a pork-pie.

"Have you been okay?" Steve asked.

"Absolutely fine." his wife smiled. "Just been chilling and reading and watching the world go by. I had a bit of a tidy up as well."

"You take it easy now, Penelope." Jefferey put his arm around his daughter. "You need to look after little one there. Don't overdo it."

"I'm pregnant dad, not disabled. And I'm not daft. We're doing fine thanks. Bun in oven is cooking away nicely and is expected to be ready on time."

They finished lunch in silence and just in time to start work on the next lock. Steve was beginning to feel the effects of the lagers that they'd been working their way through. He resolved to take a breather and drink only water for the next hour or so. Jefferey was also feeling the effects, but that wasn't a bad thing as it resulted in him relaxing and easing off on the orders he so liked to give. His workplace worries were all set to be resolved tomorrow, and a night in a hotel was just what he needed. Mick's investment had been more vital than he'd like to admit and a potentially catastrophic cashflow problem had been averted. No, Mick wasn't such a bad person after all. When he returned from the smoke, he'd make sure they made the most of this rare time that they had together. In short, it had been an eventful and frustrating first week, not least because of the Bottomley situation. It would be better from now on. For the first time since being aboard, he allowed a genuine smile of contentment to pass over his face.

That smile lasted only briefly. An old friend intervened to wipe it away.

"Take her up." Jefferey gave Steve the thumbs up and watched as his son-in-law worked the next set of lock paddles furiously. It had taken a while for him to get used to working uphill in a lock, what with the unusual effects that underwater turbulence could have, but he was now confident that a heavy application of forward or reverse thrust, as required, would work to keep the boat as central in the chamber as possible. Not all locks were the same though and at Lock 53, the nonchalant thumbs up that was given was a little hasty as the boat was threatening to smack firmly into the front gates. To compensate for this, Jefferey threw the Morse control into reverse, a little too enthusiastically and for just that little but too long. From the danger at the front, a new danger at the rear appeared and there was nothing that Jefferey could do to stop the boat heading swiftly backwards and into the rear gate.

It hit with a thud and a clunk that reminded the skipper that the fender on the rear wasn't the only thing behind him. The Firestorm 5000 absorbed whatever forces that the fender failed to and promptly concertinaed itself to half of its original width.

"You okay?" Steve asked, barely able to hold in the smile that forced to push its way through.

"That bloody buggering barbeque!" Jefferey shouted. "I wish I'd never brought it along. Don't worry though, Steve, the damage is done. Carry on doing your stuff."

Once they were clear of that lock, surveying the damage, Steve's only suggestion was that they ditch the Firestorm once and for all.

"No, no." Jefferey insisted. "That beasty cost me a fortune and I won't let it beat me. Come on, we'll pop it back on the roof now. There's no wind today and it isn't exactly going to hit any bridges now, is it?"

They undid the ropes that held the barbeque and used them to retie it to the roof. It certainly looked less impressive than when it had first been up there, but it also presented less of a threat since it was now half of its original thickness.

"Come on then, let's crack on."

"You're being remarkably calm, Jeff." Steve replied.

"One sometimes has to simply take a step back and go with the blows. It's only a barbeque after all. Only six more locks to go. You up for it?"

Off they set again, working as a team through the first five of those locks and wearily-satisfied at their progress. They were looking forward to relaxing and welcoming the others back, and to a pleasant evening of family bonhomie.

Chapter Thirty-Four:

At the last of the locks, an unexpected queue had built up, presumably from boats that had been moored between the locks and were now heading towards the tunnel at Harecastle. Stephen walked from Lock 48 to Lock 47 watching as Jefferey manoeuvred the boat out of the chamber. Two other boats were waiting. Jefferey had to ease the throttle back and prepare to pull in and wait.

Stephen missed most of the fun as he was helping the next crew with the lock. It was only the shouting that alerted him to anything being wrong. By the time he walked back to check, he could do nothing to help his hapless father-in-law.

The prequel to the sight of Jefferey flat out on the ground, being helped up by other boaters who grabbed the centre-line that he'd dropped and pulled his own boat in, was a series of events that might have been avoided with a little careful planning. Exiting the lock, Jefferey had seen the other boats waiting ahead of him and steered the boat carefully to the towpath. Having grabbed the centre-line, he held the boat loosely as he edged to the back of the queue. Settled in this position, he felt that he had the boat under control and began to enjoy the brief rest from activity. That is, until the next boat came down the lock behind, generating a surge of water that caught the stern and started to apply increasing pressure to the rope he was holding. Matching that pressure with a stronger pull of his own, Jefferey failed to notice that the line was hooked around the Firestorm 5000 on the roof. It was too late to board the boat and free the rope, so all the captain could do was pull harder and trust that the barbeque was secured firmly enough that it would take the strain. Applying increasing pressure as the boat threatened to take itself away into the lock pound, Jefferey cared little for the Firestorm as he pulled against it, feeling it buckle some more as he did so. Built to last, it withstood the pressure. Sadly, the ropes that held it were less reliable, especially as the farthest one was being chaffed and scraped by one of the many sharp edges that its adventures had left it scarred with.

Just when he thought that things were back in control, that rope gave way, the Firestorm 5000 flipped off the roof and swung down against the side of the boat, stopping as it smashed through the galley window. Jefferey meanwhile had some momentum still to lose and found himself flying backwards into the hedges that bounded the lock pound. He let go of the rope, continued his backward somersault and came to a rest in a thorny bush that tore at his clothes.

That was the point at which Steve was able to observe the action. He watched as others heaved the boat safely in, whilst Jefferey tried, unsuccessfully, to extricate himself from the foliage that embraced him.

"Are you alright?" Steve really didn't know what else to say as he helped Jefferey up.

"Yes, yes." He muttered impatiently, wincing as he pulled loose thorns from his clothing. "I'm fine. Thank you anyway. You go back to the lock, I'll sort things down here."

Steve complied, not quite sure about his father-in-law's state of mind as he perceived a strange kind of madness behind his eyes. He looked back as he reached the lock gates and couldn't quite believe what he was seeing. Jefferey, having thanked the other boaters, had taken the necessary step of untying what was left of the Firestorm 5000, since it would only act as an obstruction if they went into the lock with it in-situ. Thinking that he would simply put it back on the roof, Steve was surprised to see Jefferey lay it carefully on the towpath before disappearing inside the boat.

When he emerged a short time later, he was carrying the boat's mooring mallet, a heavy and substantial piece of kit designed to drive pegs into stubborn ground. Calmly and carefully, Jefferey moved to stand next to the barbeque from which position he seemed to be addressing it in the sternest terms. The verbal onslaught over, the mallet was raised and in a psychopathic frenzy watched by all, Jefferey proceeded to demolish what was left of his beloved Firestorm, rendering it into a flattened shadow of itself within minutes.

None of those witnessing the attack on the helpless piece of equipment were brave enough to intervene. Besides, it was the sort of spectacle that you had to make the most of, even though it was quickly over; with blood seeping from the numerous scratches and his clothes torn to shreds, few would have pegged Jefferey as a sane and sensible man. That said, once the onslaught was over, he brushed himself down, picked up what was left of the barbeque and returned to the boat that was now ready to enter the lock.

"Let's see you cause any more trouble." He muttered to the remains that he threw back on the roof, before easing the boat off and into the lock chamber.

Fortunately, the moorings at Church Lawton had plenty of vacant space. Steve and Penelope tied her up but remained seated at the stern of the boat, neither having the courage or inclination to encounter Jefferey who hadn't been seen since that last lock had been completed. Penelope had been ordered out onto deck whilst her father sorted things out.

From inside the boat they could hear the sound of running water as Jefferey bathed his wounds. That was followed by a brief pause, followed in turn by the sound of the small, battery-powered vacuum cleaner that the boat came supplied with. Silence after that and then...

"That all seems to be in order now." Jefferey joined them on the deck, a large tumbler of whisky in his hands. "We'll have a go at patching the window when Michael returns. Nice mooring spot. Well done."

Afraid to refer to the events of the day, and keen to avoid one subject in particular, Steve and Penelope took themselves for a short walk to look at the nearby church which was a fascinating example of hybrid architecture. Its tower was as expected, but the nave behind that was a modern addition that looked more like a Methodist chapel that had tried to mate with the other. Whilst the church was interesting, what got their interest more was the builder's skip that sat in the car park. They knocked at the vicarage, explained their situation and were given the necessary position to lay the fated barbeque finally to rest amongst the bricks and rubble and old doors that welcomed their new companion.

As they were returning, they heard the rattling of a well-used diesel engine and watched as Mick, Helen and Alicia piled, giggling, out of the taxi.

"Looks like they've had more fun than us." Steve whispered to his wife as they went to approach the new arrivals.

"Just watch what you say, Stephen." Penelope hissed. "I mean it. Best behaviour."

That injunction, being followed, only made it a more enjoyable experience when Mick walked down the boat and had to look several times before he realised that the galley window wasn't just immaculately clean but missing.

"Bloody hell, Jefferey." he put his head through the window and shouted into the boat. "Looks like you've had a smashing time. Not a bad idea though, get a bit of ventilation going. Might be a bit nippy at night though."

Needless to say, he received no reply.

Like several others in the past week, that evening was a little subdued, although Jefferey was less hostile than expected and was able to look at the whole thing with a wry smile. Mick didn't help with a constant barrage of comments that Steve, under the watchful eye of Penelope, refused to accompany. Alicia was vaguely sympathetic, although in a semi-distracted way that the others put down to her having had one glass of Pinot too many over lunch.

"I'm going to get an early night." Jefferey informed the crew as the conversation lulled. "Been a busy day and I need to head off early tomorrow. I've booked a taxi for seven. If I don't see you before I go, I'll be back on Tuesday morning. I'm even going to take Don Quixote with me and try to make progress on the train. He continues to beckon me."

"Nighty, night then Jefferey and you have a good rest." Mick told him. "You look shattered!"

"That's enough, Michael." Alicia chastised him. "Before you go Jefferey, I should tell you that I won't be here tomorrow either. You remember Patricia?"

"How could I forget her." Jefferey replied, casting his mind back to the fraught night when one of Alicia's oldest friends had cornered him in the bathroom.

"Well, she lives locally. I thought it might be nice to catch up with her and didn't think you'd want to be there. I'll be staying with her tomorrow. I thought about it when we were at the pub and it works out perfectly as she's recently split up with Daniel."

"Anyone else abandoning ship?" Mick looked around the table.

"Don't be daft." Helen shut him up. "You have a nice time Alicia and you Jefferey, I hope your meeting goes well. We can regroup on Tuesday and we'll still have a few days together. I'm turning in too, so, goodnight all."

Alicia accompanied Jefferey and Penelope followed her mum, leaving just Steve and Mick to crack open a bottle of whisky and see the night off. Mick was still in pain but not so much that he couldn't enjoy the next episode of the story of Jefferey, one that his son was able to tell him in full and delicious detail as they watched the sun go down and heard the gentle flapping of the temporary window that they'd fixed in place earlier with plastic and duct tape.

"This is a pain in the butt." Mick raised his broken arm as he spoke to Steve. "And I should be booked into some sort of mental health facility for treatment given all the grieve that that man's caused me. But, you know what? I wouldn't change any of it. It's been like watching an ongoing soap-opera. I might miss him tomorrow. I'm certainly looking forward to what happens on his return."

It was that comment that inspired his son's next move.

Week Two

Day Three, Monday:

Church Lawton to Barlaston

Chapter Thirty-Five:

Not being used to taking much exercise, Stephen grunted and groaned as he stretched his weary muscles, trying to shake off the pains that the previous day's exertions had caused him. He was alone in the galley, having been unable to get back to sleep after Jefferey had inconsiderately let the door slam as he dashed for his taxi. Mind you, a little bit of peace and quiet was well worth the lost hour or so of sleep.

"Ow!" he muttered to himself as he stretched up for the tea bags that were kept on a high shelf to keep the damp off them. "I'll need a holiday after this holiday to recover."

"What are you moaning about, love of my life?" Penelope sidled up close to him and rested her protruding belly against his back.

"Morning, angel of my pants. Not moaning, just groaning. I could do with a massage. Later on, perhaps?"

"You may be in luck. If your mum and dad go for it, that is. You still want to go ahead?"

"Of course." Steve replied, now keener than ever to progress the plan they'd discussed in bed last night. "You go ahead and book it. Now, leave me in peace so that I can prepare the morning's repast."

The smell of a full English began to fill the boat, bringing the rest of the crew into the main saloon within minutes of the first sausages hitting the pan.

"Ay up lad." Mick patted Steve on the shoulder. "Don't forget the black pudding and haggis. No Jefferey means a free-for-all and I intend to make the most of it."

"I wish I could disagree with you." Alicia slipped onto the dinette's bench. "And, whilst we're all gathered here and in the absence of his nibs, let me say how sorry I am that he's been a little bit challenging. I knew he'd struggle, but not as much as he has."

"Don't you worry, Alicia, love," Mick slid in next to her. "We've been through tougher times and if one broken arm and a smashed window are all we have to get upset about, I'm not complaining."

"Don't forget the flattened Firestorm." Steve shouted above the sound of hot oil. "and the flooded engine."

"Don't encourage him Steve." Helen sighed.

"So, what are the plans for today?" Penelope didn't want to hear any more about her father's difficulties. "Mummy, are you still set on visiting Patricia?"

"I am." Alicia replied. "But don't worry, I'll set off a little early and have a mooch around the old town before meeting up with her. That way, you can set off in good time."

"Thanks." Steve had plated up the food and begun handing the breakfasts out. "I don't think we're planning a long journey today, but there are some locks involved and, for your own particular delight, father, a long tunnel to get excited about."

"Eh, that's right!" Mick replied excitedly. "The Harecastle Tunnel. Three thousand yards of blackness and damp. I've been looking forward to that."

"You may have been." Helen carefully cut around her egg yoke in a way that was unique to the Roberts family, none of them wanting the various foodstuffs on their plate to mingle. "But you can count me out if you think I'm doing anything other than hiding inside."

"Me too." Penelope added. "Let the boys bounce around but I'm staying where I can't see how close they get to disaster."

"But," she continued. "Steve and I know how hard you've been working lately so we've got a little surprise for you later. Provided Mick gets us through safely."

"Sounds intriguing." Mick said. "Nothing dodgy I hope?"

"You'll love it dad." Steve told him. "As sure as Toddington Heath still stands!"

Having washed up with Helen, Alicia packed a small overnight bag and left to meet her taxi just before ten. Mick and Steve did the engine checks whilst Penelope and Helen set up their morning camp on the bow deck.

"Will Mick be alright?" Penelope asked.

"Oh, he'll be fine, love." Helen told her. "And if he complains, I'll just remind him of the time he discharged himself from hospital against doctor's orders just so he could go bowling. I can still see him now, taking the match easily, despite the stitches that criss-crossed his leg."

"How did he get the stitches?"

"Football.", Helen sighed. "And if it wasn't that, he'd be on the cricket field. Mind you, I think our marriage has survived because of our regular absences."

Steve reached across from the towpath to undo the front rope.

"You hold tight now ladies." he smiled. "Napoleon's going to try driving this thing with one hand. I'm on lock duty. Again!"

Mick had practised moving the throttle with his broken arm and was confident that it would be fine. Which is how it proved to be as he eased the boat away from the moorings and towards the first of the six locks that would see them at the entrance to the tunnel.

Neither Helen nor Penelope were called to assist, although they occasionally made a foray to the stern of the boat to offer words of encouragement and the obligatory liquid refreshment, before returning to their lazy morning in the sunshine. There were a few other boats about, all of whom seemed equally relaxed in the morning sunshine and passed the time of day in that wonderfully amicable canal way, whichever member of the crew they spoke to.

All were headed to the tunnel and only one seasoned traveller saw it as a chore rather than an exciting interlude.

"You go past us then." Mick told him as they waited at a lock. "I'll slip in behind you and follow you, if that's okay?"

The other boater was happy to go with that but did warn Mick that he wouldn't be dawdling.

"Mind you," he explained. "once you get past the entrance and into the swing of it, you'll soon pick it up. Just keep your mouth shut. A drop of pure, filtered rainwater may be nice, but you can't be sure that that's all that's dropping down from the roof. Oh, and put a hat on."

More snippets of advice were picked up from others and stored in Mick's memory banks. Steve missed them all as he worked the boat through the locks. Mick wondered which, if any, he should share with his son.

At the tunnel entrance, a line of boats waited to be given the all clear to enter. Each boat was checked to ensure that its light and horn worked before the crew were handed a leaflet explaining how to navigate this tricky part of the system. Mick was halfway through reading that leaflet when the boat in front of him moved off and he passed it to Steve to finish off.

"I don't think it's rocket science, son. You just keep an eye on the ladies and I'll take us through safely. I've never had a problem slipping through a passage before. No matter how tight!"

"You're a filthy man, Michael Roberts." Steve replied. "And you've already broken the first rule of getting through this tunnel without being a predictable prat. Make sure I can't tick off the others, such as shouting 'echo', pretending to be a ghost or turning the lights off. They've all been done before and they've never been funny."

Despite his outwardly relaxed demeanour, Mick was properly terrified as the entrance loomed ahead. He was almost ready to hand over to Steve, having been rendered temporarily blind by the shift from sunlight to darkness, but he just managed to get his bearings and was soon settled in and watching the boat in front.

"Argh..." Steve shouted as a drop of water fell onto his face. "They should warn you about that. Tell you to wear a hat or something."

"Speaking of which," he looked at Mick's wide-brimmed sun hat. "you seem remarkably well prepared."

"Just had a hunch, son. Just had a hunch!"

For a first-timer, six knocks against the tunnel walls, only two of which were hard enough to scare the crew inside, was a pretty good result. Father and son exited the tunnel and blinked in the sunlight, giving each other a high-five as they did so.

"Are we out?" Penelope stuck her head out of the doorway.

"I bloody well hope so." Mick chuckled, "'cos if we aren't then the tunnel roof's collapsed."

"Be careful, Michael." Helen joined them on the deck, waving a piece of paper at them. "Or you won't get this."

"I think he's earned it." Penelope took it off Helen and passed it to Mick.

"Eh, look at this son," he opened the folded paper and saw the fruits of Helen and Alicia's distraction activity. "A 'Certificate of Tunnel Completion', and it's awarded to 'Mike and Steve in recognition of their skills in transporting their loved ones through The Harecastle Tunnel'."

He passed the badly-scribbled 'certificate' across to Steve who thanked them both graciously.

"Which reminds me." Penelope said. "Our little surprise. Sorry we haven't got anything printed but … drum roll please, husband dearest …"

Steve obliged a little too enthusiastically.

Chapter Thirty-Six:

"…we are pleased to announce," Penelope continued after Steve's trumpet voluntary finally came to an end. "that you are booked into a nearby spa hotel for an afternoon of rest and relaxation and a night of luxury accommodation. I'll book a taxi when we get to Longport. They can pick you up there."

"A hotel?" Helen asked. "Are you sure?"

"Well," Steve explained. "we figured that with the others away, you may as well have a bit of a break as well. No pun intended. Dad, you can chill in the spa and the pool and rest your arm. Mum, you can have a long bath. We'll sort a taxi for tomorrow to bring you back to Barlaston."

"Well done lad. I'm impressed." Mick was almost lost for words.

"Oh, it's not just about you." Steve replied. "It'll give Penny and I some time together."

"Like father like son, hey, Helen." Mick leered at his wife.

"Rest and relaxation Michael Roberts." She replied. "That's all."

In the same uncharacteristic way in which it had accompanied the crew of the hire-boat on their journey, the sun continued to shine for most of the time as the weather stayed fairly predictable. With the blue skies above and the rippling waters all around, Steve and Penelope waved goodbye to Mick and Helen as they waited on the towpath for their taxi.

Lunch had been a relaxed affair in a local pub and all bar the unfortunate mother-to-be had topped up their alcohol levels. For Steve and Mick, it was the prelude to a happy day of boozing. For Helen, it was a rare indulgence and would be followed by soft drinks until maybe a glass of some liqueur or even a cocktail, before bed.

"Your mum and dad are great." Penelope passed Steve a fresh glass of lager and sat down beside him as he steered the boat gently and slowly through the urban sprawl of the Potteries. "So much less complicated than mine. Easier to get on with."

"I know." Steve sighed contentedly. "It's only when you see them up against others that you appreciate who and what they are. You nailed it with 'uncomplicated'. Love them or loath them, what you see is what you get."

"And they really appreciate the value of money." Penelope continued. "I grew up in a world where money was always plentiful. At least, it seemed like it was. Your parents though, they aren't ashamed to be careful with every penny. I couldn't believe how hard it would be to get them to take a taxi to the hotel rather than waste a couple of hours of their holiday cruising with us. And then…"

"Go on." Steve knew what was coming.

"There's this mystery side to your dad. Everybody seems to know him and love him. Did you see the other people at the pub pointing and nudging towards him? Are you sure he doesn't have some sort of alter ego?"

"Not him. I think he's as baffled as any of us. You'll have to try a facial recognition search later and see if there isn't some new celeb that looks like him. Or some short-arsed Northerner who's become a hit banging the spoons on a talent show."

"You never get that with my dad." Penelope spoke softly, reflectively. "Never has been like that. Sure, he'd tell you he had a huge circle of friends, but they're more acquaintances. Even at the golf club, it's all about back-scratching. Different worlds I suppose."

"He ain't so bad, is he?"

"Oh, Jefferey's fine. I could have done a lot worse. He's always been that bit distant with me. Like I'm more of a character in his life than his own flesh and blood. He's got the house and the Merc and the Gold Amex. A pretty and boarding-school educated daughter seems to be just another box to tick. That's why I like Mick so much. He seems to genuinely care for me."

"That's just Jeffery for you."

"No, I'm not sure it is. There's still that bit too much distance between us. I wonder if I wasn't a disruption to his carefully planned life. I was a shotgun baby. And I've always wondered why, if mum and dad really wanted kids, didn't they have others? They've told me that they struggled but, well, I'm not sure."

"What a cheery pair we are." Steve smiled at his wife. "Come on, enough of the deep and meaningful stuff and let's enjoy having a bit of fun while the cats and the mice are away. Look at these beautiful surroundings. How can this not make you feel good to be alive?"

Needless to say, Steve's sarcasm was of the least sophisticated form and raised only a groan from his wife. They were in the heart of the Potteries now and its present revival coupled with its past history left very little room for nature to have her way. Where derelict wharfs and run-down areas were strewn with graffiti that was difficult to love, newly-developed areas were similarly unlovable but for their modernity and the traffic and the people they generated.

"I bet that cost a few quid!" Steve pointed to the newest of the glass-clad buildings. "I said, I *bet* that cost a few quid."

"I heard you the first time. Not one of your best though." Penelope had had to put up with Steve's quips for too long now and this one was a very lame reference to the headquarters of one of the nation's most successful online betting companies.

And, like his dad, she now realised, silence was a rare commodity with Steve. Whilst Mick was more for reading out the paper to all and sundry, Steve had to read who loved who and who did what to whom on the various sprayed missives that they passed. When none were near, he read the signs that they passed. When there was nothing to hitch onto, he'd make up a stupid song as a special gift for his wife. One which was rarely appreciated.

"Oh dear, what a shame." Penelope breathed a sigh of relief. "Time for you to get off and do the first lock. Off you go, boy."

"And," she shouted after him. "don't you dare even think of asking me if I'm okay to drive this thing. Remember, a first-time pass for me, five attempts for you. And no, little sprog is not a disability."

In fact, Penelope proved to be the most competent so far of all the crew who had had a go at the tiller. Steve was quietly impressed, although a few bystanders looked at him as though he were the nastiest and cruellest of slave-drivers.

The Etruria locks were big, ugly affairs, fully functional and bedded into the industrial landscape like old familiar scars. There was some safety in the presence of other boats but this wasn't an area you wanted to hang around in after dark. If the drinkers and the users who left their rubbish behind didn't get you, then the pigeons would. For the pigeons here had even less to redeem themselves than the barely adequate homing pigeons which at least seemed some way useful. These pigeons hid in the rafters of bridges that spanned the canal, their droppings thick above you and their cooing causing you to work the gates twice as fast.

"Now wasn't that a scenic jaunt!" Steve jumped back on the boat and let Penelope cruise them out of the city of five towns. The last landmark they passed was the home of Stoke City FC, which set Steve off on another annoying bout of singing, even though he had always been a rugby fan.

Gradually, they returned to a more scenic landscape passing the huge edifice of the Wedgwood factory and Visitor Centre, before coming in to moor at The Plume of Feathers.

"First rule." Penelope told him as they headed to the pub. "If he's there, not one word from you. No silly impressions and no jokes. Okay?"

Steve readily agreed. He'd wound his wife up about the witty comments that he had in reserve for the celebrity owner of the pub, but he'd never intended to use them. If he was there, so be it. He was more excited about the Plum Porter that they were reputed to sell. And rightly so, as it lived up to its promise and made a stunning pub-grub meal into a really enjoyable evening. That said, with the rigours of cruising and locks and the food on top, the Plum Porter also acted as a very effective soporific which saw Steve off to bed before nine, giving Penelope a little bit of peace and quiet.

"Now then," she thought to herself as she treated her and baby-on-board to just the smallest glass of sherry. "Let's see if we can't get to the bottom of this Michael Roberts fame and recognition thing."

Chapter Thirty-Seven:

Whatever that mysterious 'thing' was, it continued to work its magic for Mick as the young lad behind the reception desk gave him a knowing wink before upgrading their room to one of the hotel's best suites.

"I think we can make an exception for you, sir." the receptionist smiled as he made the necessary adjustments. "Give you a little time to rest and relax away from the crowds."

Still confused about the whole situation, but happy to go with the flow rather than follow Helen's demand that they confess to some sort of mistaken identity, Mick slipped the key-card into the lock. Any doubts were silenced by what they saw as the suite opened up before them. Aside from the extra space and the lavish furniture, the bowls of fruit and the vases of flowers, it was the bathroom that left them speechless. Accessed through a door off the bedroom, with a four-poster bed that Mick greeted with a typically lewd comment, the bathroom was bigger than any they'd seen before and was dominated by a sunken bath, beside which, a small hot-tub bubbled gently away.

"Hey up, love." Mick nudged his wife gently. "We could have a bit of fun here. You still want me to tell them it's a mistake."

Though a small part of her wanted to come clean, the suite had worked its magic on Helen and a greater part of her was now happy to accept the upgrade without raising any further questions. Before she'd had time to answer, Mick was already peeling the foil off the champagne. Sometimes life threw you a little treat like this. Whatever else happened, they were going to make the most of it.

Jefferey too was finding the day to be working in his favour. The train to London had been fast and comfortable, so comfortable in fact that Don Quixote was overlooked for a nap instead. Added to that, the tube had been surprisingly empty and the bank that was his first call had been respectful and efficient in completing the transaction he'd asked of them. By mid-morning, he had all that he needed to proceed to the next part of his plan. He hadn't been entirely honest with Alicia about the details of his excursion, but the anticipated outcome was the same nonetheless: the business needed help in releasing the shipments that had already been sold, and the means of doing that were secondary.

Having converted the loan that Mick had so kindly given him into the contents of the briefcase that he now held in his hand, Jefferey returned to Euston to embark on the second stage of his mission, arriving at his destination just before his scheduled three p.m. appointment.

"Jefferey Williams to see Anatoly Rostov."

"Certainly, Sir." the hotel receptionist replied. "I have a note of your meeting here and of your reservation. Mr Rostov has asked that we send you straight up, but would you like to check in first? As Mr Rostov is a very good client of our hotel, we've taken the liberty of upgrading you to an adjoining suite. I trust that is acceptable?"

"Very." Jefferey replied, feeling a little more like the important businessman he knew himself to be. "And thank you, much appreciated."

"Our pleasure entirely, sir." the receptionist smiled as she passed the key across. "Enjoy your stay and if there is anything we can do for you, please don't hesitate to ask."

As Jefferey was escorted to the bank of lifts by one of the uniformed porters, his movements were watched with a certain degree of surprise and incredulity by one of the many customers seated in the busy bar area of the hotel. On recognising the familiar face, the penny had dropped for PC James Cartwright who understood immediately why the connection hadn't been made before. The booking on the hotel's system had Jefferey as Geoffrey. It was a common mistake and one which Jefferey had been willing to overlook this time, given the upgrade that he'd received. Of course, Williams was also no unusual surname.

"Well, well." Cartwright muttered to himself as he wrote a note of the incident in the diary he was pretending to peruse. "This could be interesting."

As the lift doors opened, the porter stepped out and introduced his charge to a heavy-set man who was standing before them. The man eyed Jefferey up and nodded to the porter who slipped quietly away.

"Please, follow me."

The two men walked a short distance along the richly-carpeted floor before stopping at a door marked 'Presidential Suite'. Just off to the left was another door to the 'Minster Suite' which Jeffery noted as this was his own room. A knock on the door was followed by the appearance of another large guy, almost a twin of the first, who beckoned Jefferey into the room.

"My friend." Anatoly Rostov's heavily-accented voice greeted Jefferey. "So nice to see you after such a long time."

"Likewise." Jefferey took the proffered hand and gripped it firmly. "You're looking well."

"Ah, the fruits of the good life." Rostov beckoned his visitor to sit in the armchair next to his own. "We may not, as you say, burn the candle at both ends like we used to, but I am certainly making sure that the candle continues to burn brightly. And you, you seem a little less relaxed than usual? Maybe you need a holiday?"

Rather than explain that his weary countenance was actually the product of his current holiday, Jefferey simply offered a non-committal 'maybe', before sitting down.

"For you," Rostov smiled as he called the other man across. "I have a very special treat. Anton, please, a glass of my special vodka for our friend."

"This," he continued, after the two drinks had been poured and set before them. "is the finest vodka you will ever taste. That I own the distillery is by the by. In fact, I only own it because it was one of my life's ambitions to do so. Please, let us raise a toast to a successful meeting."

The vodka wasn't Jefferey's particular cup of tea, but he played along and made the right noises as the fiery liquid disappeared only to be replaced by another.

"I see you have a gift for me too." Rostov pointed to the briefcase that had been set on the floor between them.

"As requested." Jefferey pushed the case towards him. "Used notes, untraceable and all as clean as can be. And the case is a gift from me to you."

"You are too kind my friend. I shall not do you the disservice of counting it. We are, as you might say, too far down the road for mistrust. And so, to business. A certain problem shipment that you need a little bit of help with unsticking. That is right?"

"In a nutshell, yes." Jefferey replied. "You already have the details of the shipment in question. Sadly, a minor hiccup in our cashflow is impeding its release. The product is all sold, my customers are desperate to get it into their shops, but I can't get it to them. Hence my coming to you."

"An unfortunate situation indeed." Rostov replied. "But not one that need present too much of a problem for us. Anton, please, come and sit with us."

"This is a confidential meeting?" Jefferey eyed the other man with suspicion.

"My friend," Rostov smiled. "it is because this meeting is 'off the record' that Anton must be present. Trust me, he is both a safe pair of hands and an extraordinarily gifted man. Neither of us wishes to make notes of any agreement we might enter into. Anton will be our record keeper. Believe me, every word that is said in this meeting will be stored in Anton Petrov's faultless memory and can be recalled word-for-word at any time. And so, let me outline the solution that I am proposing."

The three men sat for over an hour as they agreed a deal. True to Rostov's words, Anton was able to fill in any gaps and refresh his memory every time the minutiae of the proposal needed clarifying. In essence, Rostov would 'buy' the disputed cargo and import it under the guise of a shell company. Once it was released and on the market, Jefferey would receive a share of the proceeds, less Rostov's own commission.

"You see," he concluded. "with my help, you recoup enough to tide you over, whilst I make a profit on the risk I am taking. In my country, we have a saying that goes something along the lines of, 'better a partridge in the pot than a field of pheasants that have flown'. You shall have your partridge. I shall catch the pheasants."

"Believe me." Jefferey replied. "I'm happy to get what I can in this instance. It's a good deal for you, but it smooths my own cashflow problem. You win some, you lose some. I'm happy to let the profits from this one pass to you."

"And I, in turn," Rostov said quietly. "am happy that we have a ready-made opportunity for me to wash a little of my wealth clean. You know that this is not a strictly legal transaction. I don't want to exploit you too greatly, but the money that we shall be using here has something of a past. My risk is great. My rewards must match that risk. We shake, no?"

The two men shook on the deal and Rostov rose to escort his visitor to the door.

"I shall be out and about this evening." he told Jefferey. "I understand that you have the delights of one of these beautiful suites, so, my advice is that you enjoy yourself. Your problems are solved. Go wild!"

"And," he continued with a wink. "if you feel the need for a bit of company, or maybe a special pick-me-up, please, allow Petrov to help you out. He has a varied and interesting catalogue of pleasures that he can supply you with. On the house, of course."

Once inside his own room and having familiarised himself with the luxury of the suite, Jefferey toyed with the idea of taking Rostov up on his offer. But such thoughts quickly passed. It had been a long day. He was tired and the whole business transaction, though successful, had been immensely stressful. No, tonight he'd pamper himself with more traditional luxuries. Beginning with a short nap.

Chapter Thirty-Eight:

Cartwright smiled as he finished putting the last of the day's observations into the e-mail that his temporary superior had requested. His smile was more than just the product of a good job done and of results that were beyond even his own expectations: his was a smile that recognised the combination of factors that had placed him where he was. Officially, he remained a lowly Constable. There was nothing to complain about in that, since he was only in the early stages of his police career. From the day that he'd first joined up, his ambitions had always lain in the prospects the future held for him, prospects that might one day see him rising to the rank of Chief Constable. If that was what he wanted. As a fan of crime fiction, it was the intermediary stage that he looked forward to. Yes, he knew that for every chapter that hit the pages there were numerous other ones that were too dull to be given voice to, but that didn't worry him. He wanted to make a difference and if part of doing that meant the dull drudgery of paperwork and statements and dead-ends, then so be it. That said, he was smiling now because fate had put him further along in the game then he'd thought possible.

He credited his good fortune to the dogs that he'd shared his formative years with. One by one, they'd appeared as waifs and strays needing a home that was never denied them, and one by one, they'd been nurtured back to health and given him invaluable lessons in the art of sacrifice. On top of which, they had also filled his life and surroundings with numerous invisible visitors who temporarily brought sickness with them, but who left behind a legacy of an immune system that could cope with most invaders. A widespread bout of a flu-like bug having recently worked its way through his local headquarters, he was one of only a few still standing and had therefore been swiftly seconded to 'Operation Hawk'. He knew it was only a temporary assignment, but it was a great opportunity to get a taste of the future and to impress the people he needed to impress. All of which gave him good cause to smile.

Naturally, the unexpected sighting of Jefferey Williams had helped to add a little amusement to proceedings. The man was a buffoon, but a well-connected one, and it had taken a lot of effort on his own part to have to eat humble pie and apologise to him. Still, that was another priceless lesson that he'd learnt and his compliance to his Chief Constable's request had at least put his name up front and centre. It all worked out in the end, provided you did your bit and went with the flow.

He was just packing up his laptop and the notebooks that he'd spent so long filling up, when the final surprise of the day presented itself. He saw her fleetingly at first as she passed him by on the way to the ladies. Having waited a few minutes and having set himself up in a better position to observe, he was rewarded with a much better view on her return. Hers wasn't the sort of stunning beauty that meant that, once seen, she could never be forgotten, but he recognised her nonetheless. After all, it hadn't been that long ago that he'd first met her and noted the carefully sculpted and precisely presented figure that came from a good, middle-class background.

On first impressions, her presence was surprising but hardly unexpected. What didn't make sense was her return to a table in the hotel restaurant and the amount of unrestrained flirtation she bestowed on her dining companion. That it was Alicia Williams was unquestionable. What she was doing with another man was less understandable. Jefferey might not be Cartwright's cup of tea, but he didn't have him and Alicia pegged as being active participants of the swinging scene. Besides which, the other man was familiar and not the sort of person you'd place in a threesome. Still, each to their own. It wasn't illegal and it wasn't relevant to his own work. He made a brief note of the development and prepared to leave the bar that had been his home for most of the day.

Halfway to his car, he paused for a moment. What if the presence of Alicia *did* prove to be important? Better to overegg the pudding than be found wanting.

"Thanks for your help today." Cartwright leant closely over the reception counter as he spoke quietly to the Assistant Manager who'd been more than willing to play his part in the surveillance being conducted before his own eyes. "I'm not sure where we go from here but keep it all to yourself and try and stop your team getting too excited."

"Only too glad to be of service." the young man replied. "I'll brief the team on the need for discretion. Mind you, it is part of our company policy."

"Just before I go." Cartwright resumed. "I just need you to check a couple of other things. This 'Geoffrey Williams' you have, he did book in as sole occupancy?"

"That's right."

"Okay, but can you check if you have an Alicia Williams in for tonight?"

"Nobody by that name." the reply came after a few quick keystrokes.

"Your restaurant bookings then?" Cartwright asked.

"No, still no Williams, not if you discount Mr Williams who's booked in at seven-thirty this evening."

"Try not to stare, but can you see the couple over by the far window?"

"The lady in the red dress?"

"Yes, that's her. What name have you got for that reservation?"

"Oh, I can tell you that without having to look it up." the manager told him, "I know him from old. Not that he recognised me when he checked in. Then again, he must do hundreds of Christenings. That's Reverend Mackintosh, a local vicar. Don't recognise the woman though. That said, he's not married. My wife and I had him down as being gay when we met him. Maybe he's getting bored of rattling around that big vicarage on his own."

The mention of Mackintosh's name filled in the gaps for Cartwright. He'd seen him around too and the information he'd been given only added to the strangeness of the situation. Perhaps it was all about the sex after all. Why shouldn't a vicar be bisexual? And if he wasn't married, maybe it was alright in the churches eyes. Still, it made an interesting end to the day.

Chapter Thirty-Nine:

Alicia's world, already more precariously balanced than anyone but herself understood, had been tipped into turmoil from the moment that she saw the Reverend Jonathon Mackintosh barely more than twenty-four hours ago. She had only ever known the man who'd been her first and only love by the name of Tosh. The circles she moved in at that time were short on the niceties of social norms and had a certain need for the anonymity of nicknames. She'd been Angel, at times. In fact, she'd been whatever they wanted to call her.

"You know I never stopped loving you, don't you?" she leaned forward into the vicar's personal space. "You were the only one who ever showed me genuine compassion. You were different somehow."

"Cheryl." Mackintosh spoke in a thoughtful, slow and steady tone, more real than a cynic might have believed it to be. "Can you really say that? It was so long ago. We were different people. And, let's be honest, we weren't exactly in control of things, were we?"

"I know all that. But it doesn't change anything. What we were was all about the surface. I could only survive by retreating inside, and you were there with me. It was more than just the physical. I gave you space in my heart and you were there. Just tell me one thing."

"Go on."

"You never married. Coincidence, or something else."

The vicar placed his hands on Alicia's, holding them gently as he composed his reply.

"I could tell you that I'm married to the church." he began. "And, to some extent, that's true. I know it sounds a bit happy-clappy, but my first love is Jesus. I follow him. He saved my life, after all. There are pros and cons to marriage, but it's not something I allow to distract me."

"But," he continued after a pause. "my faith also precludes me from lying. Ever since that night you left, I think of what we could have been together. Yes, I loved you then and yes, I love you still. What we're doing now, in so many ways, it's so wrong. And yet, it seems so right as well. I don't get what's happening, but that doesn't mean it isn't happening."

"Oh, Tosh." Alicia let the tears flow as she spoke. "It must have been so hard for you. I had it easy with the new life I created. But you've borne it all on your own. I don't want you to have to do that anymore. I want us to be together."

"Easy! This whole thing's a little fast for a parish priest. Let's at least enjoy our meal. First off, tell me what happened to Cheryl Atkins, aka Angel."

Holding nothing back, Alicia complied. She didn't need to describe the background to that final day they had together, they were both fully aware of the depths they'd sunk to. Tosh was probably the best mule that the Bradford Syndicate employed. They gave him the goods, they told him where they wanted them and when, and he delivered. His reward was his own supply of the heroin to which he had long been addicted. Somehow, he managed to balance that addiction with an ability to function well. He was one of the few people in the close-knit group who could do that.

Angel was at the top of her game too. Less in control of the addiction that ravaged her young body, she had come up through the ranks thanks to her willingness to do anything to anyone to get her fix. A brief stint in hospital after a minor overdose saw her return to the group with much of the submission gone.

"I thought of only two things while I lay in that so-called drug-dependency unit," she explained. "Firstly, how best to blag a quick recovery and get out to get my next fix. And, secondly, you. When they released me, I grabbed Polo and told him that I wasn't giving my body away anymore. Before he had a chance to deal with me, I explained my alternative solution, and he went with it. I would move from being his best whore to being his best pimp. And it worked. The girls trusted me because I was a woman. I got him the pick of the crop and he seemed happy with what I was doing."

"After that, well, you know how it went. We were an item. Granted, we were both damaged goods, but that didn't stop us finding solace in each other."

"Then you disappeared." Mackintosh replied.

"I had to. You know what I did to Polo. It wasn't like I could stick around after that."

"But why on your own?"

"You remember that night? We had the best sex we'd ever had. I was coming down and trying to stay in control, but what we had then was better than the highest high I've ever experienced. That's why I couldn't share my plan with you. I had to leave you there, or else they'd have been after you as well. After you'd fallen asleep, I packed my things, checked that Polo and the others were out of it, which they were. Then I helped myself to the money. They'd told me a few days before that they were pooling funds to buy a big shipment. That same day, I broke in a young girl of thirteen and, for the first time, I felt sick with myself about what I was doing. I put two and two together and realised that that money would be my ticket out. I stole it, brought myself a new identity and checked into a private clinic. Within a fortnight, I was clean and nobody would have recognised me. Gone was the pasty, heroin-ravaged wreck. In her place, a slightly plump and heavily made-up young Conservative appeared."

"And that's that." She concluded. "A week later, I'm at a Golf Club do, I meet Jefferey Williams and I reel him in with my seductive charms. He didn't know what had hit him. I found myself pregnant, he married me and Penny was born six weeks premature. But enough of me, what about you? Why the change of heart and the new career?"

The vicar explained to her how he'd resolved to get out of the game as soon as Angel had left. His exit was aided by a spiritual epiphany which Polo and the others could see was genuine, and which left him free to work his way to the priesthood.

"The details are boring." He told her. "But the transformation is real. I was 'saved' and 'born again'. I had no choice but to give back. And now, I don't know where it leaves us."

"It leaves us with our feelings." Alicia accompanied her words with a sultry smile. "I know which way I want to take at this crossroads. But the choice is yours. Jefferey and I are over anyway. I've seen too much of his dodgy deals and cowardice to want to stay with him. Which leaves the choice down to you. You know which room we're booked into. You stay here and make your decision. I'll be waiting."

With that, Alicia slipped away from the table and was watched closely by Mackintosh as she walked the steady middle-class walk towards the lifts. Alone with his own thoughts, the vicar called the waiter over and ordered a large whisky. It was true, this was a crossroads. Unfortunately, they only ever offer you a mutually-exclusive choice. That was why prayer was such a useful tool. Would God really be interested in this one?

Chapter Forty:

Rostov having taking his team for a well-earned night on the tiles, the charge of monitoring comings and goings on the hotel's exclusive floor had been passed to a third member of his entourage. Paul Flynn was a man of slight build but not the sort of person you wanted to get on the wrong side of. Ex-army and ex-mercenary, he commanded a high price for his service but gave good value for money. He recognised Alicia from the images he'd scanned on the hotel's CCTV, access to which had been granted to Rostov in return for certain favours.

"Evening." he smiled politely as Alicia exited the lift and headed to her room.

"All quiet?", Alicia enquired.

"Yes, ma'am."

"Goodnight." Alicia spun flirtatiously as she slipped through the door to her own suite – a present that she had consciously treated herself to from the bank account that Jefferey knew nothing of, even though he funded it.

As that door closed and Flynn's mind began to concoct a potential sex-scenario for the evening, in which Alicia would play a major part, the sound of another door opening snapped him back to professional duty.

"Ay up, love." Mick nudged Helen and nodded to Flynn. "You'd better be on best behaviour tonight. No sneaking out of the dorm after lights out!"

"Evening." Mick continued as he greeted Flynn whose finger had already stopped the lift's closing door and who was the epitome of courtesy as he beckoned the couple to enter.

"And thank you. Don't you worry about Helen here, she may look like a troublemaker, but I'll keep her in check."

"Will you stop embarrassing me." Helen whispered as she slipped past Flynn who, to his credit, gave her the sort of smile and wink that told her he knew just what she had to put up with.

The couple were in good spirits having enjoyed the luxury of a room-service meal, along with the bottle of champagne that had been presented with the compliments of the management. Though they would have been content to sleep the rest of the evening off, they knew that the sort of treat that they were currently enjoying was to be made the most of and had resolved to chill out in the hotel's spa for an hour or so.

"Looking forward to the sauna." Mick chuckled as he led Helen down the side of the restaurant towards the 'Health & Fitness Centre'. "You never know, we may be on our own in it. What do you reckon? Swedish saucy fun?"

"Dream on!" Helen tutted. "I remember the last time you tried that. You want another scolded willy?"

"Oh, yeah. Bloody hell, I'm glad you reminded me. That thing were sore for weeks!"

Next in line on this bizarre parade of coincidence and crossed-paths, Jefferey greeted Flynn with a condescending air of superiority as he waited for Rostov's man to call the lift back. On its arrival, he slid out a hand to the guard and slipped him a folded five-pound note.

"Thank you, Sir." Flynn acknowledged the gift with a practised gratitude. "You have a good evening now."

"I will." Jefferey replied as the doors closed. "I most certainly will."

On the lift's arrival at the Restaurant, the final encounter inevitably took place. Jefferey stepped out and into the path of the Reverend Jonathon Mackintosh. There then followed one of those awkward two-steps as each tried to give way to the other, throughout which, both men laughed at the situation.

"A little early for a dance!" Jefferey offered.

"Absolutely." Mackintosh replied. "Perhaps later!"

It was one of those brief exchanges that happened and that should really mean nothing to the participants. But the length of the interaction had given Jefferey time to look closely at the other man and into his eyes. There was something strangely familiar about those eyes. Where had he seen them before?

"Mr Williams?" a voice behind him caused him to forget his musings and turn around.

"Yes."

"Your table is ready, Sir." The uniformed porter advised him. "Please, follow me."

Jefferey did as he was instructed and was led through to a cordoned-off section of the restaurant, where several couples dined in opulence and enjoyed the best views available.

"My name is Jeremy." a perfectly-polite waiter took Jefferey off the hands of the porter. "I shall be your waiter for tonight and have been asked to advise you that you are Mr Rostov's guest and must treat yourself to whatever you like at his expense."

Which Jefferey spent the next couple of hours doing. Although no stranger to dining in much more exclusive restaurants than this one, the saving of his vital shipment had put him in a good mood and he resolved to share a little of that good humour with the team who were bending over backwards to help him. He followed the waiter's recommendation for the crab mousse starter and complimented him when the empty plate was retrieved. Choosing to opt for a medium-rare fillet as his main, he deferred to the waiter again over the choice of wine. That course being finished, he cleansed his pallet with a fine sorbet before calling the waiter over with the universal finger-scribble sign that indicated it was time for the bill.

"Was everything okay?" the waiter asked as he placed the slip in front of the diner.

"Wonderful." Jefferey sighed as he signed the bill with a flourish. "A credit to yourself and the team. Well done. Well done."

Those final words were accompanied by a discrete placing of two twenty-pound notes next to the bill.

"Thank you, Sir," the waiter bowed and stepped around to help Jefferey out of his chair. "May I recommend a cocktail in the lounge to finish with?"

"You may indeed, young man. You may indeed."

Fast forward an hour or so and that first cocktail had been joined by several others. Tomorrow it would be back to the boat and the final few days of the holiday that he'd not really been able to get into so far. Maybe he was a bit boring and over-powering. Maybe he should lighten up a little and enjoy the strange journey they were on. With the business wobble over now, and with Mick's loan secured, perhaps now he could show the rest of the family that he wasn't always a killjoy. With that newly formed resolution in his mind, he slipped a fiver under the empty cocktail glass and bid goodnight to the barman.

Week Two

Day Four, Tuesday:

Barlaston to Stone

Chapter Forty-One:

The noise got much louder at two o'clock in the morning, causing Jefferey to wake from the deep and satisfying sleep that had enveloped him soon after he'd returned to his room. The suites were all of an ample size, but the bed in which he lay was backed against an adjoining wall to the bathroom of the suite next door, through which, the sounds of the activities going on in there came to him, amplified by the many tiled surfaces of that other room. At first, his instinct was to bang on the wall and tell them to shut up. That was the natural thing that pre-wakefulness urged him to do, but he let that feeling pass and chose a different route.

Jefferey was not a highly-sexed man. Marriage to Alicia had brought with it some memorable nights of passion, prompted on many occasions by the desire to birth a sibling to Penny. That had never happened. Alicia was honest with him about their lack of success in that area after visiting a specialist and advising him that she wouldn't be able to give him what he wanted. That news was followed by several years of unabandoned sex, which in turn was followed by the natural complacency that comes with familiarity. Jefferey too had stopped feeling as passionate. He put it down to age and was content with the status-quo, assuming that Alicia was too.

Every now and then though, Jefferey's loins stirred. It was a part of the male condition: unannounced and often unwelcome, lust reared its head and began to take over. Placing a glass against the connecting wall, the sounds of passionate lovemaking were fuel to the fire. He listened for a few minutes before giving in to temptation and picking up his phone. Gone were the days when a momentary succumbing to self-pleasure meant an embarrassed look at the points of checking out of the hotel. Nowadays, a few taps on a smartphone, a connection to the hotel's free wi-fi, and you were into the seedy world of internet porn. He chose a video that matched his own situation – one where a couple invited a stranger to join them in their hotel room. With that playing before him and the sounds increasing from the bathroom Jefferey didn't think he'd last long. Sure, he knew he'd hate himself as soon as he was finished, but that had never stopped him before. Nor indeed, had it stopped any man in a similar position.

"Harder, harder, harder!" the woman's voice helped Jefferey along.

"Oh, yeah, slap me, baby, slap me!"

That was almost too much. With each resounding smack on the woman's flesh, followed by a squeal of delight, Jefferey felt himself drawing closer to the end. That was, until the woman shouted again:

"Oh man, oh man, oh man!" she screamed. "Oh man, oh man, oh man."

To anybody else listening, those words would have been mere icing in the cake. To Jefferey, they were as effective as a cold shower. Not only did he recognise the words. He also felt convinced that he recognised the voice.

"Alicia?" he muttered to himself. "It can't be."

Any thoughts of finishing what he had started were gone now, replaced by a closer scrutiny of what was happening next door. They were close to finishing but the woman continued to share her pleasure recklessly and every word that she uttered confirmed Jefferey's suspicions. That the man called her 'Cheryl' or 'Angel' meant nothing. That it was the most unbelievable coincidence imaginable was by the by. It was his own wife in that room and he was being well and truly cuckolded even as he masturbated to the sound.

Some men would have thrown caution to the wind and knocked on the neighbouring door until it was answered. Others might have shouted for silence and banged on the wall.

Too stunned by his own suspicions, Jefferey chose simply to move out of the bedroom and away from the noise. He slid the balcony door open and sat in the cool darkness with a small cigar in his hand, trying to compose his thoughts. Sure, he'd not been as open and honest with Alicia as he should have been, but there were reasons for that. His had only been a little white lie. And yes, he could understand why Alicia wasn't satisfied, but he did his best. It wasn't easy doing what he did and working out ever more complex ways to patch up the holes in the finances that threatened the lifestyle that he'd promised Alicia. No, she was the one at fault here. She was the one who'd pretended that she was off to visit an old friend. Her lies were bigger than his. And, if she had lied about that, how much more of their marriage was nothing more than a convenient falsehood?

Until he knew for sure, he resolved to hold back on any action. The wait wouldn't be for too long, although it wasn't a wait that he was inclined to go through in such close proximity to the situation. Dressing quickly, he slipped out of his room and walked towards the lifts. Flynn remained on duty. That presented Jefferey with an unexpected advantage.

"Couldn't sleep." he told the bodyguard. "Thought I'd treat myself to a nightcap."

"Have one for me." Flynn replied with a smile.

"Just one thing though," Jefferey drew closer to Flynn and withdrew his wallet from the suit jacket that he was wearing. "Have you seen this woman before?"

Flynn took one glance at the photograph and nodded towards Alicia's room.

"Not a problem, I hope?" he asked.

"No, no," Jefferey stepped into the lift. "Just wanted to make sure. It's good. I'll see you later."

Down in the bar, the night porter was just finishing his cleaning duties when his eye was caught by movement on the CCTV that he constantly monitored. He was back in position before Jefferey arrived and enquired about the availability of drinks.

"Whatever you want, Sir." the young man replied. "Except for cocktails. Company policy, we don't serve them after midnight. But anything else should be fine. What can I get for you?"

The requested single malt having been passed across the bar to him, Jefferey downed it in two goes and asked for another.

"Difficulty sleeping." he explained. "The people in the room next door are banging away like rabbits. Only not so quietly."

"I'm sorry about that, Sir. Would you like me to ask security to check it out and request that they be a bit less enthusiastic?"

"Yeah, that would be good." Jefferey smiled at the small victory that this would bring him and listened as the barman radioed through for help.

"You get much of that sort of thing?" Jefferey asked. "You must see it all in your job."

"You wouldn't believe most of it." the night porter smiled as he replied. "It's not as frequent as people think. Most of the time I'm left alone with only simple requests and early check-outs to keep me going. When they do happen though, boy, can they defy explanation. It's usually when we have a wedding."

Encouraged by his customer to share more detail, that same customer seeming to want something to distract him, the young man shared his tales, always professionally, but holding nothing back.

"My best one," he continued after Jefferey slipped him a fiver tip with the next round. "is the ex porn-star who broke her boyfriend's penis. Not too over-the-top for you, I trust?"

Chapter Forty-Two:

The whiskies helping him forget the problems he knew he would have to face later in the day, and the night porter's openness, broke down the usual barriers that Jefferey put between himself and the 'servant' classes.

"Please, go on." he said. "I'm intrigued."

"Well, I'd just finished up down here after a long night and nipped outside for a cigarette. Must have been about five a.m. That's when I see this woman wandering around the grounds. I called over to her and she waved her room key at me to show she was a resident. I let her in and she explained that she'd been at the hospital all night. I wish I hadn't asked, but I casually enquired if everything was okay."

"'I broke my boyfriend's penis' she told me. "Just like that, as though it were something that happened all the time. Well, what could I say? I commiserated, more with him than her, then I started to lead her to her room, but she asked if the bar was still open. Who am I to argue with a guest? So, she starts drinking glasses of champagne, at a tenner a pop. The more she drinks, the more uninhibited she becomes. That was when she showed me the photograph. Seriously, it's not something you want to see and it will be with me forever. After that, we go into her life story and she tells me that she runs a high-class escort agency, having retired as a porn-star. A few celebrity gossip tales later and my boss turns up to relieve me. The look on his face was priceless. Especially when she showed him the photo without any prompting. I was due to head off then, and she casually enquired about whether she could get some food to take to her boyfriend in hospital that evening. I explained that the chefs could put together something for her, suggesting something light, like a pasta dish. 'Oh, no,' she says. 'he won't want that. He's a meat and two veg man.'"

"I know I shouldn't have," the barman smiled as he finished the tale. "But I really couldn't resist it. 'Not any more, he isn't', I told her. Luckily, she was too far gone to take offence. I said goodbye to her and handed her over to my boss. Apparently, she carried on with the champagne until lunchtime, at which point she staggered back to her room, only to be found minutes later wandering around the corridors stark naked. That was one to remember!"

"I know I've had my share of embarrassing moments." Jefferey replied as another drink was passed his way. "But even I can't trump that. Goes to show, doesn't it? You think your own life is a bit strange, then you come across another even stranger."

"Funny how rare those nights are though." the barman said. "People think you see all sorts as a night porter, but most of the time it's very quiet. Weddings are fun, sometimes. Although, when the groom wets himself on the way to the bedroom and the new wife spends the night ordering takeaway pizza, you do wonder how many of these marriages will last."

"You ever get scooped up into counselling conversations?" Jefferey asked, genuinely interested in the man behind the bar who had an open and relaxed manner and whose presence was helping him put the noise from his neighbours out of his mind.

"Sometimes. I try and avoid it for obvious reasons. But you can't ignore a guest's conversation. It's strange though. The times it happens are when you have the highest profile people in. Not necessarily celebrities. They make no bones about being messed up. No, it's the ones who seem so 'together' who surprise you. It seems that being alone in a bar in the middle of the night, with a stranger whose job implies discretion, breaks down a lot of barriers. It usually starts with them asking about how I started here. I tell them that I jumped off the rollercoaster and opted for an easy life, doing this to pay the small bills that a downsized life brings. They see how happy I am with it and that's when they pour it all out. The pressures of keeping up appearances, the struggle to pay school fees etc. I just listen and take it in."

"I'm not surprised." Jefferey sighed. "So many lives seem to be what they're not. I can get where they're coming from though. You look really happy. There must be something in your way of life. But it's hard to break out of the cycle. I should know. I'm a successful businessman, but even I find that parts of my life are built on sand. Seems like the harder you try and build the life you envisage, the more fragile it becomes. Maybe I should let things go a bit."

"I'm not the one to come to for advice." the barman laughed. "Not after the mistakes I've made. And I don't know if I can claim to be any more right in my lifestyle than anyone else. I guess we all have to find our own level and settle there. I've chatted with miserable millionaires and wonderfully happy people who have nothing. And vice-versa. I can only answer for myself, but, my thinking is that if your current situation doesn't bring you peace, you should change it."

"And," he continued. "Not worry about what other people are thinking of you. Because, most of the time, they're not!"

"You don't mind me staying down here?" Jefferey asked as he waved for another drink. "Not all, Sir. You're a resident and this is the resident's bar. Mind you, I may have to leave you for a few minutes to do some of my routine tasks. You look trustworthy enough."

"Oh, by the way." he continued. "Security have been in touch to say that it's all quiet in the room next to yours, so you should be okay to go up if you want to."

Jefferey didn't take this as a hint that he should go back to bed. The information was offered simply as a routine update. The drink wasn't making him any sleepier, and the thought of having to hear what he didn't want to hear ever again was enough to keep him downstairs. He knew what he wanted to do and he had every intention of staying up through the night to bring that plan to fruition. When the night porter disappeared to do an hourly check, Jefferey grabbed a couple of magazines from the reception desk and settled down to read them. He chose his seat carefully. It gave him a clear line of sight to the lifts and to the restaurant where breakfast would begin to be served in an hour or so's time.

For all his good intentions, it was a gentle whisper from the night porter that woke him. Terrified that he might have missed something, he apologised for falling asleep and asked if breakfast had started yet.

"Half an hour ago, Sir." the reply. "You want to go through?"

"Yes, yes. Please." Jefferey staggered to his feet and walked quickly through to the restaurant, where he declined the proffered table and chose his own spot from where he could watch proceedings. He wasn't hungry, but the coffee was welcome. All he had to do now was wait. His tiredness would be no barrier to what he wanted to say. Despite the hope, deep down in his heart, that it was all some sort of strange mistake.

Chapter Forty-Three:

Jefferey ate very little, drank numerous cups of coffee and finished several of the morning papers without seeing anything untoward. The first wave of breakfasters was always the businessmen and businesswomen who had places to go and people to see. They began to thin out and make way for the leisure guests. Expecting to be rewarded in his observation mission by witnessing certain strange but true facts that he had to be certain of, it was nonetheless a shock and a surprise when he saw Helen and Mick strolling into the restaurant and settle at a table not far away. He remained out of sight, hidden by a high-backed partition that was topped with plastic flowers. Mirrors gave him a view of the familiar couple, but the newspaper that he held up before him, hid his own presence.

"This is a bit of all right, isn't it?" Mick's voice was recognisable anywhere and never kept at too low a volume.

"It's wonderful." Helen replied. "A perfect end to our mini-break. And look at this menu! How many ways can you cook an egg?!"

"One." Mick laughed. "Fried and sitting on top of pile of sausage, bacon and black pudding. You order what you like, love, but I'm too old to change my habits."

"Do you not want to start with some fruit?"

"Fruit goes in pies, love, and only ever for afters with custard! You go for it though. Just don't expect to change anything when we get home. Now, excuse me."

Mick walked across the restaurant and piled a plate high with every traditional foodstuff that was laid out on the buffet. Meanwhile, Helen ordered poached eggs on toast, preferring to make her own way to the buffet after Mick returned.

"You are embarrassing at time, Michael Roberts." Helen watched as her husband worked his way through a breakfast big enough for six. "Thank goodness we're only passing through."

"And that there's no-one watching, eh?" Mick replied with a wink. "Come on, allow me this one blow-out before we go back to the boat-trip from hell. Besides, I've done a damn good job so far. I deserve this."

Helen smiled and patted Mick's hand.

"You have done well. It won't be much longer now and I think that we might make it through without strangling certain people. You never know, he may be delayed in London. We might have another Jefferey free day."

"Wishful thinking!" Mick poured tomato ketchup onto the remains of his breakfast and wiped the plate with buttered bread. "I tell you, if that's how the other half live, they can keep it. I've never known such an arrogant prat in all my life, and one who hasn't the cause to be arrogant. I reckon his business is about to go under and we'll see another side of him soon. All I want to be sure of, is that Steve and Penny come through okay. Imagine their kid becoming a mini-Jefferey?! Doesn't bear thinking about."

"Or a mini-Mick!" Helen replied as her husband belched his approval of his breakfast. "Somewhere in-between will be fine. God forbid that those two try and buy the baby's affection."

"That's all they do." Mick slurped his second cup of tea. "Buy friendship, buy favours, buy company. Without the money, who'd really want to spend time with those two? He's so far up his own backside he bangs his head on his teeth, and she's the perfect example of 'fur coat and no knickers'!"

"You think so?"

"Aye, I do. She's too perfect to be real."

"You may be right. I quite like her though. In small doses."

"Well," Mick whispered, leaning closer to Helen. "You'd better get ready for one of those small doses. Look what the cat just dragged in!"

Helen turned and nearly choked on her toast as she saw Alicia and the vicar she remembered from last Sunday walking arm-in-arm into the restaurant. She was speechless. Mick, however, was not.

"Aye up, Alicia!" he shouted across the room. "What the heck are you doing here? Come and join us."

Looking like a cat that was frozen before headlights, Alicia paled at the sight of the other couple. Whispering something in Mackintosh's ear, she took a moment to compose herself, before straightening up and leading them to the others' table.

"What a pleasant surprise!" she squealed. "But, how come you're here?"

Helen explained that Steve and Penelope had brought them a little gift.

"More important than that," Mick interrupted with a wink. "What brings you here? And who's your friend? Not playing away from home, I hope!"

"Jeffery." Alicia gave him a look that threatened to knock him off his chair. "I will have you know that this gentleman is a man of the cloth and this isn't what you and your dirty mind think it is. Now, are we to be civilised, or do Jonathan and I choose a different table?"

Mick apologised and waited for the explanation that was readily offered.

"As you well know, I spent last night with my good friend from the old days in her flat. Given the proximity of her dwelling and the pleasure that I had got from the service on Sunday, I decided that I would like to chat with Rev. Mackintosh again and he very kindly agreed to meet me here for breakfast. That's all there is to it."

"Whatever you say, love." Mick smiled and winked as he replied. "Mum's the word with Helen and myself. Besides, we can share a taxi back to the boat, so there's a few quid saved there!"

"Perhaps I should leave you to it?" Jonathan Mackintosh wanted out of this whole situation for good reason.

"No, Jonathan." Alicia replied firmly. "You're my guest. Allow me to introduce you to my daughter's in-laws, Michael and Helen."

"My pleasure," Helen smiled as she took the vicar's proffered hand. "And may I say how much I enjoyed the service on Sunday. You have a church to be proud of."

"Thank you." Mackintosh began to relax and compose himself, shifting into respectable parson mode seamlessly. "Our church is going from strength to strength and we are truly blessed in our ministry. I hope we'll see you again there soon."

A period of small talk followed. Helen was genuinely interested in hearing about the church, whilst Mick remained a tad sceptical about the whole situation. Alicia played her part perfectly and all might have been settled quietly had Jefferey not been so near. He listened to the lies that his wife was spinning within his own earshot, and he watched as closely as he could without being seen.

It was an unexpected turn by the vicar that changed the whole dynamic. He was obviously one of those people who liked to look others in the eye as they spoke and he shifted a little to hear what Helen had to say. In that shift, Jefferey got a full and clear look at his face and found himself staring into eyes that he had seen before. They weren't just the eyes that had caught his attention by the lift doors. No, he finally realised where he'd seen those eyes before and that realisation sent his world crashing around him.

"Enough of the pretence." he whispered as he moved away from his own table, walked quietly towards the familiar grouping, slid out a chair and sat between the other speechless couples, his face reflecting the shock of a new understanding and his lack of sleep.

"Morning." he spoke quietly, nodding to the others.

"Morning Jefferey." Mick felt like he'd won the lottery, the way things were panning out. "It's certainly a very small world. If things go on like this we'll need to book a minibus instead of a taxi."

"Morning." Helen couldn't think of anything else to say. Her only concern was to shut her husband up.

"Jefferey?" Alicia just about managed to mumble.

Chapter Forty-Four:

"Yes, Jefferey. Your husband." he emphasised his reply by dropping his room charge-card onto the table before him. "And your very close neighbour last night, I believe."

"Funny, really, vicar." he continued. "Aren't I suppose to love my neighbour? Well, it isn't always easy, is it?"

"I'm not sure what you're implying." Mackintosh replied. "But you should be very careful in what you are saying. Alicia and I ...."

"Forget it, Tosh." Alicia sighed. "I'll not have you making a liar of yourself for my sake. You're right, Jefferey. Jonathan and I stayed the night here. I'm sorry."

"You're sorry!" Jefferey stayed remarkably calm, the revelation being no more than a confirmation of facts that he'd spent the night reconciling himself to. "That's all you have to say. You're sorry. Well, I'm sorry too. Sorry that you're not the person I thought you were."

"Well, what are you doing here?" Alicia went on the defensive. "You were supposed to be in London?"

"Leave it." Jefferey sighed. "This isn't about me. It's about you and him. And ... it's about Penelope."

"What's Penelope got to do with all this?" Helen asked.

"Can't you see it?" Jefferey pointed to Mackintosh. "Look at the eyes. You recognise them?"

"Oh, that's a dreadful allegation!" Helen almost shouted back. "How dare you?"

"Aye," Mick butted in. "You're out of order there."

"Well?" Jefferey turned to his wife. "Do you want to come back at me?"

The silence around the table lasted for several minutes. Alicia gazed at the faces around her with a coldness that none of them had ever seen in her. That coldness dissipated as she looked at Jonathan, stopping him adding his own contribution with just the slightest shake of her head.

"It's time," she began, pouring herself a cup of tea and dropping in a lump of sugar that she stirred carefully into the drink. "for a bit of honesty. I'm sick of all the pretence. You're right, Jefferey. Your suspicions are well founded. There's no easy way to tell you this but our marriage is over. Such as it was."

"On the basis of a quick fling?" Jefferey couldn't believe that she'd disarmed his righteous anger so quickly.

"No, Jefferey. Not on the basis of last night. On the basis that our whole life together has been a sham. We've had our moments and we've had some good times together, but I never loved you. You were a convenience for me. And, to your credit, a good father to Penelope."

"Are you sure this is what you want?" Mackintosh touched Alicia's hand gently.

"Yes," she whispered in reply before taking a deep breath and opening up to the others.

"I'm not the person that you think I am. Alicia Williams is an imposter. I started life as Cheryl Atkins. Cheryl Atkins, became a whore and a drug addict and a pimp. I've done things you'd never believe a woman capable of doing, and I've been to places you wouldn't even believe existed. That's the reality, Jefferey. That's the woman you married. And now, it's all over. Call it serendipity, call it fate, or just call it a natural end. Very much a part of my sordid past, and with his own past to add to it, I'm afraid that despite all that, Jonathan is the only man I've ever loved. Seeing him again reminded us both of what we had between us. And I'm not giving it up again. I'm sorry."

"And you, vicar, what do you have to say?" Jefferey almost spat the question out.

"I can't speak for Cheryl." he sighed. "And believe me, this isn't how I planned things. Cheryl, or Alicia, has to make her own choice. I won't persuade her either way and I have a lot of praying and seeking guidance to do myself. But, if she comes to me unencumbered by marriage, I'm not going to let that opportunity pass. Our love seems to have been ordained. What else can I say?"

"I'll tell you what you can say!" Jefferey shouted. "You can say that your calling to the church means more than your cock and that you'll leave her well alone. If you steal my wife, I'll kick up such a fuss with the papers and with your bishop that you'll regret ever having meddled in things. Some example you are!"

"Jefferey." Alicia spoke softly. "It's not Jonathan. It's me. Even if it never happens between us, I'm not coming back to you. I'm fed up of a life of lies and of trying to be a manufactured person in your middle-class world of golfing and dinner parties. It's never given me the sort of peace that I know I can find elsewhere. We'll work out the details and I'll be as amicable as possible, but it's over. I'm sorry."

"And Penelope?"

Alicia simply shrugged her shoulders and looked towards the vicar.

"You bitch!" Jefferey spat out the words. "You evil bitch. I brought that girl up as my own and now I find out that even the daughter that was the only good thing in our marriage is a lie. You must have loved it, mustn't you? It all makes sense now. You were already pregnant when you snared me. She wasn't premature. You snared me as a cash cow and you led me down the aisle carrying another man's child. And all those years of trying for another. What about them? Tell me you weren't on the pill."

"I've told you, no more lies."

"Well, I hope you know what you're doing. And don't even think about coming back to the boat with us. I never want to see you again. Go home, pack your stuff and piss off out of my life. We'll make the divorce as clinical as you made the whole marriage. But..."

The other hotel guests had, for the most part, stopped eating, choosing instead to enjoy the unexpected cabaret that was being played out before them. Jefferey calmed himself and spoke more quietly as he continued.

"...don't you dare even think about breathing a word of this to Penny. You can have it all, and I won't stand in the way, but don't you dare take her away from me."

"And as for you," he turned to Mackintosh. "you'd better start praying. And you'd better not think about going near *my* daughter."

Alicia slid her chair out and started to walk off.

"That's it!" Jefferey shouted, eyeing the security guard who was walking towards their table. "Get out of my life and make sure I never see you again. The whoring I can live with, the past life of drugs means nothing. It's the lies that I can't stand. My whole life with you has been one long lie and I have to find it out like this. You're not worth thinking about anymore."

"You want to talk about lies?" Alicia turned on her heels and shouted back. "You want to tell everyone about the state of your business? You want to share your dodgy dealings with the audience? Why are you here now? I'll tell you why, because of another of your lies. What was the deal this time? A bribe, a bung, a little cash payment to smooth a licence? Judge me as guilty as you want to, but don't ever believe that you're not as bad as me. If I'm nothing but a whore, then you're no better than a spiv. Thanks for nothing."

The guard waited to let Alicia leave the restaurant, before drawing closer to the table.

"Sir, we really need you to keep your voice down." he whispered diplomatically to the unruly guest.

"Oh sure," Jefferey shouted in reply. "got to keep some more pretences up, haven't we? Don't you forget that I'm a paying guest of this place. I'm paying your wages and if I want to tell the world what a shit my wife, sorry, ex-wife is, then let them hear it."

"I've asked nicely." The guard replied, joined now by the restaurant manager. "Now, I'm afraid that we will need to escort you off the premises."

"You keep your hands off me. And don't worry, I'm going. I wouldn't want to spend another minute in the same building as that bitch that just left and this mock cleric here."

Pushing the hands that tried to restrain him away, Jefferey flung himself off his seat and stormed away, joyfully telling all the watching diners how wonderful it was to find out that your whole life was a lie.

"Michael," he shouted. "I'll be outside when you're ready to go, I'll sort a taxi out for us."

Amongst those watching, police constable James Cartwright sat quietly at a corner table, glad that he'd decided to start his shift early and avail himself of the management's offer of a free breakfast.

With Jefferey and Alicia out of the room, Mick, Helen and the vicar sat in silence as the table was cleared away by a stumbling waiter. The chatter in the room died down, but all eyes remained tilted towards that table. Finally, and inevitably, it was Mick who broke the silence.

"More tea vicar?" he asked.

Chapter Forty-Five:

Nothing was said as the taxi took Jefferey, Mick and Helen back to the boat. The only words they'd shared as they checked out of the hotel, was a request from Jefferey that he be allowed to explain Alicia's absence to the others, and that nothing else was said on the matter. Still too numbed by the whole thing to even consider further discussion, the others had readily agreed and Helen knew that even Mick would follow orders this time. If he didn't, there may well be another divorce in the offing.

The moorings outside The Plume of Feathers were spacious enough to allow Steve and Penelope the luxury of a relaxed breakfast, sprawled out on the pub's tables. A slap-up meal there the night before was enough to justify their using the outdoor furniture. Besides, the pub didn't open until lunchtime.

"This'll be them." Steve pointed towards the taxi that rolled into the pub car park. "So long sanity!"

Little did they know how prophetic those words were. The first sign of something not being quite right was the sight of Jefferey climbing out of the passenger seat whilst Mick settled up the fare. Adding to the confusion, but not a major concern at the time, was the absence of Alicia. Three different taxis had been expected. One must surely be on its way.

"Morning kiddies!" Mick waved a cheery hello to the youngsters. "Hope you behaved yourselves last night."

"Hi Dad." Steve waved back. "You have a good time?"

"Aye," he sat down next to them. "You mum and I had a wonderful time. Thanks a million, to both of you. But, Penny, love, I think you need to have a word with your dad. Things have gone a little wobbly for him."

"Wobbly isn't quite the word I'd use." Jefferey joined them and they immediately noticed the weary look of defeat on his face. "But Michael's right. We do need to have a chat."

"Is mum okay?" Penelope asked, not quite sure what was going on.

"She's fine. Nothing to worry about. But she won't be joining us today. Look, why don't we go inside and I'll explain."

Helen already had the kettle on and was rinsing out the teapot when the others clambered aboard. Steve handed her their breakfast plates and together they washed and dried.

"What's happening?" Steve sked.

"You'll find out soon enough. Just don't worry. Everything will be fine. Penny will need some support though. You make sure that Junior remains number one priority. Now, go and make yourself useful and help your dad with the ropes. You two can navigate today. Jeff's a little out of it."

"Are you going to tell me anymore about what's going on?" Steve asked his dad as they started the engine and headed away from Barlaston.

"Buddy," Mick patted his son with his cast-covered arm. "If I told you, you wouldn't believe me. Let's just say that Jefferey and Alicia have had a falling out."

"But he was supposed to be in London, and she was with a friend. Come on, you've got to give me something of a heads-up."

Lacking any particular loyalty to Jefferey and realising that actually Steve did deserve to know more, Mick filled him in on as much as he could about the morning's activities. If he hadn't loved Penelope so much and if she wasn't carrying his grandchild, he would have added the juiciest bit of the gossip and the telling of the tale would have been a lot less sympathetic. Over time, it would morph into a fascinating story that was ripe for drunken nights out. Just now, it felt more tragic than comic, and Penelope would be protected to his dying day.

"Bloody hell!" Steve whistled as the tale was told and the first of the Meaford Locks came into view. "No wonder they're so long in there. Thanks for telling me, I'll make sure Penny's okay."

The end of the peak boating season coupled with continued mild weather, had brought out a lot of boats from marinas, crewed by a variety of people who shared only the desire to avoid the busiest time on the water. Paradoxically, such thinking made the waterways as busy as ever and the queue at the first lock testified to that.

Holding the boat by the centre-line, using his good arm to take the weight, Mick did what Mick was made to do and started chatting to the next boater in line to use the lock. As he made a new friend, Steve played his part and gave a hand at the locks where as many boats were waiting to come up as go down. In-between bouts of windlass use, he too chatted to the crew members charged with doing the harder part of locking. Neither his nor Mick's conversations were profound, revolutionary or particularly memorable. They were simply canal conversations, where stranger met stranger and shared pleasantries before moving apart into their own separate lives.

On board the boat, Penelope had finally stopped crying. Helen had been asked to stay with Jefferey as he explained to his daughter what had happened. That request was a mark of the genuine respect that Jeffery had for Mick's wife; a respect that had grown since the morning.

"I can't tell you where things go from here." Jefferey concluded. "What I do know is that you and Stephen have bigger priorities than your mum and I. Please, put the baby first."

"The truth is," Penelope settled herself and replied in a surprisingly calm way. "I'm not really surprised. Mind you, I thought you'd be the one to leave. It happens all the time. It's weird, in this case, but, hey, it's happened. Are *you* sure *you're* alright?"

Jefferey paused before answering.

"I will be. I'm not where I thought I'd be, but it's happened and I have to accept it. That's why I've come back here. We still have time to make something of this holiday. We should give it a go."

"And that's not just you being stubborn?" his daughter asked.

"No, really, it's not. I know I'm a bit of a prat sometimes and yes, I dig my heels in and demand that things go my way. But after what's happened ...well, I just want us to try and have a bit of fun despite what's happened. You don't think that's heartless of me?"

"No, dad." Penelope put her arms around Jefferey. "As long as you're not playing your games again. That was always the problem. When you are being you, you're a great dad. I wouldn't change you for the world. It's when you try and manufacture this façade about your life that you seem to stumble along a negative spiral and drag us all down. Hey, why not make the most of it!? I'm sad about mum, but you were always top for me. Not that I don't love her. No, it's just, well, dad's and daughters. You may not understand it yet, but I love you to bits. You're the best dad I could ever have hoped for."

Jefferey wasn't too far distant from the man he pretended to be just yet, so the swell of tears that he began to feel rising up in him prompted him to thank Penelope and Helen and excuse himself. He needed the sleep he'd been deprived of last night and he really wanted to begin work on Don Quixote, the book having been laid aside several times at the hotel. It seemed like he'd never get past the first page. Who would have predicted the strange goings on that were preventing him from escaping into what would seem a more realistic world?

"Wake me at supper time." He asked them as he slipped through to the bunk that still smelt of Alicia's perfume, the book staying unopened beside him as he escaped into much needed sleep.

"It'll always be 'supper' at least." Penelope laughed. "Good to see some things never change. Come on, let's join the others."

.

Chapter Forty-Six:

The small flight at Meaford consisted of four locks that were closely followed by the elongated flight of a further four that covered the length of the historic, if presently down-in-the-mouth, canal town of Stone. They could have chosen to moor anywhere within those lock pounds, but decided to get the hard labour out of the way on this short day's cruise and moor at the far end of the town, filling up with water before they slotted into a two-day mooring space.

If much of the ethos of the boating life was about escaping the madding crowd, Stone was one of those exceptional places where such aspirations were put on hold. It was built around the canal, had the wharves and the remnants of the old brewery to support its links to the waterways, and it had the pubs. More importantly, and the reason it continued to be a popular mooring spot, were the modern conveniences that were all within walking distance. These included a supermarket, a high street and a mix of restaurants and takeaways. Granted, the high street was little more than a succession of charity shops, but that's what happens when a town is earmarked to take an overflow of sink-estate inhabitants. Politicians may aspire to the half-baked notion of assisted upward social mobility, but the truth would always be that it was easier to drag something down than lift it up.

Most of the boats that had accompanied them through the Meaford Locks were to be found moored up at Stone. Mick, mysteriously, continued to be recognised by a frightening number of them, making him more and more convinced that he had a doppelganger out there who had achieved some minor level of celebrity. With the boaters, it was all good-natured and restrained. Once he and Helen were pushing a trolley around the supermarket, the attention was a lot more invasive. So much so that they hurriedly bundled a minimum of shopping into their trolley and exited as promptly as they could.

"I'm getting bloody sick of it!" Mick complained. "I'll be glad when we're back home and away from all this."

Helen let him have a rant. After all, he'd been on best behaviour all day and she'd seen the best of the man she'd married and was proud to still be married to. They'd left Jefferey sleeping, whilst Steve and Penelope had opened a bottle of wine and were sitting out on the towpath enjoying the fine weather. They didn't talk too much about what had happened. When Penelope needed him to, he'd listen. Meanwhile, they had a few days of holiday left and weren't going to waste it.

With a well-built towpath beside them and a good long length of visitor moorings, two worlds collided in front of the old scout hut that loomed over the boats. Cyclists raced by, bringing out the more vocal members of the boating community who either shouted insults or stood deliberately in their way. For the main part, the cyclists toed the line; not only did they have those mysterious 'others' on the water to worry about, they also had the many locals who enjoyed a walk by the water and who also refused to have the space hijacked by Lance Armstrong wannabees.

"Hello flower." Mick smiled at the flamboyantly dressed woman who was chatting with Steve as he arrived back, arms laden with groceries that he passed through to Helen.

"Nice day for it." Mick let his gaze wander from the woman's shapely legs, up past her tennis skirt and onto a tight-fitting blouse that did nothing to hide shapely breasts and firm nipples. "Are you on a boat?"

"Yes, I was just telling Stephen here, that's mine two spaces back." She smiled in a jaunty and flirtatious way at Mick. "He was saying that you were having a bit of a hectic holiday. Still, it's good fun isn't it."

Steve and Penelope sat back and watched as they handed their new friend over to Mick who was doing very little to hide his interest in her. They smiled as he played the real gentleman, always keeping his eyes on her figure and rarely looking closely at the face that was predominantly covered with a large pair of sunglasses. It was only when the light summer scarf that was draped loosely around her neck was removed, that Mick understood why his son felt no threat from their new acquaintance.

"I'd better help put the shopping away." he blurted out before running inside to tell Helen that he was going to kill Stephen for not telling him that the 'she' that he was chatting to was actually a 'he' in a skirt.

"And I bet that he or she is a nicer person than most of the people you've ever met." Helen replied, throwing a loaf of bread it him. "Have you learnt nothing yet? Tolerance. Respect. I'll start calling you Jefferey soon!"

"You come in for a glass of Pimm's, dad?" Steve laughed as he pushed into the galley and grabbed another bottle of wine. "I reckon you're in there. Just be careful though, you may end up fighting over the electric shaver in the morning!"

"Bugger off."

"With pleasure."

Jefferey joined them as the evening began to set in.

"By jingo!" he smiled as addressed the remaining crew. "I feel properly refreshed by that sleep. Seems I've got some catching up to do on the alcohol front, and I know just the place to do it. We're booked into The Star at seven."

"Well, take me home, Mummy!" Mick replied. "You seem in fine fettle, man. We'll take you up on the offer, and then, you and I will work our way through the pubs of this town and forget all about what's happened. Not too soon, Penny, love?"

"Not at all." Penelope replied. "And The Star's perfect. I checked out before, and they have free wi-fi. You just wait until Steve and I show you our own little surprise."

The Star wasn't just a good choice for its food and the availability of an internet connection. It was also a pub that was made for Mick, situated as it was between a number of information plaques that he memorised and repeated verbatim to all, and with its own claim to fame as a record breaker.

"So, the Trent and Mersey canal was first planned from this very pub." He informed the family as they settled into the cosy snug. "Just imagine, Brindley and the others might have been sat in this very room. Makes you think doesn't it. A couple of jars, a dirty ditch dug out by hand and wham! The Industrial Revolution begins. Amazing."

"But," he continued before anyone else could get a word in. "That's not all I've discovered about Stone ..."

He went on to tell them a contrived and only partially accurate tale about the name of Stone being something to do with two medieval princes who were beheaded on a stone for being Christian. That comment brought a semi-bitter interruption from Jefferey who said that some vicars should be beheaded as far as he was concerned. After this came the tale of Christina Collins, whose statue, beside one of the locks, had elicited a comment about her not looking too good which Mick regretted when he got to know the story of that 19th century traveller who was raped and murdered after paying to take a fly-boat to London. Then, finally, the last fact he could remember:

"And, of course, this place is in the Guinness Book of Records as the pub with the greatest number of different levels. Now, aren't you all glad that you have me for company?"

"You are a veritable encyclopaedia, Michael." Jefferey didn't even try and hide his sarcasm. "A Google of the North, indeed!"

"But that's nothing to what we know about this place." Steve gave a wink to Penelope.

"You're right." She took over from him. "You see, this is the pub where Michael Roberts finally learnt the truth about why people keep staring at him and treating him like a celebrity."

Cruelly, the young couple left it hanging there as they ordered more drinks before explaining.

Chapter Forty-Seven:

"You see," Penelope told her captive audience, "the fact of the matter is, he is a celebrity. If we've all finished eating, please permit me to show you the evidence."

"Yeah, right!" Mick chuckled. "Never mind me being a Google, Jeff, it appears I'm now an Elvis!"

"Hurry up then, love." he told Penelope, who was connecting the tablet they'd brought with them and bringing up the necessary links.

"Have you heard of You Tube, dad?" Steve asked by way of introduction.

"Aye, of course I have. Never used it though. Not really my scene the whole interweb. Too many tits popping up when you don't want them for my liking."

"You'll find a lot of tits on You Tube as well." Jefferey made another joke, adding to the surprise that the others were feeling about his new character.

"Forget all that." Steve butted back in. "Let us explain. People video things on their phones and then post them to You Tube. As Jefferey rightly said, a lot of it is rubbish. But, occasionally, a video goes viral. Which, before you make some stupid comment dad, means that it spreads like wildfire over the internet. And that's what Penelope's discovered. Shall we have a look?"

Penelope placed the tablet on the table in front of them, turned the volume up full and let the video play. The quality was surprisingly good, both of audio and video. Mick's smiling face was there for all to see in high definition. He appeared to have just finished singing a song that the audience had loved, a borrowed accordion hanging limply from his shoulders.

As the applause died down and the shouts for more were acknowledged, Mick's viral performance began.

"And now, ladies and gentlemen, a little number I wrote myself, called 'Ophelia'." His voice was slurred by the numerous pints that had been consumed at The Shroppie Fly only a week or so ago, but that didn't seem to affect his performance as the accordion came to life and the song with it.

"*She was only the vicar's daughter,*" it began. "*but she lay her hands on my heart. She touched me one day, as I knelt down to pray, and I thought, 'well, that's a good start!'*"

Then the chorus began.

"*Touch me, touch me, Ophelia. I feel ya want me to feel ya. Touch me, touch me, Ophelia, I feel ya the girl of my dreams.*"

And so, to the other verses:

"*She was only the vicar's daughter, and I was the poor boy next door. Her wink said her spirit, knew no normal limits, and I thought, 'now I'm pretty sure'.*

She was only the vicar's daughter, but she oozed Celestial Bliss. We hid in the choir as she shared her desire, and I thought, 'I'll have more of this'.

She was only the vicar's daughter, a pair made in heaven were we. But something went wrong and a third came along, and I thought, 'A kid? Bugger me!'

She was only the vicar's daughter, I was obsessed and so weak. We were wed by her dad, but the marriage is bad, and I think next time I'll go Sikh!"

"Well, I don't remember that." Mick shook his head.

"You were well gone." Steve reminded him. "And so was I. But the camera never lies, eh!"

"You are such an embarrassment, Michael Roberts." Helen gave her husband one of her killer stares. "There's another thing I'll never be able to live down. You wonder why I didn't let you bring your stupid musical instruments on this holiday? Where did you get that one from?"

"I must have borrowed it." Mick replied. "Still, it were a pretty good song that one. I don't see what's so special about it though."

"That's the whole point of You Tube!" Penelope explained. "It's not about the merit of the videos. It's about what taps into the mood at the time. And, somehow or other, you managed to do that. You really need to understand how big this thing has got. The You Tube video has had over ten million views and it's growing exponentially. Beyond that though, because nobody knows who you are and nobody can track you down, there's an air of mystery about the whole thing. I've started drawing the various weblinks together and I've put up an official website with a hint of who you are, and already that's gone massive."

"Aye, but who wants to be famous?" Mick finished his pint and waved to the barmaid for refills.

"It's not just about fame." Steve replied. "This is a serious money-making opportunity. It'll probably be just a flash-in-the-pan, but you can milk it just the same."

"That's why we've set up a website for you." Penelope took over the explanation. "And remember, that was only yesterday. Since then, I've had enquiries from all over the world. From the media, from record labels and from every crackpot and his son. This is big, Michael."

"Aye, big it may be, but what if I don't want that?" Mick asked. "I'm happy as I am. Fame's never interested me."

"Don't worry," Penelope reassured him. "I've left it all very vague just now. The next steps are up to you. Even the website name keeps you anonymous. It's www.touchmeophelia.com that's all. There's a shadow picture of an anonymous face and the strapline, 'Who is the Mysterious Canal Crooner?'. That's all just now. Mind you, there have been quite a number of speculative identities put out there and some of them name you. We can get around that though. And, if you want, I can easily take the site down."

"It's a huge opportunity, Michael." Jefferey spoke up. "Potentially very lucrative too. Don't dismiss it just yet. I think the kids may be onto something."

It was left that way. Attention soon shifted to the dogs that had entered the pub and which took an instant liking to Jefferey. Preparing themselves to divert them away, the rest of the family watched in amazement as he petted and cuddled the inquisitive beasts, no longer the man who thought they were vermin, but now a man who seemed to understand the genuine love that was in their nature to give.

"Sheba, get away!" the dog's owner called firmly.

"She's okay." Jefferey told him. "Aren't you Sheba, girl?"

"Well, that meal was lovely Jefferey. Thank you." Helen yawned and stretched as she spoke. "But this has been a bit of a hectic day, and I'm ready to turn in."

"We'll go back with you." Steve told his mum. "What about you Dad?"

"I'm not quite ready." Mick replied. "I need a few more jars to get my head around this whole fame and fortune thing. Jefferey, how about we check out the watering holes of Stone?"

"A splendid idea, sir." Jefferey replied. "Starting, I think with The Borehole. It's a little place attached to a brewery near here. I checked it out before we came here and looks like it might be an awful lot of fun. Sound like a plan?"

"As sure as Toddington Heath still stands." Mick replied. "And awfully good of you, old chap, to find an awfully fun place. I just hope it doesn't prove to be bloody awful!"

Stumbling a little as the fresh air hit their already beer-soaked frames, they left The Star and walked the fifteen minutes to their first stop, where they found a cosy and simple building that carried the full range of the beers that were brewed in the buildings behind the pub. For a weekday night, it was packed full of people. That said a lot for the reputation it had.

The two men were in fine fettle, despite the broken arm that still plagued Mick and the broken promises of marriage that plagued his companion. It wasn't all doom and gloom. Jefferey's company had been able to ship out the much-delayed Tiger Claws and the companies they supplied were easing off on the pressure. That release of stock, and the help of Rostov, also meant that Mick's loan could be repaid with interest. An easy ten-thousand profit in the bank was enough to explain Mick's own good mood. The impending storm from the web wasn't enough to cheer him in himself. It remained a mysterious mixed blessing and he was able to put it out of his mind.

Chapter Forty-Eight:

As something of a hidden gem, The Borehole attracted a majority crowd of locals. They were polite enough to Mick and Jefferey but happy in their own company; the sort of familiar grouping that came from years of gentle, low-commitment companionship. Given their age profile, it was no surprise that the mystery of The Canal Crooner seemed to have bypassed them, as none of them gave Mick as second look. A secondary, smaller group of drinkers were the regulars from the boats that knew the area, and the crews of passing boaters who'd been tipped off about the place.

That particular band of brothers, for all were male, were huddled together in one corner of the bar, in hot debate about the way the waterways were being managed and the things that were being done by the Canal and River Trust, the authority that oversaw them. It had been British Waterways until a political sleight of hand transformed it from a quango into a charity. That change had been reluctantly accepted by most boaters. A sceptical bunch for the most part, and certainly an opinionated grouping who had affectionate memories for what the waterways had once been, even if their memories were tinged by false-nostalgia, for the most part, they'd taken the transition in their stride and waited to see what the new organisation would do. After several years of maintaining the status quo, things had begun to move in a way that raised some concerns. What they were finding it more difficult to accept was the CRT's focus on everything around the canals and not the canal itself.

"Cyclists', Anglers' and Ramblers' Trust." Mick and Jefferey heard as they settled in on the edge of the debate. "Three times this week I nearly been run over by a lycra-clad twat. Twice, I've been held up by a seemingly never-ending stretch of anglers having a competition, and I've lost count of the number of chavs with cans of booze gathering near the boat. You advertise that the canal is the place to be and that's what you get. The proper walkers, the people who appreciate the cut for what it is, well, they already know it's there. I despair some times."

"Nice new logo though." a different voice spoke with just a hint of sarcasm.

"No! Don't mention the logo. That'll get me onto canal poet's and floating sculptures. Why don't they have a go at fixing some locks, sorting out the lock landings and dredging the water? We need to be careful. They'll have us all in marinas and the boats will disappear from the water."

"Are you guys on a boat?" one of the younger members of the group turned to address Mick and Jefferey.

"Not sure we should admit it." Mick laughed. "We're on a hire-boat."

"Hey, that's fine mate." the other man replied. "We need more of your sort out there. It keeps the water moving."

"Provided you stick to the rules." the first speaker interrupted.

"Oh, give it rest Tommy. We know your views on hire-boats. But, even you've got to admit they drive more carefully than the shiny-boat brigade."

The other conceded that point and Mick and Jefferey were included in the rambling discussion that saw them through several pints each over the next hour. It was an insight into a part of the canal system that they hadn't seen before. On holiday, they'd enjoyed the scenery and the whole experience and had met some great people. What they hadn't been party to was the politics of the cut and the shift in focus that was stirring such dissension amongst those who loved the canals more than any faceless bureaucrat sitting in a land-locked office ever would.

"Time for your input, Roger." somebody shouted.

"Well …" Roger began. "I may be no expert on running a big business, but I do know the waterways and I can see what I can see. It's as simple as this. Forget all your moaning about the marketing gurus and the daft initiatives like the canal poems and cut to the chase. I don't care what they do, so long as they do the basics. You see a hole in the ground by a mooring and you fill it in. You don't cover it with that bloody red netting and then spend five years doing a survey about the effect of any work on the Lesser Spotted Bong-Worm, or whatever it is their concerned with. If a lock paddle isn't working, you fix it. You don't cover it in yellow tape and wait for a time when a team of ten can attend to consider what needs doing. And forget all the health and safety rubbish. One man can clear a blocked channel. He doesn't need two buddies to ensure that he doesn't fall in. And…"

He paused to finish off his pint. The assembled locals and boaters all waiting on his next words.

"…when a bridge is starting to fall down, you don't just measure it every week. You fix it. That's my biggest bug-bear. I was in Penkridge a few days back and I was terrified as I went under the bridge at Otherton. It'll take the death of a boater to make them wake up. You get a hire-boat, no disrespect, tapping that dodgy bridge as you pass under and the whole lot could come down on you. No, that's all I've got to say. If they get the basics done, let them do what they want. But, they ain't doing those basics and the network's suffering as a result. That's all I've got to say…"

"…although," he continued. "a quick word about hire-boaters. And all due respect to our visitors here. In general, they're damned good at what they do. Sure, they don't get enough training to handle a beast like a barge, but they try and they follow the rules a lot more closely than the marina-millionaires who think the cut belongs to them. That's all."

"Centre-ropes." another participant joined the debate with his cryptic input. "Just one thing that they should all be told and it would help us all out. I live by my centre-line. How many times do you see hirers thinking that you pull the boat in with a crew member at the front and one at the back? You do it that way and chaos is bound to happen. Why don't they tell them when they hire these things that your centre-line is all you need? It's your best friend and it only needs one person to operate it. It would save us all a lot of hassle."

"You and your bloody centre-lines." Roger laughed. "But, sound advice anyway."

"And talking of sound advice," he continued, speaking directly to Mick and Jefferey. "if you're out to make the most of Stone, you want to try The Swan next."

Advice which they heeded and which saw them staggering back to the boat at midnight, having sampled more varieties of beer in one night than they had in the past year. The Swan had been all it promised to be. It allowed dogs but barred children and it had a dozen or so real ales, proper cider and quirky shorts on offer. On top of which, it had a clientele that brooked no pretensions and who welcomed Mick and the new, improved version of Jefferey into the fold immediately. Realising how little respect he'd had for others, that welcome helped cement the change that Jefferey was now determined to effect in himself. Sod the past. He'd missed out on so much.

Chapter Forty-Nine:

"Just hang on here a moment." Jefferey told Mick as they arrived back at the boat. "Got a little something special stashed away on board."

Mick settled on a bench just a few metres from where the boat was moored. When Jefferey returned he was waving a bottle of Glenmorangie at his friend.

"Nice one, Jefferey." Mick took the proffered bottle and undid the foil.

"Thought it would be a nice end to the day." Jefferey took the opened bottle and poured generous measures into the glasses he'd brought with him.

"Cheers, mate." He said as they toasted each other and downed the fiery liquid.

"Cheers, Jeffery. And thank you."

"For what?" Jefferey asked.

"For the money, for starters. And for the pints you paid for tonight. But, most of all, for not being your usual pompous self. You're alright when you take the stick out of your arse!"

"Well, that's a compliment indeed." Jefferey refilled their glasses. "And I'm taking no offence. But all the thanks go to you. Not just for the loan of the money. I owe you more than that, my friend. You've taught me how to chill out and relax, and how not to be the prat that I was."

"Although ..." he was struggling now to make his thoughts and words coherent. "It's not quite as cut and dried as you think. Being the old Jefferey was good to me. Sure, it came back and bit me in the backside, but it paid a lot of bills. Mind you, at what price? You and I, we should spend more time together. When the little one comes, we'll do that. You up for a monthly blow out?"

"I'll drink to that." Mick replied.

For both men, the world was spinning slightly and the words they were sharing had more than a hint of a slur to them, but they didn't care. They were bonding in a way that was beyond the temporary bond that alcohol forged.

"No, let me finish." Jefferey continued. "I always thought I was better than you. I had the money, the business, the houses and cars. I had everything I'd ever dreamed of. You were okay, but we always thought of you as some sort of rude mechanical. I was wrong. My whole life was built on a lie, whereas yours was truer than any. You and Helen have it right. You work hard, enjoy what you have and appreciate it. And you don't pretend to be people you're not. You've taught me a lot, Mick, and I thank you for that."

"It isn't difficult." Mick replied. "In fact, the hardest part of being me is trying to cope with people like you. I used to envy you all the money and the toys, but I wouldn't have changed anything to get hold of them. Mind you, that whole Alicia thing was a bit of a twat, wasn't it?"

"You could say that. And you'd be right to think that it knocked me for six. But I had a chance to think about it and I'm happy to have found out now. We'll split the money, Penny will be fine with it, and we'll both get on with our lives. I know it seems really soon, but I'm going to live every day now and not care about what others think. A toast to new beginnings!"

Already, the whisky bottle was half-empty. Idle chatter carried on for a few more minutes, Mick and Jefferey trying to remember the dirtiest jokes they could, each one bluer and funnier than the other. So engrossed were they by their own company, the blue light that flashed behind them was ignored.

"Now then, Michael." Jefferey put his arm around his new buddy. "What about this song of yours. Let's have a go at it."

They'd just completed the first chorus of 'Touch Me Ophelia', when the flashlight that shone into their eyes stopped them in their tracks. They looked up to see a male and a female police officer standing over them.

"Gentlemen?"

"Ah, Officer. Good evening." Mick waved at the new arrivals. "Can I tempt you with a quick drop of the finest whisky ever made?"

"I don't think so." The female officer spoke first. "In fact, I would suggest that you pop the cork back in and put the bottle quietly to one side."

"Is something the matter?" Jefferey just about managed to keep the words slur-free.

"It is, I'm afraid." the male officer spoke this time, his voice as youthful as he.

"Aye up," Mick chuckled. "It's true! They are getting younger."

"Please sir, be quiet." he replied. "And listen."

The police officers waited a moment as Mick and Jefferey hushed each other as only two drunken men can, putting fingers to lips and trying desperately to stop giggling.

"This area is designated as a no-drinking zone." the female officer took over. "There is a sign just above your heads telling you that. And a breach of the law can bring a fine of up to one thousand pounds. So, may I suggest that you sober up a little and listen."

The two men sat quietly on the bench, heads hunched like naughty schoolboys.

"We would be within our rights," the officer continued. "to fine you on the spot, or even arrest you. This is an area that has had its share of problems and the rules are there to help solve those problems."

"Fortunately, for you," the male officer took over. "We are only here on a routine patrol, so we're not responding to a complaint. That puts a slightly different complexion on things."

"I should think so too." Jefferey tried to stand but ended up falling against Mick and causing them to burst into another laughing fit. "We are not, as you can clearly see, the sort of people for whom that law was intended. Good on you for driving the chavs and the tramps away. But I can assure you, we are respectable and upstanding citizens. So, thank you very much and goodnight to you."

"Sir, I don't think you quite get this situation. You don't say how this goes and you don't tell us what to do. I would be very careful if I were you. There is a certain law concerning being drunk and disorderly. Do you want us to go along that route?"

The exchange continued for a few more minutes, during which names and addresses were taken and the boat the men were from was identified. Believing that they were due a slap on the wrists, the two men relaxed. Mick managed to keep himself in check, but Jefferey was enjoying his new-found freedom.

"Officers." he declared. "You are certainly Britain's finest and I applaud the work you do. Good on you. Now, as a gesture of my thanks, might I be permitted to give you a little something?"

He stood and opened his wallet, pulled out a couple of notes and tried to pass them to the two police officers. The speed of his standing up, coupled with the effect of the whisky caused him to stumble and fall against the younger male officer who promptly fell down on the towpath. In trying to help him up, Jefferey gave in to the stirring in his stomach and succeeded only in vomiting on the officer's shoes. Watching all this, the other police officer swept into action and Jefferey was handcuffed and pushed back onto the bench. It didn't look promising for the two friends. That is, until there was an unlikely intervention.

"Michael Roberts and Jefferey Williams, what the hell do you think your playing at?" Helen stormed towards them wielding the kitchen broom that was one of the practical utensils supplied by the hire company.

"Ma'am." The female officer tried to stop the new arrival. "Please stay away. We have this under control."

Her words were ignored by Helen who began to use the broom to beat the two men soundly.

"I have never been so disgraced in my life."

Keener to wash his shoes in the canal than intervene, the male officer smiled as Helen vented her wrath.

"You are like little children. Now, apologise to these two officers."

The apology was duly accepted and the handcuffs were removed.

"Please, take them away and lock them up." Helen said. "It's what they deserve and it will be a hell of a lot more pleasant for them than what I have in store. This is absolutely beyond the pale. You have a young couple inside who are waiting on the birth of your grandchild and this is the way you behave. I will never let you live this one down ..."

As Helen's scolding continued, the officers talked amongst themselves. To take the two men into custody was probably the right thing to do, but it would involve a lot of paperwork. Besides, if imprisonment was the punishment, how little it was compared to what that vixen had in store for them. They approached Helen and called her over.

"Ma'am?" the female officer asked quietly. "If we leave these two in your care, will you ensure they go to the boat quietly?"

"Yes, I will."

"And," the male officer added, "can we be assured that they will not suffer an assault?"

"Aside from a verbal one, I assure you they will be unharmed."

The police officers were happy with that. They watched as Helen ushered the staggering and stumbling men aboard the boat and started walking back to their car. The church bells chimed the end of another day as they drove away.

"Did we do the right thing?" one of them asked the other.

"James, believe me." his partner replied. "Nothing we could have done would have been anywhere near what they will have to put up with from her. No, we can let this one be. Call it a just end to the affair. Come on, let's go and do some real policing."

Week Two

Day Five, Wednesday:

Stone to Radford

Chapter Fifty:

Had Helen known the lengths to which Alicia had gone to in order to control her husband earlier on in the holiday, she might have counted herself lucky that the previous night's escapade was the worst that she'd, so far, had to endure. Granted, it was embarrassing. And, of course, extremely annoying. After everything that had gone on, the last thing she'd wanted was to be denied a much-needed sleep. Having been married to Mick for a good long time, she was used to his occasional forays into drunken stupidity, but that didn't make it any better. She almost wished that the police had arrested them. Maybe that was the lesson they needed. That said, thoughts of vengeance were not in Helen's nature, so the much-feared tongue-lashing that the men expected over the breakfast table simply became a staring silence. One that Mick tried his best to break.

"We're both very sorry." He told the family as he passed around the sausage and bacon baps that he'd got up early to prepare. "It was childish and stupid and there are no excuses. We just had too much to drink, that's all. We are very, very sorry."

"Michael has said it all." Jefferey added. "I know an apology seems a lame response, but we genuinely mean it. And thank you for keeping us out of custody."

"We're going to give this day completely to you, love." Mick continued. "You can do whatever you want and Jefferey and I will make sure you have a lazy and relaxing day. There aren't too many locks, but we'll do them all whilst you and Penelope and Steve chill out."

"And lunch is our treat." Jefferey took over. "I've already booked us into the Saracen's Head in Weston where the menu looks stunning. They do rooms as well, but I didn't think you'd want to go along that route. Not after the last hotel debacle."

"That would be interesting." Steve spoke mischievously. "We could see how many more family members we can lose in a night."

He stopped there, having been poked in the leg by his wife.

"Dad," Penelope turned to Jefferey. "You really upset Helen. I know it's not easy for you, but please make sure that doesn't happen again. We're only got a few days left of the holiday, let's make sure we make the most of it. Are you certain you're both up for that and capable of delivering?"

"I am." he replied. "I told Mick last night. The situation isn't perfect, but it is what it is. New beginnings and all that. Maybe that's why we went over the top. I'm up for some fun and I'm going to learn from these two wonderful people how to be the best granddad I can."

That was enough for Helen to recant and soften her look. She had to put up with a lot with Mick, but Jefferey was right, they had a good marriage and he was a decent bloke. Despite everything, she knew she was lucky.

"You can start with the washing up then." she told the two transgressors. "After that, you can get us moving and keep us supplied with tea. Meanwhile, Penelope and I are going to look at this ridiculous phenomenon of Mick the Superstar! Whatever next!?"

The late Summer weather was perfect for cruising. A light wind kept the air flowing under clear skies, and the trees and hedges that lined the route were showing the last of the peak, fecund beauty before it would give way to Autumn's death-song and Winter's mourning. The journey itself took them away from the relative urbanity of Stone and out into the most stunning countryside. As they descended through Aston lock and cleared the marina there, all around was farmland. Granted, the through road ran near at times and trains rattled past every half hour, but other than that it was peace and relaxation.

"I can't remember when I last saw mum that mad." Steve had joined the other men on deck, firmly on their side, but not in a way he'd dare tell Helen. "I'm impressed that you're both so with it this morning. No side effects?"

"Aye, a few, lad." Mick replied. "For me at least. It seems that Jefferey there is less of a lightweight than I am. Mind you, I managed to keep all mine down!"

"Don't remind me." Jefferey shook his head. "I didn't think anything of it at the time. I thought it was funny actually. Now I realise how close I was to the cells. And those handcuffs bloody hurt."

"They handcuffed you?" Steve asked. "I'd love to have seen that."

"Luckily your mother came along." Mick told him. "Otherwise, we were on very dodgy ground. They were only kids as well. I wish I'd had my camera with me. Jeff there in cuffs and the young copper dipping his feet in the cut to wash the puke off."

"Yes, well, it's not something I want to dwell on." Jefferey said. "Not really a moment to be proud of."

"You're a pair of legends." Steve laughed as he took over the tiller from Jefferey. "One of you an internet superstar, the other an old lag!"

The banter continued for a while as the canal opened up towards Burston. Once every permutation of gentle ribbing had been exhausted, they settled into a comfortable silence as they meandered through the stunning landscape. It was a brief respite that lasted only half an hour, before the next lock appeared and Mick was left to steer the boat through as Jefferey and Steve worked the paddles and gates.

"He's a different person." Steve whispered to his dad as he boarded the boat ahead of Jefferey. "I could almost like him."

"I think he may have had a Damascene conversion to humanity." Mick whispered back. "We had a cracking time last night. He's alright once you strip away the façade."

"I wondered why Penny had a soft spot for him." Steve sighed. "Now I know. He's different, certainly, but he seems to have been a good father to her."

Fortunately, Jefferey arrived before Mick had to reply. He knew the guilty secret of Penelope's parenthood and it would be a burden he'd carry with him for a long time, all of which would be a desperate attempt to ensure that it remained a secret.

Arriving at Weston shortly afterwards, Jefferey pointed out the hauntingly gothic Weston Hall that had been one of his options for the lunch treat. He'd opted against it when he'd seen the photos of the Saracen's. On a day like today, it should tick enough boxes to ensure that Helen's forgiveness was complete.

It didn't let them down. They were able to moor just a short walk away from the pub and arrived in plenty of time for their reservation. Inside, the pub was fresh and cool, beautifully furnished but practical enough that it allowed dogs in. In fact, they even had a dedicated dog menu. Surprised at his own change of heart, Jefferey liked that idea and was seriously contemplating a canine companion to replace the wife who would never be returning. That was all for the longer term though. Now it was about keeping Helen happy.

"I think we'll sit outside." she told them. "If that's okay with you?"

"Bloody hell," Mick chuckled, knowing how much his wife felt the cold. "That's a first for you."

Ignoring her husband, Penelope and Helen walked through the pub and into the garden, settling themselves in bright sunshine at a table that looked directly towards Weston Hall and onto the field where the Saracen's kept their unusual resident pets.

"Herd of llamas!" Mick shouted and pointed as he joined them.

"Of course, we have." Steve and Jefferey replied simultaneously, rising to Mick's joke.

"Ignore them." Helen muttered to Penelope. "They're like three naughty schoolchildren."

Starting with gin and tonic's, the ladies made the most of their upgraded status. Whilst the gin fad was soon to give way to a whisky one, the Saracen's had a great range and both Penelope and Helen knew that there would be more to follow.

"Fish and chips for me." Mick glanced only briefly at the menu, ignoring the masterpieces that the Chef's were proud to present as 'pub food squared'.

"No surprise there." Penelope muttered. "No doubt the rest of us will be a tad more adventurous."

Not only was the gin menu extensive, the beers on offer included some of the best that Staffordshire had to offer.

"Look Mick." Jefferey pointed to one of the pumps. "Titanic brewery. I bet that one goes down well!"

"Aye, I could sink a few of those!"

"I wonder if it comes with ice?" Steve joined in.

Still laughing at their jokes, three pints of Plum Porter were quickly followed by three more.

"You just watch yourselves now." Helen admonished them as they returned from the bar.

Chapter Fifty-One:

The food at the Saracen's was stunning and ample. The gin and tonics hit the spot and the Plum Porter was a dangerously easy to drink drop of ale. Feeling relaxed and sleepy after their meal, it was something of an effort for the crew of the Harriet Knot to make the necessary journey back to the boat, but a comment from Steve helped them along.

"I see your guys have finally shipped the Tiger Claws." he said to Jefferey as they drained their last drinks.

"I told you not to worry." Jefferey replied, resisting the urge to tell Helen how she'd missed out on the opportunity of a quick buck. "Everything's back on track now and I've got another shipment on the way."

"I told you, Stephen." Penelope gave her husband a hard stare. "You just turn your work phone off and enjoy the break. Tiger Claws! How old are you?!"

Stirred again by their various involvements in that mysterious late shipment, the crew made it back to the boat and set off on the last leg of the day's voyage.

"You're not planning on telling her?" Jefferey asked Mick.

"Would you?! No, I'm going to keep my little nest egg for a project that I'm planning. Please, don't breathe a word to her."

"Don't worry." Jefferey reassured him. "Your secret's safe with me. Mind you, if the kids are right, you've got more money coming your way."

"I'm not banking on it. Let's see what happens. It'll probably all be over by the time we get back."

That was wishful thinking on Mick's part. The reality was that Penelope and Helen had spent most of the day talking about how to make the most of Mick's unusual fame. Not a great one for technical things, it had taken the morning for Penelope to bring Helen up to speed on the basics, but by the time they moored for the night at Radford Bank, she was fully aware of the various ways of making money from social media. Her only concern was the lack of privacy.

"You can keep that under control." Penelope told her. "We just need to limit the exposure of the real Mick. It's the Canal Crooner they're all enthralled by."

"I'm sure you're right." Helen conceded. "But please do everything you can to keep it low key. Mick's a delicate creature under all that bluff."

Radford was a convenient stopping point with a number of plus points to it that made it a natural stop for boaters of every ilk. The towpath had no time restrictions, other than the statutory fourteen days and it ran below a cycle path, making it a tad less precarious than most. Given its proximity to Stafford, liveaboard employees found it an ideal place to commute from and the pub that adjoined the canal would allow them to park their cars there if necessary. In recent years, a budget supermarket had joined the attractions and it was to that supermarket that Jefferey was despatched to top up the boat's essential supplies. Whilst it would have made more sense for any of the other crew members to make that journey, Steve and Mick had encouraged Helen to allow Jefferey the treat of shopping at an Aldi for the first time.

"He'll be standing forever at the till, waiting for someone to pack his bags for him." Steve quipped.

"Or he'll be calling the manager over to ask where he could find the duck eggs!" Mick added.

"It'll do you good." Penelope told her father when the suggestion was made. "You need to learn to shop by yourself now, and it doesn't matter that it's not a Waitrose. You'll find they have perfectly good food there and at great prices. I'll give you a heads-up on the basics before you go."

His mind filled to overflowing with the rules and conventions laid out by his daughter, Jefferey nervously poked his pound coin into one of the supermarket's trolley handles and smiled at the small victory of it coming free in his hands. The shopping list he removed from his pocket had been carefully written by Helen to both ensure that he brought all they needed, and that he did so without having to worry about navigating through the various aisles. That was the beauty of Aldi; the stores were the right size and their layouts very much the same.

Like many a single man in a supermarket, Jefferey muttered to himself as he began dropping items into the trolley. And, like many a man before him, he couldn't resist checking over every shelf for other items that were of interest. Shopping with Alicia had only ever involved a request or two as she placed their online order, or the occasional foray into Waitrose or Marks and Spencer's to pick up a forgotten item. Now, set free into an Aldi, where a trolley full of goods would cost little more than what he'd been used to paying for a decent burgundy, the scope for add-on purchases was huge.

He'd just placed a cordless drill in with the groceries when he felt a tap on his shoulder.

"Excuse me, young man." the woman who addressed him was seventy years old, if she was a day, and was wearing the flimsiest of summer dresses. Fluttering her eyelids and drawing closer to Jefferey she asked him if he would be so kind as to reach a special-offer hand cream that had been placed high above sundry other offers.

"There you are." he smiled as he handed it to him.

"That's so kind of you." she smiled back. "I could do with taking you home with me."

"I'm not sure my friends would appreciate that." Jefferey mumbled an excuse. "We've already lost one crew member and the boat's supplies are dangerously low in alcohol."

"Oh, are you on a boat?" The woman replied. "How convenient. So am I. I'm moored on the bank there. You?"

Wary of giving too much away, Jefferey admitted nothing more than that, yes, they were moored there as well.

"Come on then, sweetheart." the woman held his arm as she continued, drawing Jefferey a little closer and forcing him to inhale the unusual aroma of cheap perfume and stale alcohol. "Let's go around this place together and we can carry each other's bags back. You look like you could do with a hand. I'm Carol by the way."

"Hello, Carol by the way, I'm Jefferey."

"Delighted to meet you, Jefferey. Now, shall we shop?"

Aside from his new companion's excessive use of touch to express herself, Jefferey appreciated the help that Carol gave him. Explaining as eloquently as the most highly qualified retail analyst, she explained how the discounters had given the big supermarkets a 'kick in the balls' with their simple shopping offer, friendly staff and great prices. She also guided him through the own brand choices to make, detailing how some of the looky-likey products were to be avoided whilst others were better than the product they so cleverly emulated.

"It takes a while." she told him. "But I wouldn't go anywhere else by choice now. After all, it's only a shop. Who wants to spend all their life buying groceries, when there are so many more fun things to do?"

The most challenging moment came when they were approaching the checkouts and Carol whooped with joy at a special buy line of lingerie that promised to be a 'sensually seductive secret'.

"What do you think Jefferey?" Carol held a bright red basque up against her torso. "Sensually seductive enough?"

Jefferey mumbled something non-committal and watched as Carol placed it in her trolley.

"Last stop." She giggled as she directed them to the tills.

Having been used to the slow but service-oriented process that was favoured by his preferred retail outlets, watching items being scanned and pushed back into his trolley at lightening speed was a new experience for him. Before he had time to think, the tally had been added up and he was expected to have his card ready for payment. Wondering how it could possibly all be included in the total he saw flash up on the screen, he paid and was escorted by Carol to the packing area.

"No queues, you see?" she told him as they began to unload their trolleys and bag up their purchases. "And no hassle. Once you're here at the packing place, you can take as long as you want and make sure your bags are properly sorted."

"Makes sense." he replied, relieved that he'd survived the ordeal and pleasantly surprised by how friendly such a functionally efficient retail system proved to be.

They walked slowly back to the towpath, Jefferey carrying as many of Carol's bags as he could manage. His own bags were laden with all the necessaries and a number of impulse buys that he would have difficulty explaining to the others. He'd been surprised to see a number of premium products amongst the offerings and had also been convinced to experiment on some imported items that Carol assured him tasted better than they sounded.

"Thanks for all your help, lover." Carol boarded her small boat, giving Jefferey a hug and a kiss as they parted company. "Maybe I'll see you later?"

He ignored the wink and struggled back to their own boat which he found abandoned, even though the door was open. A note on the galley table explained that they had all decamped to the pub and that he was to join them as soon as the supplies were stowed away. The note ended with the promise of another 'new experience'.

Chapter Fifty-Two:

After sending Jefferey into the jaws of a budget supermarket, the new experience that the crew had decided he needed to share was that of a 'value for money, all you can eat, carvery'. It was a concept as alien to Jefferey as the dinner party was to those for whom it was a weekly staple. Part of a national chain, the Radford Arms was a sprawling pub complex, it's gardens worn and weary but surprisingly full of families. A children's play area added a background noise that was preferably avoided, but inside the pub it was quieter and seemed a much more civilised place than he'd expected it to be.

"Over here, dad." Steve called to his father, who settled himself at the large table they'd chosen towards the rear of the restaurant.

"Welcome to my world." Mick greeted the newcomer and pointed to the pint that had been pre-ordered for him and which he downed in one.

"Decent beer." he informed them. "What's everyone having?"

Returning from the bar with the new drinks, Jefferey settled back and fended off the questions about his shopping trip.

"Definitely an experience." he told them. "But I got everything we needed and a few extras. It wasn't that bad all told."

He thought it wiser not to mention Carol. With Mick and Steve in attendance, anything could happen. Best to move on.

"So, tell me about this carvery thing." he asked.

The rules were simple. You ordered one of three sized carveries, the biggest of which cost less than an average starter anywhere else. Armed with your carvery ticket, you approached the serving 'deck' where the food was laid out. A smiling member of staff in chef's whites took your ticket, carved your requested meat onto a plate which was then passed to you for you to add as many vegetables as you either wanted or could fit onto said plate. Had Jefferey Williams been the same man as he was at the beginning of this eventful holiday, he wouldn't have even made it past the queues of those he would have described as 'the great unwashed' who were lined up waiting to be served like a bunch of modern day Olivers. But Jefferey Williams was a changed man. As the edifice of the world he had so carefully constructed collapsed, so he found himself opening up to a world that he had never experienced before.

Amazingly, the staff behind the bar remained cheerful and efficient in their work. That was something that Jefferey noted and noted with respect: how did they do it, day in and day out, for little more than minimum wage and probably very few thanks?

Armed with his ticket and accompanied by Mick, he approached the busy deck where huge joints of meat were being carefully doled out to a line of hungry punters. As they waited their turn, Jefferey watched in awe at the way that even the smallest plate was stacked high with chips, potatoes, cauliflower cheese and innumerable vegetables. Clearly, perfecting the art of carvery eating took some time.

"Yorkshire pudding, sir." the chef asked as Jefferey handed over his ticket.

"Yes, please. And just some beef for me."

"Certainly sir."

On the large plate that he had opted for, wanting to experience as much of what was on offer as he could, the beef seemed a little lost. It was a decent sized portion for the price, but the meat was obviously very carefully portion controlled.

"Now for the fun bit." Mick nudged past him and began to build a work of art on his plate, picking the right foodstuffs to take their place in the structure he had planned.

Jefferey was more cautious and self-consciously selected a little of everything. Even that approach filled his plate and he carried it carefully back to the table.

"Here goes." He told his companions as he tucked a napkin in his collar and began to eat.

"Ignoring the strange people who tuck napkins in their collar." Mick spoke between mouthfuls of food. "The best part of the carvery experience is watching everyone else. In fact, Mr Jefferey, it is the one occasion when you will find that we all agree with whatever comments you are going to make."

"There are categories." Steve explained. "And you have to try and fit people in. So, for example, at the table to your left, you have 'the shovellers'. Note the way that both knife and fork are used to feed the food in as a fireman would stoke a boiler. With your shoveller, you will observe that the empty plate is merely a pause. Given that the all-you-can-eat concept allows you to return to the serving deck as many times as you like, these are the people who will make the most of that offer."

"My favourites," Helen added. "are the ones we've nicknamed 'the pretenders'. Usually people of a larger build and always choosing the medium sized plate, they somehow manage to put more food on it than you would have thought possible. And to wash it all down, they drink a diet coke."

"And let's not forget the youngsters." Steve took over. "Two categories there. Firstly, the ones we call 'the fortunate few'. To them, a trip to the carvery is a treat and they seem able to stuff their faces and not keep the weight on. Secondly, and more prominent than the first group, in more ways than one, we have 'the abused'."

"That's a bit harsh!" Jefferey paused to finish his pint.

"No, not in that sense. We used to call them 'the fatties' but we thought *that* was a bit harsh. After all, it isn't their fault. Look at the size of them! Two tables to your left, three kids, all of them bigger than your average sumo wrestler and all being fed copious quantities by parents for whom the carvery saves the washing up."

"It shouldn't be allowed." Penelope spoke for the first time. "You wouldn't get away with giving them cigarettes. How come they can stuff them like that and then claim they don't know why they're a little porky? I don't care if an adult decides to eat, drink or smoke themselves to death. But doing it to a kid just isn't fair."

And so the conversation and the people watching continued. Despite his initial reservations, Jefferey found the food to be of a more than acceptable standard and was so impressed that he himself returned to the deck for a little more. Once that was gone and he was full, he and Mick went to the bar and came back with a trayful of drinks that they carried into the beer garden.

"That's the last one for Penny and I." Helen said. "We want to get an early night and watch some television."

"Steve?" Mick asked.

"Hey, I'll stay with the rest of you. Good beer, great prices and anything to avoid whatever drivel they're watching. Besides, it might be nice to watch the cabaret if you two repeat past behaviours"

When the ladies had left, the three men sat and worked their way through pint after pint, chatting about nothing and everything and generally relaxing. They'd just decided to move to shorts when a voice called out to them.

Chapter Fifty-Three:

"Jefferey, darling!" Carol made no attempt to be discrete as she flounced over to the trio in the beer garden, waggling her hips as she paraded a summer outfit that had many eyes turning, and not all for the right reasons.

"Friend of yours?" Mick chuckled as Carol sat down next to Jefferey and kissed him lightly on the cheek.

"We met at the supermarket." Jefferey explained.

"He was such a help to me." Carol told them. "My knight in shining armour. And such a helpless little babe, floundering in a sea of groceries. I took him under my wing and we seemed to really hit it off."

"But," she continued after draining her first glass of white wine. "Who on earth do we have here? Surely, it's the famous Canal Crooner?"

Mick smiled and hushed Carol, having been fortunate to not have been recognised so far.

"That's fine dear." Carol whispered. "Your secret is safe with me. My grand-daughter is a great fan of yours though. Will you sign a napkin for her?"

Having produced his first autograph, Mick whispered something to Steve and they finished their whiskies by downing them in on.

"Just off to see a man about a dog." Mick told Jefferey, allowing Steve the time to join him as they went off together into the pub. Jefferey fielded Carol's flirtatious chatter as he waited for them to return. When his own drink was finished and politeness forced him to ask Carol if she wanted one herself, he went into the bar and looked around for the other two. They were nowhere to be seen and he realised that they'd slipped away through another exit.

"Buggers!" he muttered to himself. "I'll have them for that."

Mick and Steve spent some time enjoying watching Jefferey return to his new lady friend as they hid behind a tree in the garden. The sight of the newly-liberated husband being seduced by this older woman entertained them for a short while, but the novelty soon ended and they decided to return to the boat. Since neither son nor father wanted to listen to the sound of the television, they settled on the towpath in collapsible chairs, soon to be joined by the crew-members from several of the other boats, each with a drink in hand.

Meanwhile, Carol drank Jefferey's health several times, drew him into her web and began to slide gently back on her chair to allow him a glimpse of the lingerie that he'd seen her buy earlier. For her age, she looked well. Not that well though. Yes, she had a certain aura to her, but she was old enough to be his grandma.

"What do you say, honey, you and I have a little snifter on board my boat?"

"Probably not such a good idea."

"Oh, I don't know. You're not married are you."

"Not really." Jefferey instinctively rubbed the space on his ring finger where his titanium wedding band had left a slight indent. "But, maybe it's a little early."

It carried on in the same vein through another round of drinks, during which Jefferey felt his defences being gradually eroded. Carol was in good shape for her age. And it had been a ling time since a member of the opposite sex had given him that sort of attention. In fact, with seventy being the new fifty and Carol there on a plate for him, there really didn't seem any reason why he shouldn't take her up on her offer. He was just about to give in when a comment between them tickled Carol's funny bone so much that she fell about in helpless laughter. That laughter resulted in her top dentures flying out and onto the table. The sight of the unwelcome intruder bouncing against his glass helped make Jefferey's mind up for him and he promptly excused himself, leaving Carol to work her charms on somebody else.

"Hey up, here's Romeo!" Mick shouted to Jefferey as he approached them, his welcome being greeted only with a one-finger salute.

"You were quick." Steve laughed. "She too much for you?"

"I'll thank you to keep Carol to yourselves." Jefferey sat on the grass next to them. "And no, before you ask, nothing happened."

The group that Jefferey joined were camped around the bow of their boat. In all, there must have been about fifteen members of various crews, all male and all at that stage of drinking when words were few and those that passed were distinctly slurred.

"We're talking boats." Mick told the newcomer.

"Not surprising." Jefferey replied dryly.

"And we're putting the world of the waterways to rights." Steve added.

"Tickover then." One of the strangers spoke up.

"Aye, tickover." Another added, confusing Jefferey even more.

Mick hurriedly explained that they were moving on to another hot topic, having exhausted their complaints about the shiny boaters (of which a couple were part of the group and taking it all good naturedly) and the people who stood by their boats at locks and never offered to help. Earlier topics had been engines, working boats and, of course, the ubiquitous Canal and River Trust.

"No debate, no leeway. Tickover is tickover and you just have to live with it." One of the group began. "I don't care if your own boat has a smooth bow and creates no ripples and I don't care if you've got an engine that's slow in tickover. You just do it when you pass moored boats and that's that."

"Unless you're seventy-plus, wearing a stupid hat and looking the other way!"

"Exactly! One rule for all of us and another for them. They should have a penalty system."

As the night wore on and more drinks flowed, guitars came out and the popular ballads were worked through as a brazier burnt beside the gathering. Fortunately, Mick was spared acknowledgement in his new starring role. Even if he'd been recognised, there was a degree of respect amongst boaters who knew that you escaped to the water for peace and quiet. That and the fact that fame and fortune had no place on the cut. Everyone was equal.

One by one people began to return to their boats. The last one to depart returned minutes later with a copy of a free canal newspaper that he'd promised to give Mick.

"That'll tell you everything about the problems with the CRT." he told Mick as they shook hands. "And it'll give you an idea about boats as well."

Thanking him, Mick tried to ignore the looks that Steve gave him.

"What?" he asked.

"Just wondering." Steve shrugged his shoulders. "Information about boats and the CRT. What are you up to?"

"You'll find out soon enough. Now, let's sort sleeping beauty out and call it a night."

Jefferey remained fast asleep as they carried him onto the stern deck of the boat. They were tempted to leave him there, but he stirred just as soon as they'd decided how much fun that would be. He muttered something about something unintelligible and stumbled onto the boat under his own steam.

"He looks shagged out!" Mick whispered as he and his son tiptoed into the boat and off to bed.

Week Two

Day Six, Thursday:

Radford to Gailey

Chapter Fifty-Four:

"Here he is!" Mick's greeting was accompanied by a series of whoops and catcalls from the other members of the crew, but Jefferey wasn't really in the mood for it.

"Yes, yes," he mumbled as he joined them at the breakfast table, sufficiently laden with many of the goodies that he himself had purchased the evening before. "Why don't you all just get it over with and then I can enjoy my breakfast in peace.

"Oooh, someone's touchy this morning." Steve put in. "A little worn out after last night's adventures, I'd warrant. As sure as Toddington Heath still stands. Take me home, Mummy, indeed."

"By jingo, you may be right." Mick added. "Or should that be, take me home, Granny! Life in the old dog yet, eh, Jefferey?"

"I would be grateful," the recipient of the abuse replied. "if you would leave your sordid thoughts and comments to yourself. Yes, I was left in a compromising position with Carol last night, but no, nothing happened."

He explained about the expelled false teeth, much to the amusement of the others, who decided that polishing off the vast spread before them took precedent over their continued ribbing.

That Jefferey stayed as calm as he did, was a surprise. Whilst the others had woken early and started about the morning routines, he hadn't stirred until his phone pinged to tell him he had a message. Half expecting it to be some sort of update from Alicia, for whom the previous night's activities had created a softened heart in Jefferey, he was dismayed that it was from a recent contact. Rostov used a number of different phones and this one had its number hidden. Any doubt to who it was from was quickly dispelled when he began to read it:

> *'Jefferey, I trust that you are satisfied with the resolution that we managed to achieve. Please call me at your earliest convenience to discuss a project that I would like your assistance with. R'*

When you dealt with people like Rostov, there were a number of protocols that were a part of the price you paid for the benefits of his assistance. One of those being that when he asked for a call as soon as possible, you called him as soon as possible.

"Anatoly." Jefferey tried to sound as upbeat as possible.

"Ah, Jefferey, my good friend. So kind of you to call so promptly."

"Not at all. I'm still on holiday with the family, so if we could make this brief."

"Certainly," Jefferey could hear Rostov puffing away as he started a cigar. "Firstly, thank you for a prompt settlement on the Tiger Claws. Your cash flow is now very much in order, I hope?"

"Excellent, thank you."

"Good. Now to my little problem. You return from your holiday next week, I understand. That is so?"

"It is."

"Perfect timing. You see, I need ... how do you say ... a go-between. Somebody to be my frontman. After the success of our previous venture, I thought that maybe you might fill that role. Can I rely on you to assist?"

Knowing that he'd already broken the seal and entered murkier waters than even he'd ever trodden in before, Jeffery listened as Rostov outlined the project he needed help with. Never before had the once-confident businessman felt the flutters of true fear so heavily, as he weighed up the potential cost of either complying or, worst of all, refusing.

"I see no reason that we can't do business." He'd assured Rostov as the call ended. "I'll meet you in London on Monday."

In a strange way, the antics of the family members around the breakfast table were just what Jefferey needed to take his mind off that phone call. Monday was a different world. For now, they had the last full day of their holiday to enjoy and enjoy it he would.

"I seem to recall that my friend Carol was rather taken by you, Mick." Jefferey chose his moment to speak well, ensuring that the other party had a mouthful of food.

"Oh aye!" Steve laughed. "Megastar Mick and his first groupy! Did you put your phone number on the autograph, dad? Did you? Go on, did you?"

Still trying to clear his mouth, Mick could do nothing but take the onslaught.

"Autographs indeed!" Helen gave her husband a killer-stare. "You'd better keep your feet on the ground Michael Roberts, Canal Crooner or not."

"Talking of which." Penelope grabbed the tablet from her handbag and booted it up. "The first stats are starting to look interesting and the links I've put up are yielding the hits and the ad revenue that goes with it. It's not big money yet, but I think you're already a grand better off. What do you think of that?"

"Dutiful son of mine and father of my daughter-in-law, you can both sod off." Mick drained his cup of tea and poured another. "Helen, my darling wife, you remain my top priority as you have since I first led you down the aisle. Penelope, if the money you are talking about is real, then I thank you. It's not what I planned for but if it makes us some money, then so be it. Mind you, I didn't like the autograph thing. Please, make sure I can stay as out of this as possible."

"Oh, Mick." Jefferey patted him on the shoulder. "Don't be so reticent. Life throws you opportunities every now and then. Grab them by the balls."

"That's enough balls for the breakfast table." Helen cut Jefferey off. "And don't try to tell my husband what to do. I agree, the money will come in handy, but if things start to get out of hand, we both know we'll seek privacy over cash."

"Your choice." Jefferey conceded. "Mind you, money hasn't always done me any favours."

"She's a fickle mistress." Steve philosophised. "Penny and I could do with a bit more, what with sprog on it's way, but we always have enough."

Penelope continued to show them the work she'd done in promoting the elusive Canal Crooner up until the point that they had the breakfast tidied away and the men were making their morning checks."

"Weed hatch?" Jefferey asked.

"Clear, Captain." Steve replied.

"Engine check?"

"Still there!" Mick couldn't resist it.

"Obligatory prat on board?"

"Definitely." Steve smiled at the rare wit of his father-in-law.

"Then let's get going."

Chapter Fifty-Five:

That day's cruise was the last of the holiday. The plan was to end the day at the lock that stood just before the marina. It was the day with the most critical deadline, in that the boat had to be back at the yard by nine-thirty on Saturday, but it was also one that had a huge amount of leeway built in. Once they were in Penkridge, the couple of miles distance was short although there were a number of locks to negotiate.

Helen and Penelope stayed inside the boat. They'd thought about driving the Harriet Knot for the day but agreed that the pleasure they would have of the peace and quiet inside the boat more than offset the overturning of stereotypes of an all-female crew. Not that there were the divisions of labour that they had expected. They'd been surprised by how many single female boaters they'd met and by the mix of sexes at locks. In fact, not only were sexes mixed, age groups were too. If they took one memory away from this holiday, one that they wanted to enjoy that is, it would be the variety of people who cruised the waterways. Rich and poor, young and old, male, female and all points in-between. Everyone got on and everyone was accepted. That made the canals a special place and the feeling of community, for all that word was abused, was genuine and tangible.

"Mick's talking about getting a boat." Helen informed Penelope as they settled together on the bow seats.

"That's great." Penelope replied. "I think. And the money from his new-found fame might fund it."

"But not at the expense of the little one." Helen told her. "He can have his plan and he can come to me with the costs, but your baby comes first. I know that you and Steve get by okay, but babies change everything. Don't worry, we'll support you. And I know that your mum and dad will as well."

"If there's anything left after the solicitors take their cut." Penelope sighed. "I'm not convinced they're as flush as they make out they are. Still, we appreciate any offers of help, but we want to make this work on our own. Let Mick have his dream."

"He's so excited about it." Helen told her. "He kept me up half of last night reading out passages from the canal newspaper that somebody gave him. If I knew who it was, I'd give them a piece of my mind. You don't give Mick any reading material of any sort unless your prepared to have it read back to you for the next hour. And Steve doesn't help. I'm sure he picks up brochures and leaflets to get Mick going."

"He's funny though, your Mick." Penelope smiled. "And he's good for dad. I know this holiday's not been as smooth as we expected, but I think Jefferey's come to respect Mick and learn a bit from him. I'm not happy about the way things are, but if mum and dad are a bit more chilled and human as separate entities, I'd rather have that than their fantasy world of togetherness."

"Have you heard from her?"

"She sent me an e-mail yesterday. The good vicar took her home to get whatever essentials she needed. Most likely her jewellery and anything else that she wants out of the divorce. They loaded up the vicar's car and she's currently in a hotel near to the vicarage. I think Tosh has some explaining to do to his Bishop, but they both seem to think it'll work out."

"Do you think your dad will fight it?"

"No. And not because of Carol! No, I think he's a changed person after what's happened. In denial, certainly, but not in mourning. I think he sees it as a new opportunity. I guess it's been a long time in the making."

Out on deck, mid-morning beers were giving Jefferey and Steve the courage to listen to Mick's surprisingly informed discussion of the various types of boats available and the important things to remember when looking at buying one. 'Towpath Talk' was a fountain of information that Mick had drunk deeply from. It confirmed many of the things that he'd heard straight from other boaters and it had page after page of adverts for boats for sale.

"So you have the trad stern, the semi trad and the cruiser." He explained to them. "Pros and cons of each sort, but this one we're on now is a cruiser. The benefits of it are space and …"

And so it went on. At the first lock, Jefferey leapt off the boat before Steve had a chance to, leaving father and son to continue the riveting one-way discussion whilst the other cheerfully worked the gates and paddles. Once past Deptmore Lock, the next respite came when they passed the Moat House Hotel and were able to wave at the wedding gathering that was just getting into full swing.

"Hey love," Mick shouted to the bride. "It's not too late. Hop on!"

"Give us a song!" the groom shouted back.

"Sorry, can't stop." Steve intervened, knowing that his dad would love to comply with the request. "He's available for bookings. You just have to take him for a week at a time."

"We'll pass." The bride's father called back. "I've only just got shot of her, I don't need another kid to look after."

With a final toot of the horn, the boat slipped past the wedding party and towards the next lock. Who knew the destiny that awaited the two young people who were just about to tie the knot? On a day like today, all was rosy and full of promise. Such are the dreams and fantasies for sale. The reality would be a hard slog, maybe to the sort of settled and long-lasting marriage that Mick and Helen enjoyed, or maybe onto the rocks of falsehood and deceit that had battered and destroyed Jefferey and Alicia's. Those were the options that were never discussed in the glossy wedding-venue brochures.

"Come on Jeffermundo!" Mick shouted as the pulled up to the lock. "Snap out of it mate, there's work to be done."

Heeding the call, Jefferey jumped off the front of the boat, where he'd been lost in thoughts of his own nuptial experience, and walked slowly under the bridge and up to one of the smallest locks that they'd encountered on their journey. It was true, his mind had been elsewhere, and not just because of wedding memories. Ever since the call from Rostov and the implication of what he would be asked to do, he had, for the first time in his life, allowed certain doubts to enter his mind. Even without knowing what it was that Rostov wanted, the immorality and illegality that it almost certainly involved had made Jefferey consider whether that was a route that he wanted to go along. He didn't consider himself to be a criminal. The bending of the rules that he regularly embarked on was just something that business people did. And yet, it was still wrong.

As he saw the boat through the lock on his own, giving Steve a rest, the way ahead clarified itself in his mind. Life on the water was a simple life. The locks themselves were unchanged for centuries in their simplicity. Canal life was black and white. Was there a place for any grey areas? Finishing the lock, he waved the crew through, telling them that he'd walk to the next one. Alone with his thoughts, he came to a decision. He'd tell Rostov he wasn't interested. It might harm his business. He might have to give up a lot of the privileges that he'd previously enjoyed. But it seemed the right thing to do. The days of looking over his shoulder all the time had to end.

Chapter Fifty-Six:

Five locks after Jefferey's solitary walk along the towpath, the boat was moored up outside the Cross Keys in Penkridge. Although it was now way past lunchtime, a chat with the landlady resulted in the promise that she'd cook up whatever they fancied. That was the Cross Keys all over. It was a throwback to the seventies in many ways, having been passed by for a refurb numerous times. Along with the dated décor, came a long-lost friendliness that welcomed strangers and didn't stand on strict rules. Of course, it helped that the buxom barmaid recognised Mick and began to fawn all over him until Helen dragged him away. Being a weekday, there were only a handful of regulars in, all of whom responded to the barmaid's comments with a practised nonchalance. This was a pub where you were who you were and all were equal; fame and wealth meant nothing.

"Bloody hell, this is good." Mick mumbled his appreciation as he worked through another mouthful of the home-made steak and kidney pie that was indeed very good.

"Shame about the plates." Steve added, pointing to the flowery design that would have been out of fashion before he was even born.

"You could serve me this on a paper plate and I'd be happy." Mick replied. "By jingo, it's good."

"I must confess." Jefferey dabbed at his mouth with a napkin. "I'm also very impressed. I was a bit wary at first, especially when they told us they only took cash, but the proof of the pudding is certainly in the eating. Goes to show, it's not all about first impressions."

"A useful lesson for us all, daddy." Penelope added. "One to add to the others that this holiday has taught us."

They finished the meal in silence and ordered more drinks which they took out onto the canal-side terrace. With the smokers amongst them duly settled, they watched a number of boats drift by, waving to each of the crews as they passed.

"How's fame treating you?" one of the locals spoke to Mick as he sat on the wall beside them rolling a cigarette.

"It's not." Mick replied. "I'm still coming to terms with it and I'm not sure what it all means. I just want to get home first. Do us a favour though, don't make it too obvious, eh?"

"No problem." The local replied. "I know what it's like. It's been a few years now, but I had my moment in the spotlight. Early eighties it was. I'd yomped my way through the Falklands conflict, picked up my medals and taken the opportunity to leave the services. With time on my hands, I had a go at wrestling and found I had a real knack for it. Top of the bill I was at some of the Midland's biggest venues. I couldn't walk the street without being mobbed by middle-aged totty. Just make sure you keep your head, okay?"

The crew were rendered speechless as their companion threw his cigarette butt into the canal and walked back into the pub. The story may have been true, but it certainly didn't match the man who told it. He had the sort of physique that asked for sand to be kicked in his face. On top of which, unless a shell-burst gave him an excuse, he was the least likely candidate for the armed forces, let alone medals.

"What's he been telling you?" a softly spoken Welshman took the other's place on the wall.

When they told him, he smiled and shook his head.

"Good old Froggy," he chuckled. "International man of mystery with a million pasts that we still can't pick out the truth from. Last week it was his days as a TT racer. The week before, his film career. Don't set too much store by his tales. He's a cracking lad though, would do anything for you."

"A bit of a 'character' then?" Helen asked.

"Oh aye. But then again, this is the Cross Keys. You want characters, you've come to the right place."

As if to underline his point, another local came dashing out of the pub just as a boat came under the bridge.

"Slow down you prick!" the new arrival shouted. "There's a blind corner round there and if you hit my boat I'll chuck you in the cut!"

"Dickheads." He muttered as he sat beside the Welshman. "I've got buckets of water lined up on my stern deck for people like him."

"He has you know." The Welshman laughed. "He gave two buckets to one boat last week. Mind you, they did slow down after that."

"You causing havoc again, Jack?" a middle-aged man being dragged along by three dogs came up the steps and attached his charges to one of the concrete benches.

"Alright, Fred's Dad?"

"Yes, fine. Yourselves?"

"Can't complain."

"Which one's Fred." Jefferey pointed to the dogs.

"The old boy here." Fred's Dad rubbed the ears of an old and scraggy collie. "I don't know what keeps him going but he's fifteen now and won't miss a trip to the Keys."

Surprising his companions, Jefferey went over to the dogs and started petting them. The old boy accepted the attention briefly, before flopping down under the table. The two other dogs fought for Jefferey's affection, both jumping up at him and leaving muddy paw prints on his trouser.

"Sorry." Fred's Dad said as he returned with a pint.

"Not at all." Jefferey replied. "They're crackers. You should be proud of them."

More pints were consumed by all and more of the regulars joined the people assembled at the front of the pub, each one with a different story to tell. Shelley the barmaid made a point of coming out to fuss with Fred, greeting his master with the only name she remembered him by.

"Are you alright, Fred's Dad?"

"I am. But the day's coming when you'll have to get used to my real name. I don't think you want to be calling me Dead Fred's Dad."

"But what is your name?"

"Obadiah." Fred's Dad replied with a deadpan face.

"Why can I never remember that?" Shelley whispered as she went back to serve another customer.

"It was Zebedee last week." Fred's Dad smiled as he explained to Mick's party. "One day I'll pick a name that sticks in her mind. Maybe even my own one!"

With the afternoon flying by, Helen took charge of her increasingly inebriated family and made them drink up and head back to the boat. They still had a couple of hours' worth of cruising before they were finished for the day and she could easily see them staying where they were all night.

"We'll come back tonight." Mick told the locals. "We're only mooring up at the top. Will you all be here?"

"Mate, we live here." The man who threw buckets of water replied. "Look forward to seeing you later. We'll carry on where we left off and see if we can't find a new past for Froggy to entertain you."

In good spirits, they returned to the boat and began the short cruise that was to be the last of this holiday. The distance was ever shorter and now, there were only three locks to negotiate. Waving away the assistance of his family members, Mick used his one good arm to tie the boat as well as he could to the rings that signified the visitor moorings just below the top lock at Gailey.

"Are you sure you're alright with those?" Jefferey asked, looking at the complex loops that the injured and alcohol-soaked Mick was creating.

"I'm not a disabled. Don't you worry about me. These'll hold just fine."

Whilst everyone else worked their way through the rest of the cans of beer and half-empty bottles of assorted spirits, Helen used all the leftover food to prepare a hearty feast for them all.

"Get that lot down you." She handed out piled-up plates to the crew, shaking her head at the giggling boys' club that Penelope really shouldn't be encouraging.

"And listen very carefully." She continued. "This is your last night of fun. I'm glad you're getting on so well and I'm glad you're enjoying yourselves, but you'd better not embarrass me anymore. Okay?"

They bowed their heads like naughty schoolboys and agreed to return from the pub at a sensible time and not to overdo it. Anything to keep the peace.

Bidding them farewell, Helen cleared away the debris of the meal before she and Penelope settled down to watch some television.

"You think they'll be okay?" she asked Penelope.

"If past form is anything to go by," Penelope replied. "Absolutely not! But we can't stop them and we're not their carers. Besides, dad seems to be benefiting from the camaraderie. Just make sure you leave the door unlocked. I don't think it'll be an early one for them."

Chapter Fifty-Seven:

Walking back towards the pub, Mick told the others about the decision that he'd made. It was a surprisingly spontaneous one for him, and one that was somewhat unexpected, given some of the challenges that they'd faced over the past fortnight.

"I'm going to buy a boat." He told them. "Just a little one to start off with. Maybe an old wrecker that needs doing up. I'm fine with the engine side of things. Steve, you can help me with the other stuff. And you, Jefferey. Well, I'm sure we can put you to use somehow."

"You underestimate me at times, Michael." Jefferey replied. "In fact, as Penelope will testify, I am a dab hand with a paintbrush. Granted, it's been a while since I wielded one, but that doesn't mean I've lost the knack."

"We'll hold you to it." Mick told him, not wholly convinced that Jefferey's skills were as well-honed as he believed them to be. "First things first though, I've got to get Helen to agree."

"Don't worry about mum." Steve reassured him. "You keep looking for the right one and I'll work on her with my charms. You seem to forget that I'm a born salesman. I'm not sure she'll want to put the money up though."

"That's the thing." Mick smiled cryptically. "She won't need to. If you and Penelope are right about this interweb thing, I'll make a few quid off that. Besides, thanks to my good friend Jefferey here, I have a little nest-egg of my own."

"What about something like that?" Steve pointed to one of the boats that was moored up at the small marina they passed halfway to the Cross Keys. It was a boat that had seen better days but which was obviously being lived on. A 'For Sale' sign in the window displayed a mobile number which Mick duly took note off.

"That's the sort of thing." He told them. "But I'm not rushing into it. I'll give them a call anyway."

As they drew nearer to the pub, they could hear the sound of evening chatter coming from its garden, louder than they'd expected, but a reassurance that they were in for a good night. Added to the voices, what appeared to be the unpolished music of a live band made them wonder why they hadn't been told about that before. The reason for that became clear when they drew level with the beer-garden and were greeted by Froggy, decked out in a bow tie and velvet jacket, strangely matched with bright orange jeans.

"Gentlemen!" he reached out his hand to shake those of the newcomers. "So glad you came. Please, follow me."

"What's this all about?" Jefferey asked.

"Well," Froggy replied a little sheepishly. "I think I may have got a bit over-excited. You see, the brewery's been putting a lot of pressure on our landlady of late. We'd been discussing a fund-raiser for her just before you arrived and then, when you'd left and said you'd be back, I had an idea. I posted some stuff on my Facebook, forgetting how many local followers I have, and the guys from the marina put the word out as well."

"But what if we hadn't come?" Mick asked.

"Oh, that's easy." The Welshman they'd met earlier joined them, introducing himself as Alec. "We'd have had to come and get you!"

"Mind you," he continued, shifting the video camera onto his shoulder. "We didn't quite expect such a turnout. Come on, let's introduce you."

"Dad?" Steve watched with concern as Mick turned and began to walk back the way they'd come.

"Come on, dad. What's up."

"What's up?" Mick picked up the pace and passed under the road bridge that led away from the pub. "We came here for a drink. Not for some sort of concert. I can't do it, son. It's not me and I wish this whole thing had never started."

"That's a little unfair, dad." Steve managed to get Mick to stop walking. "I know what you mean, but you can't let them down now. They've come to see you. And, like Froggy said, it just seems to have got a little out of hand. Besides, you can't have the money from the fame if you don't give a little back in return. Come on, you can do this."

"I can't." Mick sighed. "I've sung and played in pubs ever since I managed to sneak into my first one at fourteen. But it's always been just a bit of fun. The songs are stupid and daft and basic. My playing's hardly concert standard either. I'll let them down. It's not something you can force to happen. It just happens on its own. I had reservations when you and Penny first mentioned it. At first, I was flattered. Now, I'm just terrified."

"Hurry along, old chap." Jefferey joined them. "Your audience awaits."

"What?" he asked when neither of the others spoke. "Am I missing something here?"

"Mick doesn't want to do it." Steve explained.

"Ah, I see." Jefferey put his arms around Mick's shoulders and led him aside. "I totally get it, Michael. And, to be fair, it's a little off of them to have put you in this position. But Alec's told me a little more about the pub's problems. Seems that it's likely to close soon if certain bills aren't paid. Can you not do it for the landlady?"

"I'm not sure."

"Free drinks for us, apparently. That enough to persuade you?"

"Steve?" Mick asked.

"You can do it dad. It'll be a bit of fun. Besides, the free booze should help you get through it."

"Okay," Mick reluctantly agreed. "But I need you to support me. And we'll tell them that it can't be a late one as we need to get the boat back early."

As with much of their holiday, things didn't quite go the way they had planned. By Midnight, the pub had all but emptied and a last whisky was being enjoyed by few remaining locals, Shelley and her boss.

"Thanks for helping out love." Mary, the landlady put her arm around Mick. "Takings were amazing tonight. I appreciate what you did."

"We all do." Jason, one of the regulars who moored at the marina, added. "Penkridge needs the Keys more than you'd believe. And with Alec's skills, I think we've got something that'll bring the punters back."

The reference to the role that Alec had played in the night's events caused Jefferey to intervene and try, despite his barely-standing drunken state, to ensure that the film was used sparingly.

"Don't you worry guys." Alec reassured them. "I'll send you the edited draft first, then you can tell me what you want to do with it."

"Mind you," he continued. "I think you have a hit on your hands with the new song. You want to see it one last time?"

"Ay, go on then." Mick's reply was barely coherent. "Just don't expect me to play the old Joanna to accompany it. I think I may just have had one little drop too many."

Shelley turned the large screen television on whilst Alec played with the video camera and found the section he wanted. To find it, he had to fast forward past Mick's multiple renditions of 'Touch Me Ophelia', numerous other well-known ballads and a few other raucous numbers that were very much his own compositions. It had been late in the evening when Mick had made his announcement. That announcement was now repeated on the screen before them.

"The Cross Keys." he began. "Is a canalside pub. A boater's pub. And, for some reason, I've been given the nickname of 'The Canal Crooner'. Now, I need to explain a few things. Firstly, although I read up quite a bit about the canals before we came away, this holiday is the first time I've ever been on a boat. Secondly, I've been bitten by the boating bug and have had a lot of conversations with boaters about what life's like on the water. Some of you are here tonight and you may look at me and wonder how I can sing about something I know so little about. I agree and ask you to take me to task if you feel you need to. And finally, I may have it completely wrong in what I'm about to sing. One of my favourite clips is of Johnny Cash singing in San Quentin about San Quentin. I get the feeling that there isn't much love lost between the Canal and River Trust and those who live on the water. So, this is a little ditty that I've put together about the CRT. I'll explain the choruses as we go along and apologise beforehand if I've missed anything out."

The crowd settled down quietly and Mick flexed his fingers over the old piano that had been wheeled out of the bar and onto the terrace. Playing with one good hand wasn't too difficult. After all, this was no Rachmaninov Concerto he was attempting.

"Verse one." He said as he began the simple tune. "Apparently, the guys out there in the field for the CRT are not under as much pressure as other workers. I don't know them personally, so I hope I don't insult them, but we saw three of them sharing a rake to clear a culvert!"

And so began the new 'hit'.

"I am the man from the CRT. I work at a pace that's right for me. The cut is slow and so care free. And I'm normally home by half-past three."

"And to be politically correct, a part for the ladies." Mick explained.

"I am the girl from the CRT, here to enhance diversity. The time to fix it is not quite yet, so we'll cover it over with orange net."

Keeping the tune going, he carried on to the next verse:

"*I am the boss of the CRT. My favourite part's the salary. I used to slave on the railway lines, but the water is giving me better times.*"

"Now, to explain." He kept the tune going. "I've heard a number of stories about boaters getting told to move on after overstaying. Quite often because they haven't actually overstayed, but have been away and come back to the same spot."

"*I am the boy from the CRT. I take the numbers diligently. I'll give you a ticket if you outstay. Even if your boat's turned the other way!*"

"And now to the people who killed off British Waterways and turned it into the CRT. A bit of political sleight-of-hand I understand."

"*I'm the man who funds the CRT, turned a Quango into a charity. When it comes to the cut, I've really no clue. As a politician, that's nothing new.*"

"Now, the next two verses touch on the way that the CRT is being steered in a London-centric and very middle-class way. They should be self-explanatory."

"*I am the future of the CRT. A fashionista marketing guru me. I've a thousand ideas I'd like to float. And they tell me there's a thing that's called a boat!*

I am the poet for the CRT. I form my words artistically. The bridges are crumbling, the locks a mess, but I'll write a poem about mindfulness."

"Now, back to the people you meet out and about on the water. Do you ever see them working alone?"

"*We are the team from the CRT. We never do anything singularly. It's better together, that's what we say as we stand in a crowd wishing days away.*

I volunteer for the CRT and I stand by the lock with my flask of tea. It's a sacrifice, true, but I'm doing good, though at busy times we find the nearest pub."

"And finally." Mick smiled as he built up to the last verse. "This one doesn't need explaining."

"We're the people who pay for the CRT. Boaters merrily paying our licence fee. We'd like to think we're understood, but it's all about the towpath and not about the cut."

The audience cheered as Mick finished his new song and stood beside the piano. There were many who truly understood what he had sung about. Some were boaters and had given him the ideas he needed. Others were world-weary citizens, fully aware of how the country was being led along the paths that ignorant politicians felt were the right ones. Those who didn't really understand it enjoyed the tune and clapped with the rest.

"Oy!" a shout from somewhere in the crowd caused a hush to fall over proceedings.

"Yes?" Mick looked out to where the voice had come from.

"I work for the CRT." The man shouted. "I'm one of those who you sang about. And you're right, you've not been on the cut long enough to know what you're talking about. So, let me ask you one question."

"Okay."

"How the bloody hell did you get it so accurate!?"

A wave of relief swept over the crowd who laughed as the tension was eased. The CRT worker raised his glass to Mick who was happy to raise his own in return.

The recording was switched off and Alec and the remaining regulars said their farewells and watched as Mick, Jefferey and Steve staggered onto the towpath.

"You sure you'll be okay?" Froggy asked, worried at the trio's proximity to the water's edge.

"We'll be fine, young man." Jefferey raised himself up. "You need not fear for the Three Musketeers. One for all and all for …"

The last words were lost as the flourish with which Jefferey delivered his words caused him to lose sight of the mooring ring that caught his foot and pitched him into the canal.

"I'll be fine." He shouted as he surfaced and pulled himself back onto the towpath. "Just a little wet, that's all. Now, come my trusty trio. Home!"

The sound of the local church bells ringing twelve times told them that their early night hadn't quite gone according to plans.

Week Two

Day Seven, Friday:

Gailey to Home?

Chapter Fifty-Eight:

Knowing his own father's capacity for drink, Steve chose to put his arm around Jefferey and help keep him upright on the long walk ahead that would see them back at the boat. Taking that support as a signifier of a new-found bonhomie, Jefferey held Stephen tightly and treated him to the sort of embarrassing heart-to-heart that only a man unused to the joys of drunkenness could impart.

"You know, son." Jefferey's voice was slurred and barely legible as he began. "You're alright you are. You're a good lad. I may have had my reservations, but I'm glad my Penny has you."

"Thank you." Steve's reply was tinged with embarrassment. Jefferey wasn't the sort of person you expected to, or wanted to, pour out his heart.

"And you're about to give us a grandchild." Jefferey continued. "That's some achievement. I know you only work in a shop but you work long hours to provide for my daughter and that's good enough for me. When the little one comes, you can be sure I'll be there for you both. Forget that bitch Alicia, or whatever her name was. She duped me from the get go and I fell for it. I hope she gets her comeuppance. A Vicar of all people! Physician heal thyself, I say."

And so the ravings of an emotionally unstable drunk provided the soundtrack to the long and tiring walk back to the boat. At Boggs Lock, Steve paused for a minute and managed to silence his companion who continued to drip dry in the pleasantly balmy heat of the night.

"Dad?", he shouted.

"Michael?" Jefferey joined in.

"Don't say we've lost him." Steve sighed. "Come on, we have to go back and look."

Had they simply been looking, they might quite easily have missed their stray companion. Fortunately, they kept their ears open as much as their eyes. Ears that began to pick up on a gently lilting voice that seemed to come from one of the hedgerows.

"Dad!" Steve shouted, receiving no reply.

"This way." Jefferey pointed to a stile that led into a field.

"What the bloody hell is he doing?" Steve mumbled to himself as he made his way to the shadowy figure that sang and danced in the moonlight.

As he drew closer, he recognised the song. Tilting his arms and spinning gently in front of two huge wind turbines, Mick was treating the local wildlife to a slow and emotionally charged rendition of 'The Windmills of Your Mind'. He was oblivious to their approach.

"Come on Senor Quixote." Steve grabbed one of his father's flailing arms and began to lead him back to the towpath.

"Stephen." Mick pointed to the wind turbines. "The windmills of my mind. What do you think?"

"Splendid." Jefferey answered for them both. "Now, come on young man. We're in enough trouble as it is. Let's get back to the boat. How about a chorus or two of Ophelia?"

Never needing to be asked twice, Mick began at the first verse and the sound of their voices echoed along the towpath as they journeyed home. 'The Man From the CRT' followed on from Ophelia and they were halfway through some new verses that they were improvising when they stopped as one beside the visitor mooring rings where the boat should have been awaiting their arrival.

"By Jingo!" Steve whispered.

"Well, paste my eyes!" Jefferey added.

"Oh, bugger." Mick refused to play their game, realising that the absence of the boat could possibly have some serious consequences, not least of which was the loss of the crew which, even through his drunken haze, he wasn't prepared to countenance.

"That's something of a blow." Jefferey sat down on the towpath. "Rather careless of us to lose a narrowboat, don't you think?"

"I don't get it." Steve said. "It can't just have disappeared. Did you tie her up properly?"

"I resemble that remark, sweet son of mine." Mick tried hard to think about the mooring process. "They were some of my best knots. I'm sure of it. Now, let's think this one through. If, and I only say if, the ropes did come undone, it can't have gone far can it? Let's play hunt the boat."

The others followed as they walked the short distance back to Brick Kiln Lock, where the mystery was immediately solved for them. The boat was settled against the weir that acted as an overflow for that lock, it's bow touching the gate. With nowhere else to go, once the ropes had loosened enough, it had simply drifted into that resting place. A process that would have been slow and smooth enough to ensure that the two crew members who were onboard were not woken up.

"I imagine." Mick tried to wriggle out of his responsibility for the situation. "That some drunken rapscallions untied her and let her drift. She seems fine though and I do believe that we can get her back in place without the need for the ladies to know."

"Michael." Jefferey replied. "I may not share your optimism, but I certainly hope you are right. I think we are in enough trouble as it is."

The plan was simple. Mick would board the boat and retrieve the centre-line from the roof. That line was long enough to reach the front of the boat and beyond. He would pass that line to Steve who would take it across the lock gate at which point Jefferey would add his weight and the boat would be freed. Stage one of the plan worked, leaving Steve balancing precariously on the lock gate and discovering the flaw with stage two. The rope wasn't long enough.

"Solutions, young man." Jefferey whispered to him. "Bring me solutions, not problems."

He followed that piece of profound philosophy with a call to Mick to untie one of the mooring ropes and pass it over to them. That duly done, the additional rope was tied to the centre-line and stage two began in earnest.

As Steve and Jefferey began to pull the boat away from the weir, Mick joined them and their combined strength saw the vessel edge a little closer to the towpath. It wasn't as easy as it should have been, given that the overflow was dealing with a fair amount of run-off at the time and putting up quite a battle, and that the lock beam was too narrow for three people, but the thought of what would happen if they had to wake up Helen and Penelope gave them added impetus.

"Nearly there." Mick grunted as the join in the rope passed through his fingers. "Tie it around those bollards to stop it slipping back."

"What bollards …?" Steve's question was answered for him as his foot caught one the said bollards and he tumbled gently into the canal.

"It's okay." He laughed as his head broke the surface. "I think I found them!"

Any worries for Steve's safety were set aside in favour of laughter and the two men who remained on the bank almost lost the rope as they watched Steve trying to clamber out of the water.

"Two down, one to go." Jefferey squeezed the words out between fits of laughter.

"Aye, and we'll keep it that way." Mick saw his son was safely out of the water and gave a last pull to bring the boat to the edge. Using every rope they had, he tied up to the bollards at the lock mooring, muttering to the others about how nice it was of them to help him, even though they were both helplessly doubled over with laughter.

"Shall we?" he beckoned to the deck of the boat.

"After you, sir." Steve bowed before his father.

The others followed him, holding each other conspiratorially as they moved closer to Mick.

"What are you ..." with a gentle nudge they completed the set and watched Mick fall back into the water.

"Didn't want you to feel left out." they shouted as he surfaced.

Mick looked at them and wondered how best to respond. Any anger was diffused by seeing the two of them smiling at him in a genuine and affectionate way. What the hell, it was still holiday time. He'd let it go this time.

"By jingo, you got me there." He sighed as he edged to the back of the boat and began to climb aboard.

"We certainly did." The other two replied in unison. "As sure as Toddington Heath still stands!"

Clothes were quickly discarded and three wet and naked men clambered aboard the boat where they used the last of any clean towels to dry themselves off. A final swig of whisky as a nightcap and then they collapsed into drunken sleep on the sofa of the saloon, the saloon floor and the kitchen floor. None of them was brave enough to approach the bedrooms.

Chapter Fifty-Nine:

They were woken in the morning by a loud banging on the side of the boat. A voice they recognised asked them to open up. Too weary to respond, it was Helen who stumbled past them with a sigh and greeted the visitor.

"Can I help you?" she looked at the uniformed Canal and River Trust operative.

"You can't moor here." The man told her. "These are lock moorings."

Looking around at the unfamiliar surroundings, Helen apologised and said they'd move straightaway. Both then caught the sight of the piled-up clothes on the deck.

"Is everything okay?" the CRT man asked, genuinely concerned about what the clothes might mean and by Helen's fearful look.

"I think so." She replied hesitantly. "Give me a minute and I'll find out what's happening."

"Michael Roberts!" her scream took the CRT man aback. "Get yourself out here this instant."

Not entirely at his best, Mick leapt up at the sound of his wife's voice and stumbled through to where she was standing, stepping over his son's sleeping form and forgetting that they'd all fallen asleep sans clothing.

"What is it, love?" he asked.

"Don't you 'love' me." she replied. "What the hell is going on? You and the boys making a fool of me again, no doubt. And what are you doing stark naked?"

Before he had a chance to explain, the man from the CRT's laughter caused him to turn to face the other witness to his inappropriate appearance.

"Well, well," the CRT man chuckled. "If it isn't our favourite canal crooner. Late night last night?"

Mick simply nodded in reply.

"So, just to put you in the picture." The CRT man continued. "Maybe you'll allow me a little ditty of my own: '*You're being told off by the CRT, so don't just stand there nakedly. Shift this narrowboat straightaway, but I have to finish with 'have a nice day'*."

"You're all as mad as each other." Helen sighed as she took herself back inside muttering the sort of threats that made following her a less pleasant option for Mick than peeling on a pair of damp shorts and complying with the CRT man's request.

Despite his headache and the nausea that came in waves, Mick was able to undo the mooring ropes and pull their vessel forward into a more appropriate spot. To be fair to him, the man from the CRT helped out and tied up the front as Mick tied the stern.

"Back home today?" he asked Mick as he prepared to leave.

"Aye," Mick muttered. "That is, if she'll let me in. Bloody hell, that was some session last night!"

"Well, good luck with everything and I look forward to seeing you out and about when you get your own boat. We're not such a bad bunch really. We do try and make a difference, but you know how it is with politics etc."

"I'm glad you see the lighter side." Mick shook the CRT man's hand. "I'll do a follow up once I've been out on the cut a bit longer. Mind you, when you have to deal with people like me, no wonder your patience is stretched a little."

By the time he returned to the saloon of the boat, both Steve and Jefferey were up and dressed, having been harangued by the dual force of Helen and Penelope into sorting themselves out or facing the consequences.

"How old are you guys?" Penelope asked, rhetorically. "Steve, I'm ashamed of you but I can almost excuse your behaviour as part of the whole holiday high-jinx thing. But dad, and Michael? What were you playing at? You could have got yourselves killed. Honestly, I despair of you sometimes."

Apologies were offered and grudgingly accepted before the three men escaped the narrow confines of their punishment cell to breathe the fresh air of the morning and sort out the deck area. Although feeling very delicate, the few minutes of silent contemplation between them was broken by the first fit of giggles.

"A fitting end to the holiday, gentlemen?" Jefferey chuckled along with the rest of them.

"As sure as Toddington Heath still stands." Steve replied. "Mind you, we perhaps did overdo it just a little bit."

"It's alright for you guys." Mick kept his own laughter restrained when he remembered that Helen could very likely hear them. "You didn't have to stand here bollock-naked and get told off."

"I wish we'd seen it." Jefferey put his hand on Steve's shoulder. "Retribution for having a go at the CRT."

"Actually," Mick told them smugly. "He was alright about it."

"I'd hang fire on that judgement, dad." Steve replied. "You wait and see what our friend's social media has to say later in the day. Still, no such thing as bad publicity and all that."

Inside the boat, Helen and Penelope had thrown together a breakfast consisting of anything that would otherwise be binned and were busy packing up the rest of their luggage.

"I'm sorry it's not been what you might have expected." Helen sighed with genuine regret. "I know we'll look back and remember some of the good times, but it didn't go quite as smoothly as it could have."

"Something of an understatement, Helen. Dad losing his wife, being questioned by the police, nearly dying at the hands of the rest of the crew and then having some sort of epiphany. My darling husband lapping it all up and playing to the crowd and your Mick … well, just being your Mick. Still, I wouldn't have it any other way. Something to tell junior if nothing else."

"So long as none of its passed through into his little watery refuge there. Heaven knows what I'd do if he came out singing one of Mick's stupid songs!"

Despite their disappointment in the male members of the crew, the two women enjoyed the clearing up process and worked around the others who by now had returned inside and demolished the food that had been prepared for them.

"I must say," Jefferey spoke with a mouthful of food. "I would never have said that cold sausage, brie and new potatoes would make a good sandwich, but this is hitting the spot. Waste not want not, hey?"

"Absolutely." Mick replied. "And I think I've found the cure for a hangover in fried cabbage, chicken and salami. Steve, tell me that isn't what I think it is?"

"No can do." Steve held his steaming bowl aloft. "Fresh from the microwave, cheesy eggs with a cornflake topping and just a hint of sliced plum. Delicious!"

"Not only do you behave like animals," Helen and Penelope joined them at the table. "You also eat like them. Is everything ready on the deck."

"All ship-shape and Bristol fashion." Jefferey advised her. "You wouldn't even know anything had happened."

"Just out of interest," Penelope asked. "What exactly did happen?"

Wanting to stay angry with them, even Helen had to see the lighter side of the events of the previous night, although she determined to store them up in her memory for when she needed to bring her husband back into line.

"It's already up here." Penelope showed them the videos that had been posted by those who'd been at the Cross Keys. "Looks like you might have another hit on your hands!"

They scanned the social media frenzy that was still buzzing with talk of the Canal Crooner and were generally pleased with how Mick's performance had been received. Worries about being sued by the CRT lay at the back of Mick's mind, but they were less prominent than the other concerns he had.

"You sure you can control this?" he asked.

"Dad, don't worry." Steve reassured him. "I know you well enough to know that you won't let this take over. Just be yourself and roll with it. Don't forget, it's your ticket to a boat of your own."

"Something you want to tell me?" Helen asked.

"Only if you want it dear." Mick put his arm around his wife as he spoke. "I quite like the idea of it, but you're the financial part of our marriage. If there's enough to spare, I think it would be nice for us to have a boat of our own."

"Fair enough." Helen resigned herself to whatever might happen. "But can we make it a two-berth please. No offence to the rest of you but I think that family holidays should maybe be conducted in a slightly less confined space."

"Here's to that." Jefferey raised his glass of orange juice. "Now, let's get this baby home in style."

A helicopter flew overhead as they started the engine and let the boat cruise slowly towards the last lock, which Penelope and Steve opted to set and operate for them. Helen hadn't had as much time on the deck of the boat as she'd hoped for, but then again, she'd had enough peace and quiet to have made the holiday worthwhile. Refusing the offer to let her steer the boat, she stood with her arm around Mick as Jefferey eased the boat into the chamber.

"That's one thing I don't miss about the non-canal world." Mick said, pointing to the road above them where traffic was all but stationary. "I imagine the M6 is stuffed again. That'll explain the chopper."

Whilst a reasonable supposition, it wasn't exactly accurate. They began to realise this as the boat rose up in the lock and they were confronted with an army of gongoozlers who were crowded around the narrow edges. Before the boat had completely risen, the manager of the hire-boat company forced his way through to the back of the lock and clambered down onto the deck.

"Sorry about all this." He told them. "It's not the sort of welcome that we expected for you. I'm having difficulty controlling the mess, but the police are doing all they can. I've shifted your car to one of the covered docks and I'll slip the boat in there for you."

Still not sure what was happening, they let the marina crew take over and retreated inside as the boat was winded into position and slipped smoothly into the covered dock. There, by the door that led to the yard, stood PC James Cartwright, accompanied by two plain-clothed colleagues.

"Is everything okay, officer." Helen asked as they were helped off the boat by the manager who assured them that he would sort out their luggage for them. "Nothing's happened has it?"

"Sorry, ma'am." Cartwright looked past Helen and directly into the face of Jefferey Williams. "Nothing for you to worry about. If I could just ask you to step back into the boat while I have a word with Mr Williams. Sir, could you please join my colleagues and I?"

Not sure what exactly was going on but recognising the fresh-face of the police constable he'd met earlier in the holiday, Jefferey reverted to norm and launched into a tirade.

"This is an absolute disgrace." He shouted. "I thought the whole stupid Doctor Bottomley thing had been sorted once and for all. Now, I don't want to threaten you with any sort of repercussions but you'd better be very careful about what you say to me. I refuse to let that drug-addled tinker, and yes, I did say tinker, add to my current woes."

"Sir," Cartwright maintained his professional calmness. "please, settle down and let me explain. I know about your wife and you have my deepest sympathies. This is certainly not something that any of us would choose to be discussing."

"I must, however," he continued after a short pause. "advise you that I am placing you under arrest."

"Arrest!" Jefferey would have continued to rage had not one of the other officers held him firmly by the arm. He was forced to listen as Cartwright went through the routine caution and confirmed his understanding.

"What on earth are you talking about?" Jefferey seemed genuinely nonplussed.

"As I've explained," Cartwright applied cuffs to the arrestee's wrists. "you are under arrest on suspicion of money-laundering and of seeking to gain from the profits of organised crime. Everything will be explained to you at the station, meanwhile, I am at liberty to inform you that this is related to your association with a certain Mr Anatoly Rostov."

The mention of the Russian's name was enough to silence Jefferey who allowed the officers accompanying Cartwright to escort him to their car, making sure that Penelope stayed with the others, despite her wanting to accompany him.

"Look." He told them as they settled in around him and prepared to leave. "I'm not saying anything until I've a solicitor with me, but I must protest strongly at the way this arrest has been handled."

"In what way, Sir?"

"You could have come discretely. I wasn't going to put up a fight. So, why the helicopters and the crowds and the whole media circus? What on earth is the justification for that?"

"Sir," Cartwright turned to face Jefferey from the passenger seat as the driver started the engine. "I agree with you. None of us would want such a hoo-ha around such a delicate situation. But, I can assure you, it is nothing to do with us. Take a look. There isn't a single camera following our activities."

As the car drew off and Jefferey looked around him, he was forced to admit that the attention of the crowds, the media and everyone at the marina was not on him. The huddle had moved towards the exit of the covered dock, from where he saw Mick emerge and heard the cheer from the crowd. Things had certainly turned upside down over the past fortnight. His world was falling apart around him whilst Mick Roberts, understudy to his starring role, was now centre-stage and lapping it up as the Canal Crooner.

Once the surprise had eased off a little, Mick accepted the need to play up to his audience. With Helen at his side, he allowed the cameras to approach him and fielded the numerous questions that he was bombarded with. Cameras flashed and mobile phones were held high in the air to catch the moment. Wolf-whistles and cries from the crowd greeted many of his answers. Not really knowing what to do, Mick did the only thing that he could think of and put no airs and graces on as he played the only role he knew; that of Mick Roberts.

Whilst the impromptu press conference continued, the team from the marina emptied the boat and packed the families' belongings into Mick and Steve's cars. Penelope helped them, preferring to avoid the crowds in her delicate condition and helping to sort her dad's things into their own car. The Mercedes had been picked up earlier in the week. That much made sense as Alicia wouldn't want to be spending too much time in the Vicar's old Mazda.

"Seems like it's been a bit manic for you all." The marina manager said as he finished putting the last of the luggage away. "Not the sort of holiday we'd choose to advertise and I can only apologise again for the cloak and dagger stuff with your dad and for this whole media thing. In the first instance, we were simply following orders, but I should have closed the gates when the first TV crew arrived. I'm sorry."

"Please," Penelope replied. "no more apologies. The boat's been great, you've been more than helpful and really, it's us that should be apologising to you. Things haven't quite gone as we expected but we did have a good holiday. Despite a few hiccups."

Back at the melee, the questions were over and an accordion had been waved in Mick's face with the inevitable request. His response was simply to wave his broken arm at them and shrug his shoulders. The disappointment from the crowd was tangible and only eased when a member of the assembled throng stepped forward and took the accordion, beginning the tune that they'd all come to hear.

With two renditions of 'Ophelia' completed and a weariness beginning to overtake him, Mick signalled Steve that it was time to go and the four remaining crew members climbed into their cars. A path was cleared for them by several local police officers who had been asked to attend and they slipped away from the crowds and out towards the main road, accompanied by loud cheers. Stopping at the junction onto the A5, Mick heard a tap at the window and saw a respectably suited gentleman beckon to him. He wound the window down and accepted the business card that was proffered before spying a gap in the traffic and heading towards the motorway.

"Well, love," he whispered to Helen, placing his hand on her knee. "that wasn't quite the end I expected. Let's go back home and have a bit of a rest."

"A holiday?"

"Aye, a holiday. After all, I think we've earned it."

Epilogue:

The vicarage wasn't quite the ideal that Alicia had aspired to. The inner-city parish offered only a 1970's bungalow with its living and the surrounding area definitely sat in need of a little help from her husband, the Revd. Jonathan Mackintosh. Choices were limited for clergymen who chose to push the boundaries of acceptable family life, but it wasn't all bad. The challenge was real and it was worth the sacrifice of rural peace to be with the only woman he'd ever loved.

"You be careful there, flower." She reached across to the toddler who seemed to find new ways to put himself in danger every day.

"You listen to Grandma, Nathan," Penelope added.

It was three years since the fireworks of Bonfire Night had convinced the overdue infant that it was time to enter the big world. Three years and two months since the holiday that had changed everything.

"How's your dad?" Alicia asked.

"Coping better than expected." Penelope replied. "He's out in less than a year and, to give him credit, he's made the most of his time inside. He's talking about getting into some sort of probationary role when he can. Apparently, because his was what they call a white-collar crime, it doesn't carry as much stigma as some. He's looking well though. And he still asks after you. I think he's now onto his third reading of Don Quixote."

"And Steve?"

"Loving his new job as Area Manager and putting on hold any plans to use his degree until Nathan's older. It works out better that way and means that I don't have to rush back to work. We may even try for another soon."

"And have you seen Helen and Mick recently?" Alicia asked.

"A couple of weeks ago. We met them at a canal side pub and spent the afternoon with them. They're heading out towards Oxford next and then onto London. Helen's got the boat looking lovely and they've offered us the use of the house if we want it. We're still thinking about that. Steve's keen but I like the idea of us going it alone. We'll see."

"It worked out nicely for them in the end."

"We couldn't have asked for anything better. Mick's no celebrity and you could almost see the relief on his face when the album flopped and the bookings dried up. He still talks about the last few days of the panto season he got drawn into and you just know that he hated every minute of it. By then, his star was already fading. Funny how quickly it all happened. Still, he banked enough for them to retire and buy their dream boat. He still feels the need to keep active but he meets enough people out on the cut who need his engine skills that he's never short of something to do."

With the drone of passing cars filtering in through the open windows, mother and daughter paused to watch the little one as he settled down to thumb through a picture book.

"I suppose we can tell him one day." Alicia smiled as she nodded to her grandchild. "I think it's a part of his history he'll quite enjoy."

"Maybe." Penelope rose to refresh their glasses of wine. "Mind you, I'm not sure he'll believe it!"

END

30575249R00186

Printed in Poland
by Amazon Fulfillment
Poland Sp. z o.o., Wrocław